TIES
THAT
BIND

Elizabeth Blair

LITTLE ROCK ◇ DALLAS

Ties That Bind/ Elizabeth Blair -- 1st ed.
ISBN 13 978-0692668610
ISBN 10 0692668616

Only sinners, prostitutes, and angels of death roamed the streets of Atlantic City this time of night. Deserted streets, outlined exclusively by the rare homeless body stretched out near a ventilation shaft, seemed welcoming only to the outcasts of even the city's darkest side. In the back alleys behind the third police precinct, not even an eerie yellow glow from a taxicab was available to light the way. Stumbling over one of the inert bodies in his path, Mitch considered stopping and checking for a pulse but then thought better of it. If a person had chosen to die on the steps of the local pd., it wasn't his problem. He had bigger things on his plate than worrying about the press fiasco such an event would cause.

He shivered as a biting wind cut through his silk suit, wishing he'd thought to grab a coat before the police had hauled him in for questioning. Not that he'd had much opportunity to plan for the event. Unlike usual, he'd been taken by surprise when they'd yanked him out of Sunday brunch at La Mazaran and thrown him to the asphalt without even bothering to mirandize him. He checked his Rolex, noting the day rather than the time. Three days. Three very long and very grueling days. The cops had held him in custody for over 72 hours.

He sidestepped the leggy red-haired hooker that moved to intercept him as soon as she'd seen the watch flashing under the neon lights. Even she was intelligent enough to know it wasn't a fake. He offered her an apologetic smile and continued down the sidewalk, kicking away drifts of snow that the street sweeper had brushed onto the concrete path. He grimaced as he stood in front of the casino he had been calling home in the days immediately preceding his barbaric extraction from a civilized luncheon of imported lobster bisque and French champagne. He had been scheduled on a late afternoon flight back to Vancouver, and his bags were undoubtedly still packed, waiting beside the frosted glass doors of the presidential suite he had occupied. It would be pointless to retrieve them – his reason for returning to the city now a distant memory.

Jeffrey Coppell, underworld crime lord, and Mitch's boss, had been shot in the head four days earlier. He hadn't known, of course. At least not until the Jersey cops had hauled him in as a suspect in the murder. That they would consider him a suspect was laughable – he was perhaps the one person on the planet who *wanted* Coppell alive. Leaning down, he tucked a hundred-dollar bill in the pocket of the inert form leaning against the taxi stand outside the hotel. Raising a gloved palm, he flagged down the blue city cab that was nearest him. He wasn't worried about his livelihood – he knew job offers would be pouring in soon. That wasn't the problem. The problem was deciding which family to join and then, once inside, he could bring them down to their knees.

Miles across town, a shot rang out in the night air. Jimmie Vinetti gazed blankly ahead as he watched his right-hand man stumble forward and fall to his knees. He made a feeble attempt to raise himself, his fingers wrenching tightly around the tails of Jimmie's tuxedo jacket as he knelt in near prayer, pleading for his life.

"Jimmie, I did everything for you. I loved for you and killed for you," the man gasped through pain-streaked breaths. "I gave my best to you."

Jimmie moved away, leaving the man to slump onto the warehouse floor but not before a moment of weakness and regret flashed across his face. Blurred memories, near photograph stills, of the last three years with the man now lying at his feet fired through his mind at a dizzying pace: the moment they met at a party in Brooklyn's east side; the time they got arrested in Philly when their customs agent turned fed; the month prior when Jimmie had stood as best man while he married his childhood sweetheart; the crushing heartbreak twelve hours earlier when he learned from that same sweetheart that the IOC had offered a plea under the RICO act and they had both accepted without hesitation...or remorse.

Fury burned within him again, and he stepped back toward the begging man, finding comfort in the blood trickling down to the floor and pooling into the concrete. A moment was all he had for sentiment. His business didn't allow heartfelt commentaries to fallen angels of *la familia*. The coldness back, Jimmie fired another round, wiped the gun clean, and then tossed it to the ground, the metal echoing through the warehouse with the startling jolt of a train veering off its steel track.

"Keep your best," Jimmie hissed. "It's not good enough."

Amor regge senza legge

CHAPTER ONE

Ashli Vinetti glanced up from the glass-plated desk in her New York office, dark brown eyes narrowing at the interruption. Her long manicured fingernails, polished to the perfect scarlet red, tapped on the keyboard in front of her. "What? Don't I look busy here?"

"You have a visitor, Ms. Vinetti."

"I told you. I'm working on a four-million-dollar deal here. Don't bother me." She turned her attention back to the computer screen, trying to remember the secretary's name so she could fire her at the next staff meeting. Perhaps a public reprimand would keep any other moronic blonde bimbo hired by her brother's in check.

"Ashli Vinetti?"

The voice, unknown but somehow familiar, caused her to turn from the computer in an instant. The man, pitch-black hair down to his collar with a chest as wide as her door frame, set her nerves on end. Someone had allowed a stranger admittance to the executive floor - uninvited. She reached her hand out to press the alarm but in the moment it took her to raise her hand, he was across the room and had it pressed to his lips in respectful greeting. She hesitated and her shock seemed to provide him the second of opening he desired.

"I believe I owe you a debt," his voice was silky, his piercing ice blue eyes never wavering from hers as bodyguards she hadn't yet summoned entered the room with guns drawn. He dropped her hand with no urgency, his unfettered confidence causing a smile to spread across her face as recognition settled in. He was everything she had been told he was.

She waved the guards away, knowing their presence was pointless in his company. If all things said were true, he could take them all down without even changing his position. "Debts to be paid I have time for. Please sit down."

Mitch nodded and dropped into the chair opposite her. His eyes followed her moves unabashed, watching as she slipped from behind the desk and moved to lean against it. Her slender legs crossed at the ankles, her high heels tipping toward him with practiced ease. Although she seemed relaxed, he knew better than to underestimate her.

"And just how are you indebted to us?"

"You posted bail for me yesterday. In Atlantic City."

The lack of surprise told him more than any response. Her bailing him out had been purposeful. She had sought him out for some particular reason that he could not even guess at. Although Vinetti was one of the largest outfits on the east coast and he'd run across their names several times over the years, he'd never had any direct dealings with them. He had purposefully stayed clear of the Vinettis over the years. Not out of fear, although Jimmie was known for disposing of his closest allies with little notice, but out of self-preservation. It was lucky for the IOC that preservation of self was no longer one of his priorities.

"You're Mitchell Kerlin," she nodded, her eyes now moving over him with unhidden curiosity. She extended her hand in a more agreeable introduction. "Ashli Vinetti. We've never had the pleasure, but I'm told we run in familiar circles."

"Do we?" He gave her a lopsided grin. "I do believe I'd remember seeing you."

"Would you indeed?" she asked, watching as he stood up and begin moving about her office as if he owned it.

"Are you needing my assistance with something? Or was this just a friendly gesture?" He picked up a crystal vase perched on one shelf. He toyed with it a moment and when she didn't respond; he turned an expectant gaze her direction.

"A friendly gesture," she murmured, turning away from his intense gaze. He unnerved her – there was no doubt. Power seemed to radiate from him even more so than her brother. She'd never anticipated such a thing was possible from him, of all people. She cleared her throat, moving to take the vase from him and place it back where it belonged. "Vinetti Industries tries to take care of persecuted club members. Considering the recent emotional turmoil, you've been through in losing your employer, we felt-"

He chuckled. "Persecuted?"

"You were unfairly detained in the death of Jeffrey Coppell," she hesitated. "Or am I mistaken?"

"No," he nodded without breaking her gaze, "you are not mistaken."

"I thought perhaps you might spend some time here with Vinetti Industries until you find a permanent employer."

"I'll take that into consideration. Thank you. I have…"

"People to check with first, of course. And I'm sure you won't mind our doing the same."

"By all means, Ms. Vinetti, background me to your heart's content." Mitch stepped closer to her, his face coming within inches of hers. He dropped his lips to her ear, his closeness causing a blush to rise from somewhere deep within. His voice was quiet when he finally spoke. "Thank you for the gesture."

She nodded, sucking in a steadying breath as he slipped out the door. She already had all the background information she needed. Kerlin was the top operative in the Investigations of Organized Crime Bureau. Her brother didn't know, of course. He couldn't if her plan was to work. It was only by a fluke that she'd learned the information herself. Having slept with a brand new IOC recruit, he'd spun tales of drunken admiration and adolescent idealizations of mentors and veteran officers.

Mitch had been mentioned in passing. His status as a near freelance agent with the Bureau pushed the boundaries of everything legal within the IOC, so her bedmate knew little of Mitch and his operations. But Ashli knew of him. His name had tumbled out of every mafia boss she'd ever met. He'd had connections with *la familia* since birth and that he had, for some unknown reason, changed sides without ever being caught was a puzzling yet phenomenal achievement. This alone let her know he was the one person that could help her succeed at her goal.

She intended to draw him and Jimmie as close together as possible. Then, with blackmail and begging if necessary, she planned to offer Vinetti's private books for a spot in the witness protection program. The IOC wanted Jimmie, which she could provide on a platter, while she wanted freedom. Special Agent Mitchell Vincenzo Kerlin was her last chance to get it. For once in her life, Ashli Vinetti was going to get out of her brother's shadow.

She dropped back into her caramel brown leather chair, twisting her hair between her fingers as her thoughts muddled with the best approach to her end goal. She had no problem sleeping with him if it was necessary but he had an effect on her that she hadn't anticipated. He could get any woman he wanted, she had no doubt of that, and making sure that she was the one he wanted was an obstacle she wasn't prepared for. She had never lacked in men – her last name alone caused power hungry men to flock to her.

But Mitch wasn't someone looking for a job. She had come to him, and he recognized that. She chafed, wondering if she had made a mistake by bailing him out and then thought better of it. It was the right move it just meant she would have to work harder to be inaccessible to him. He enjoyed a challenge...she could see that from the moment he strode past her guards and into the inner offices. She checked her reflection in the computer screen's monitor, debating whether or not it was time to get her hair cut. Or highlighted at least.

"New boyfriend?"

Ashli didn't bother to turn around at the voice, knowing he would notice the flush to her cheeks. She stopped fiddling with her hair and turned her attention back to the computer screen.

"No. What do you want, Jimmie?"

"Heard you had a visitor," he answered, dropping down into the chair Mitch had vacated. "I haven't seen you so edgy since we dumped that fed you were bedding in the ocean."

Her eyes narrowed, her voice a low growl. "Do you need something?"

He smiled. "I just want you happy, Ashli. When was the last time you were happy? Do you even remember?"

"It was not a new boyfriend," she relented. "If you must know, Mitch Kerlin dropped by for a visit."

"Kerlin?" Jimmie perked up. "What the fuck does Coppell want now?"

"Coppell was shot in the head last week. Where have you been?" she admonished. "Kerlin got arrested in Atlantic City for the murder. I bailed him out."

"Friendly of you." His voice dropped several notches. "Did he do it?"

"Of course not," she laughed and sent him a self-satisfied smile. "Loyalty is only absent in *this* organization."

She had hit a nerve and knew it. Jimmie had spent the last few weeks talking nonsense of loyalty and honor. She knew better – the people working for them were only loyal as long as the bonus checks kept coming in. It mattered little to her, but she didn't lead the life Jimmie did. In his one commendable action as a big brother, he had kept her far removed from the darker side of their business. She told him when she had a problem and by the next day, he had it handled. Some small part of her appreciated his gesture, but it had long since been buried with the knowledge that she was the cause of hundreds of deaths over the years.

But Jimmie wanted to believe. He wanted people loyal to him and him alone. He desperately desired a family that no longer existed solely in his imagination. Though he rarely feared for his own safety, she knew it plagued him never to have someone that he could be honest with. His unwillingness to share things with her had caused this rift, but he refused to revert to different behavior. It was his burden to bear, he told her each time she tried to get him to open up, and he would bear it alone. That was what she hoped to change.

"Please remind me, why does Vinetti Industries care about this?"

"Because Coppell left no heirs," Ashli spat, her temper beginning to rise as he questioned her decision. "And the last time I checked, neither one of us knows anybody in Canada."

"The last time *I* checked, there's nobody in Canada I care to know," he retorted, standing up and moving to fix himself a glass of orange juice from the bar. He drank it in silence, amused to see her eyes flashing at him. She hated it when he involved himself on her side of the business dealings. But considering that everything after the initial contact was going to end up his responsibility, he'd forewent placating her years before. He wanted to know what he was getting into before it blew up in his face. His facial features must have changed because her anger was now gone, replaced with what he could only imagine was sympathy.

"What?" he surveyed his suit, checking to make sure he hadn't put it on backward in his haste this morning. "You not like my tie or something?"

"We seem to be short an employee this morning. You wouldn't know anything about that, would you?" she asked, her voice that tender, worried tone that annoyed the hell out of him.

"Screw Alizondo. Probably drank too much and he and that new bride of his took off to Cozumel."

Ashli moved to his side, her fingers resting on his arm. "Are you alright?"

Jimmie straightened his shirt, tucking it tighter into his waistband and offered her a smile. "Dinner tomorrow night? You can introduce me to that new boyfriend of yours."

She didn't bother to correct him, knowing it would just be cause for more ribbing in the future. "I'll see what I can arrange."

He nodded, heading for the door but then hesitated, turning to her with a more serious gaze. "Hey, do me a favor, will you? Don't shake off the bodyguards for the next few days, okay?"

That's why the guards had run in following Mitch's appearance and why Jimmie had hurried to her office this morning when he'd been told she had an uninvited guest – they were in danger. As hard as she tried, she couldn't keep the small shake out of her voice as she spoke. "Are we expecting problems?"

"Nothing we can't handle. We just haven't been able to locate Alex's brother." He offered her a smile gleaming with confidence. "Nothing for you to concern yourself with. I'd just prefer you not go out alone."

"He's in mourning, Jimmie."

"Women mourn," he returned easily, "Men seek revenge."

CHAPTER TWO

M y wayward boy returns," a quiet voice echoed down the empty hallway, its owner hidden deep within the shadows of the abandoned apartment building. "Just where the hell have you been for the last four days?"

"You should know. Don't your superiors at the IOC tell you anything useful?" Mitch countered, ignoring the inch-thick dust and sinking onto a dilapidated desk. "I've been in the Atlantic City jail, Mike."

"You got pinched for Coppell's murder, didn't you?" he laughed. "I heard on the radio that someone had been picked up. Never thought it would be you."

"Well, thanks for bailing me out," he grumbled.

Mike's eyes narrowed, and he paced around Mitch. "How *did* you get out?"

"Ashli Vinetti did the honors. I'd hate to see what it cost her, too. She had to have bribed somebody big to get me out before the arraignment."

"They wouldn't have charged you," Mike admonished. "What does she want with you?"

Mitch grinned, straightening his collar for effect. "My good looks?"

Frowning, Mike sank down beside him. Pulling out a notebook and pen, he waited patiently for Mitch to answer. When he didn't, Mike dropped the pad onto the table. "Come on, Mitch, tell me something here. What are you going to do? Retire since Coppell bit the big one?"

"Excellent suggestion. Unfortunately, everyone seems to have other ideas. Including you, your bosses up at the IOC and *la familia*." Mitch moved away from him, sliding off his coat and tossing it onto the desk. He ran a hand through his hair, letting out an exhausted sigh. As much as he disliked the bureaucracy of the IOC, it was nice to be able to let his calm, collected facade slide for a while. If it wasn't for the constant questioning of his actions, he could almost feel like a regular guy when he met with his field supervisor.

"Where were you before you got arrested? We'd been searching for you for days."

"With friends," he returned dismissively, letting him know that he had no intention of answering.

"We thought you'd gotten knocked off with Coppell," Mike argued. "You can't just disappear like that. Keeps me up at night."

"I'm fine, Mike, but thanks for worrying." He offered him a brief smile then moved away, kicking trash distractedly from one area of the room to another. He flicked the light switches, not expecting them to work but trying to do something to keep his hands busy. The last thing he needed was having his boss see the tremble in his hands from the lack of sleep and copious amounts of alcohol he'd consumed since being released from jail. Another lecture on morality and the sins of the mafia would surely follow, and he didn't think he could sit through that without slugging Mike.

"Want to tell me about Coppell?" he asked, surveying Mitch worriedly. He knew Mitch had hated Coppell. Unlike some of his recruits who often ended up friends with the guys they brought down, Mitch had held nothing but absolute contempt for Coppell and all of his men. He knew Mitch didn't kill him or even want him dead for that matter, but nearly three years of undercover work had just been obliterated when someone blasted Coppell in the back of the head with a 12 gauge. If he wasn't upset, he damn sure at least had a right to be pissed.

"Rather not," Mitch responded.

"Then let me tell you about it." Reaching into his overcoat, Mike pulled out an oversized folded envelope and passed it Mitch's direction. "Shot in the head at close range. The weapon was a 12 gauge Benelli found at the scene."

"Registered?"

"No. But the serial number matches the one you reported when you cataloged his weapons on premises six months after you started working for him."

"Montefeltro?"

"Yeah."

"It was a 20th anniversary present from his wife," Mitch provided.

"No signs of a struggle and all guards were in the other part of the house."

"What about Garrison?" Mitch asked, flipping through the photos.

"The guard that always stayed with you and Coppell? He was asleep in his room."

"You drug test him?"

"No. Why would we?"

"I wasn't there. If I'm not there, Garrison wouldn't leave Jeffrey unguarded. The guy would never have just gone to bed."

"Everyone has to sleep."

"We don't get a nice eight hours like you, Mike," Mitch grumbled. "He was drugged. I'll put money on it."

"So, you out of the country, second hand drugged and the house is wide open for an attack."

"That house is never wide open. I turned it into a fortress."

"Yeah, about that. You know the police couldn't even get through your "fortress" to respond to the call? That was a bitch to try and explain."

"Proving my point. The guards would've only gone away if Coppell sent them away."

"You're saying Coppell knew the murderer and sent the guards away?" Mike nodded. "It makes sense. Coppell has a meeting he doesn't want anyone- even you- privy to. Something goes wrong, and his private meeting turns into a bloodbath."

Mitch nodded then paused in his review of the file. "This says two people were noted at the scene."

"A man's footprint in Coppell's blood. No lead on the tread just that it was a male. Trace evidence of a female, not enough for DNA matching. It could've been from hours before the murder even. Likely one of his whores."

"He didn't have whores," Mitch cut him off. "He was married."

"That doesn't mean-"

"You automatically assume because he's a mafioso that he's out bedding someone new every night, don't you?" Mitch growled. "I was with him for over three years. Yeah, he was a cutthroat businessman with a dozen murders to his credit, but he was a loyal husband and a damn good father, Mike. Stop with the bureaucratic profiling shit, all right?"

Mike held his hands up. "Okay, so who then?"

"Hundreds of possibilities. He has five sisters, two teen daughters and their friends, dozens of female employees with access to his house. Hell, it could be from one of the whores I brought there. Take that back to your profilers, why don't you?"

"Mitch, come on," Mike tried. "You are getting emotional over-"

Mitch yanked one of the photos out of the file and held it up. The gruesome shot was enough to make Mike recoil even though he'd seen it a dozen times already.

"He died on my watch, Mike. In his pajamas, in his own house where I've spent hours drinking whiskey and shooting the shit with him until dawn. It happened because I wasn't there to prevent it so don't patronize me over how I should be emotionally detached from this because he was a criminal. He didn't deserve this. No one does."

"Agreed, but-"

Mitch waved him off, knowing his patience had met its end. "Time to move on."

"You sure you're ready for that?"

Mitch laughed. It wasn't as if the IOC ever cared whether he was ready or not. He learned long ago that determining his own schedule was the only way to survive within the IOC. If he didn't have such deep-seated connections to the mob, they would have sent him packing years ago for his flagrant disregard for their rules. Now he only chose the assignments he wanted to...and those were getting fewer and fewer as the years went on. "When are you going to ever get another opportunity like Ashli Vinetti knocking on your door, Mike?"

His answer was almost inaudible.... but just almost. "When indeed?"

Mitch whirled on him. "What does that mean? What aren't you telling me?"

"It's nothing, Mitch. If you want Vinetti, I know better than to argue with you over something like that."

"Mike-" Mitch was over him now, his tall, muscular frame easily dwarfing his superior. He put his hands in his pockets, hoping not to look quite as menacing as he knew he probably was. It wasn't intentional – he just hadn't been able to knock the edge off since hearing the gruesome details of Coppell's death...and knowing it could have easily been prevented. He offered a half smile, but Mike was already backing away from him. "Look-"

"Just forget it," he raised his hands, palms facing forward. "Did you know James Vinetti killed a guy the other night? He'd been with him for years."

"I'd imagine Vinetti's killed lots of guys, Mike."

"This one had copped a plea with us. He and his girlfriend have been missing for days now. They were about to be relocated when some of Jimmie's men nabbed them."

Mitch shrugged, cataloging the information in his brain but then dismissing it. "That's what they get for copping a fucking plea and not high-tailing it out of town. Did they expect Jimmie just to sit back and wait for the subpoenas to start rolling in?"

"He's a loose cannon," Mike grumbled and tossed Mitch his coat, "and you have one screwed up way of looking at things."

"I look at things in whatever manner keeps me alive, Mike. Nothing more sadistic than that."

CHAPTER THREE

Soft red lights flickered overhead, blanketing the bar area of Russo's restaurant in a cloudy haze perfect for imbibing in an enormous amount of alcohol. Undoubtedly, that was what the owner Vitale Russo had counted on when he planned the upscale establishment. He'd even thought to lay an iridescent marble floor to enhance the bar's dreamy feel. To Mitch, it seemed more like a scene out of bad sleaze flick.

"Hey, Vitale, you ever think of springing for some decent lighting in this place?" he asked, sinking down at the corner of the bar.

"Mr. Kerlin, welcome. It's good to have you back in the States." Vitale dropped his apron and shook Mitch's hand, grinning widely.

"It's good to be back. I spent much more time up north, and I'd lose my citizenship, I think. Damned desolate place that Canada."

"What can I get for you tonight? Just visiting the neighborhood?"

Mitch raised an eyebrow... there was no way Vitale didn't know that he and the Vinettis were having dinner at his place. Vitale prided himself on knowing everything worth knowing that happened in a ten block radius. "Give me a whiskey sour, would you?"

"Sure," he nodded and started pouring the drink before dropping his voice. "So you and Vinetti, hm?"

"It's just dinner, Vitale," he laughed. "You're as bad as the ladies down at the corner grocery, you know it?"

"Pays to be informed around here, Mr. Kerlin. You know that."

"Alright, I'll bite," Mitch chuckled and traded the glass Vitale offered for a fifty-dollar bill. "What's newsworthy these days?"

"These days?" he leaned over the bar, closer to Mitch. "Vinetti, of course. He's taken over the whole area since Terenari moved out. With you, everyone's guessing he's aiming for Vancouver as well."

"Ambitious guy," Mitch commented thoughtfully. "But Terenari's been gone since I was a teenager. It's about time somebody tried to start getting this place organized again."

He eyed Vitale curiously, wondering exactly what part of Vinetti's dealings had already been made public knowledge. "Heard he offed someone a couple of days ago."

Vitale nodded, crossing himself before replying. "Alex, Alizondo, Masseria. Feel bad for the kid. He had a brand new wife and a child on the way. But," he shrugged, "you mess with the feds and you are always gonna get what's coming to you."

Mitch nodded and pushed his glass out for a refill. His eyes swept over the restaurant, noting a dozen or so unfamiliar faces sitting along the walls of the restaurant proper. He nodded toward them. "You having problems down here or something?"

"Vinetti's men," he murmured. "They're everywhere these days. Jimmie doesn't seem too worried, but he watches out for that sister of his like nothing I've ever seen."

"Commendable action."

Vitale laughed. "Damned irritating woman. Great business mind but she's just a bit forward for the neighborhood women, you know what I mean? Personally, I think Jimmie's just waiting to strangle her himself. The two of them fight like cats and dogs."

"You ever met a brother and sister who didn't?" Mitch asked laughing as the whiskey finally started to numb his practiced nonchalance.

Vitale laughed but dropped his head and moved away from Mitch's side. He was scrubbing the already sparkling bar as if his life suddenly depended on it. He was intent on the same spot, his ferocious scouring causing squeaky vibrations to drift down the bar. Mitch caught him glancing at him from beneath shielded eyes, his eyes a mixture of apprehension and confusion. When he opened his mouth and closed it again for the third time, Mitch could stand it no longer and chuckled out loud.

"What, Vitale?"

"Nothing."

"Vitale, you keep a secret about as well as the ladies in the beauty parlor. Come on, what gives?"

He glanced around uneasily. Seeing no one, he moved around the bar to sit on a stool beside Mitch. "You know I like you, Mitch," he said softly as if afraid others might overhear them. "I've known you since we was kids. But you got a lot of people around here on edge right now."

"How's that?"

"Coppell takes a bullet; you hold up with Markesi over in Atlantic, and now you're meeting with the Vinettis here in New York? Come on, you know Markesi and the Vinettis have got tons of bad blood between them." He fell quiet as if expecting Mitch to explain his actions.

"No, Vitale, I didn't know that." Mitch frowned then took a sip of his drink. "So much for a relaxing plate of calamari, huh?"

"Vinetti's not going to cause you problems. Hell, he's probably as curious as everyone else as to why you're back in the States, to begin with."

Mitch grinned and stepped away from the bar. "That is one of those things you'll just have to keep guessing at, Vitale. Give my best to your mother, will you?"

Mitch gave him a hug before turning towards the main doorway. Ashli and Jimmie hadn't arrived yet, but Mitch's practiced eye had seen the men in the room starting to shuffle their positions, most of them now standing along the wall rather than the relaxed seated position they had held previously. Only the appearance of their boss would have caused them to move. He made it to the door just as Ashli stepped in, her diminutive frame silhouetted in a red sequined dress that reached the floor. Even for Russo's, she was overdressed. No wonder the women in the neighborhood didn't like her – there wasn't a woman around that Ashli wouldn't overshadow. She stepped back when she saw him, caught off guard by his presence.

"Mr. Kerlin-"

"Mitch," he corrected, kissing her hand. "It's nice to see you again. Vitale already has a table waiting for us."

She nodded behind her where two men were talking quietly on the steps. "My brother Jimmie is joining us; I hope you don't mind."

"Certainly," Mitch smiled as if this was suddenly news to him. "The remainder of the restaurant seems to be your employees as well."

She frowned, but it was only a moment before it dissolved into a winning smile. "Are they? We have so many employees."

"Dangerous, that."

"What's dangerous?" Jimmie's curt voice cut in as he shuffled through the door to stand between the two.

"Not knowing who your employees are," Mitch offered.

"I keep telling her that," Jimmie sent him a crooked grin. "Jimmie Vinetti."

"Mitch Kerlin. Pleasure to meet you."

"Hey, Vitale!" Jimmie yelled without bothering to shake Mitch's hand. "Do us right here. Give us some drinks, will ya?"

"Of course, Mr. Vinetti. Marco here will show you to your table."

Mitch glanced to Vitale who seemed unnerved by Jimmie's brusque orders. He cast a sideways glance to Mitch, who waved him off with a silent smile. Even Ashli seemed tense and, as they walked into the main dining room, the atmosphere seemed to drape over the entire Vinetti group before they even sat down. Mitch considered, weighed his options, and finally decided the best approach was probably just to get the idiotic questions out of the way, to begin with.

"Mr. Vinetti-"

"Jimmie," he corrected without even glancing Mitch's direction.

"Jimmie, while I appreciate the dinner invitation," he offered a sideways smile to Ashli, but she was gazing at the wall, paying them no mind, "if I'm liable to get my head blown off for just having dinner with you I'd appreciate some advance notice."

Jimmie's gray eyes cut toward him, glinting dangerously. He stared at Mitch in unnerving silence and not until after the drinks had been served did he bother to respond.

"We have strengthened security for my sister's benefit. It's only a temporary measure. If it bothers you-"

He held a hand up. "Not at all. I just prefer to know what's headed my way."

Jimmie nodded and leaned back in his chair, nudging Ashli in the side to get her attention. "You were right. He's a good looking kid. He wears black tie well."

"Oh, just shut up, Jimmie," Ashli's voice burned with fury, causing Mitch to glance her way. She offered him a smile. "Jimmie is the world's worst brother. He insists on trying to embarrass me every chance he gets as if we were still fifteen."

"He seems to take your safety seriously enough," he countered and noticed her grimace.

"So, Mitch, tell me about yourself. What do you do?"

"I'm currently between positions," he replied, grabbing a menu and pointing to what he wanted before Vitale could disappear again.

"You do dress exceptionally well for the unemployed," Ashli laughed. "Perhaps you could give Jimmie some pointers."

Sending a scathing look her direction, Jimmie sat higher in his seat. "Where did you work?"

"Coppell Management."

"Jeffrey Coppell," Ashli provided as if they hadn't already had this conversation.

"Thank you for that timely clarification," he spat, his anger flaring. "Why don't you go fix your face or something?" He didn't wait for an answer or pay her any attention as she stormed off to the restroom. "What did you do?"

"Security."

Jimmie's face lit into a lopsided smile. "Coppell's dead."

"Not on my watch," he returned. His eyes were still on the path Ashli had taken, noting that none of the guards seemed intent on following her. They seemed much more absorbed in trying to overhear he and Jimmie than anything. "Jimmie-"

"Yeah?" he looked up from the menu he was perusing.

"I'm not one to tell you how to run your business, but..."

"But?" Jimmie waved away the waiter and dropped the menu to the table.

He nodded toward the door where Ashli had disappeared. "Ashli just-"

At the mention of his sister's name, Jimmie's face blanched. He nodded minutely then waved to one of the guards to go after her. He didn't seem to breathe until he saw them return, Ashli easing past the dining room and heading to the bar.

"You have sisters, Mitch?"

"Not by blood."

"Lucky you. Mine is determined to be the Rosie Parks of the mafia," he grumbled, swallowing his drink in one gulp. "She doesn't always agree with added protection. Makes her quite the bitch actually."

He shrugged. "Please don't take this for our normal behavior. We just have-"

"A brother intent on revenge coming after you?" he asked, his gaze steady on Jimmie. He leaned away from the table under the questioning glare. "Security, remember? It's my job to know," he shrugged.

Rather than the anger he anticipated, Jimmie was rocking with laughter. "Don't you just hate it when people gossip about you? Fucked up antiquated life when other people know your business more than your own family does, isn't it?"

Mitch didn't respond but sipped his glass of merlot, his eyes intent on the flickering candles in the middle of the table, his mind wondering if perhaps Mike hadn't been right. Vinetti, rumored to be one of the most organized, well-structured outfits on the east coast, seemed to be coming apart at the seams. It wasn't really what he heard – the internal fighting between the two Vinettis, or the federal intervention, or the inept security detail – that gave him the most pause.

Instead, it was the seclusion of the whole evening that made the hairs on the back of his neck rise. Not a single customer had entered Russo's since Jimmie's arrival. It was as if the entire neighborhood knew the Vinettis were doing business here and had purposefully kept miles away from the restaurant.

Mitch knew better than to think it was out of respect. People were afraid of the Vinettis. While fear was something he was accustomed to seeing on the streets when big named mafioso were involved, the absence of any activity near Jimmie was unnerving. Publicity, even the bad kind, helped keep Mitch safe. It was in seclusion that he could easily disappear and not even be missed for a week or more.

But seclusion held another, more immediate concern for Mitch: if Jimmie was locking the family away for safety, it meant he wasn't doing the intricate deals he was so famous for. Without deals being made, infiltrating the Vinetti organization was a pointless affair. He'd just wasted nearly four years with Coppell – he had no desire to flitter away more time on something that wouldn't lead to a successful collar.

And yet, Jimmie Vinetti intrigued him. Markesi rarely made enemies and he was curious to learn the history of the two. Vinetti seemed to be in strong control of his business, but he couldn't even keep his own sister in check. It was an oddly captivating drama that Mitch hated to admit he was finding increasingly entertaining.

His eyes drifted to Jimmie who was whispering to one of his guards animatedly. His anger amused Mitch and caused him to chuckle out loud. Jimmie's gaze shot to him as if he'd called his name.

"No offense," Mitch nodded toward the guard, "but your security lacks something to be desired."

The guard didn't look offended but, instead, nodded in silent agreement before backing away from the table. He took position a few steps away, his eyes moving to stare into the distance pretending he was no longer paying them any attention.

Jimmie's eyes focused on him, his body leaning nearly across the table, and Mitch could feel his temper flaring. "Is that why my sister came to you? She feels our security is lacking?"

"I haven't a clue why your sister came to me," he replied steadily, "I'm just observant enough to know that you are putting her life and your own in danger if this is the way you conduct your daily business."

"You don't hold back anything, do you?"

"Should I?"

"Maybe," Jimmie smiled, "maybe not. Honesty can be a welcomed trait."

"Or a deadly sin," he responded, smiling genuinely this time. It was a line from his childhood, something that Markesi spouted on a regular basis to anyone willing to listen to his late night rambles of honor and loyalty. "It's a fine line."

"You know Markesi."

It wasn't a question, merely an observation, and Mitch could detect no underlying frustration at the mention of Markesi. Perhaps the street was wrong in its assessment of the Vinetti-Markesi feud. He tilted his head toward the corner where Vitale was standing quietly with a waiter, his hands twisting the edges of his apron in unease. "Vitale's waiting for us to shoot each other or call for the food."

"Fool's probably worried about his damn hardwoods getting stained," Jimmie laughed but raised his hand to Vitale. He bellowed loudly, his deep voice echoing in the nearly empty restaurant. "Ashli, *vieni sorellina!* The piccata is getting cold." He winked Mitch's direction. "Nothing worse than cold veal."

CHAPTER FOUR

"Walk with me?"

Mitch nodded and fell into step beside Jimmie. Several paces ahead, Ashli had her arms entwined with the bodyguards. She was leaning from one to the other, whispering in each of their ears. All three were laughing softly.

"She does that to set me off," Jimmie explained.

"Your men or men in general?"

"I doubt she notices the difference."

"But you do."

"Of course. Why haven't we met?"

Mitch tightened his coat, stalling. That was the question, wasn't it? The Vinettis were the one family he purposefully steered clear of...but explaining why wasn't something he was prepared to share. "I could give you a line of shit that's believable."

"Or?"

"Or I could just tell you that your family is much more visible than I ever care to be."

Jimmie stopped, considered for a moment, and then kept walking. "You play it straight. I like that."

"It's a luxury most people don't have."

"So you don't need a job?"

"Need?" Mitch shook his head. "No, I don't need a job. I like to stay busy, but it's not financially motivated."

"That allows you a lot of flexibility in choice then," Jimmie suggested. "And an exorbitant fee, I'd imagine."

Mitch laughed. "Are we negotiating already?"

"My time is pretty limited these days. I tend to get to the point."

"Okay then." He stopped mid-stride. When Jimmie followed suit and turned to face him, Mitch's eyes darkened. "Your security is in shambles. I walked into your sister's office and could've strangled her before a single guard ever arrived. Your detail is more concerned with gossip about your business dealings than making certain a place is secure. You have hundreds of employees, and you don't know the history or background of any of them, even the ones closest to you. Your sister's fascination with angering you is taking the guards attention away from, for example, the three feds that have been following us since we left the restaurant. Now, whether I help you fix that, or someone else does it, for the safety of yourself, your sister and your future business, you need to get it under control."

Rather than the anger or at least tension he expected, Jimmie merely nodded. "That was a brutal assessment. But the most honest thing I've heard out of anyone's mouth in a decade. Your last employer ended up dead."

Mitch winced before he could contain it. "Yes."

"What's to say I don't end up the same?"

"I can't guarantee your life, Jimmie, and if that's what you are looking for, then you've come to the wrong place. No one can guarantee something like that. Especially not in the life you've chosen to lead."

"What happened with Coppell?"

"I wasn't there, so I don't know. I do know there was no way anyone could get into that house if he didn't want them in."

"He knew the killer then? And just let them in?"

"I have no doubt," Mitch nodded. "Your turn. Why did you kill Masseria? And don't tell me it's because he copped a plea."

"That's not enough?"

"To off someone? Sure. To personally shoot him in the head and then dispose of his pregnant wife? I think not."

"What makes you think that's what happened?"

"Because your crew can't be trusted."

Jimmie nodded, moving several paces away to lean against the railing. His voice was soft, requiring Mitch to move closer in order to hear.

"They were going to kill Ashli. Ashli for their freedom. Had the wife take Ashli out for a day of shopping or something in LA. Ashli had no idea she was in danger. If I didn't agree, she never would have made it home. He'd been with me for three years. Three years and the sonofabitch was threatening my baby sister."

Mitch could feel the anger rising from Jimmie, and he couldn't blame him. Copping a plea was business but bringing his sister into the deal? That went against every rule of *la familia* he'd ever known. "Who all knows?"

"You." Jimmie glanced his direction then shook his head. "And have no doubt I'll-"

Mitch put a hand up to stop him. "Threatening me isn't necessary. Financial freedom also means my allegiance is my own. Spreading your secrets through *la familia* would offer me no benefit. And, for the record? I would've done the same thing."

CHAPTER FIVE

H ere."
Mitch accepted the bottle of beer gratefully, popping it open and washing down a mouthful of pizza. He glanced at the label - Birra del Sole, bottled only in Sicily and not available for export. "How'd you get the Birra past customs? I thought your guy got pinched last month."

Sonny chuckled as he flipped through the television channels. "Had another guy in within 48 hours. I've got a business to keep stocked, remember?"

Mitch raised his eyes to the television as it settled on CNN, watching but not comprehending the news ticker is running along the bottom of the screen. Flashes of war-torn areas and even a picture of Coppell moved across the screen. A picture of him, a mug shot, stilled on the screen, his silk tie glowing under the harsh flash from the precinct's cheap camera. Had it really been a week since he got released? Briefly, he wondered if the world had ended while he was otherwise engaged but then thought better of it. He'd rather just not know. Gray pause lines wrinkled across his image, causing him to take another swig of his beer.

"Not bad. Most guys get yanked out of bed and look like death in their mug shot. You dress for the occasion."

"Fuck you, Sonny. Is that just now airing?"

"It's been on the local news most of the week. Just hit international last night when there was a problem getting his body through customs for burial."

Mitch sighed. So that's why Coppell's sister had been calling him all night. He'd ignored her calls. Knowing the cause, he felt a tad guilty. "They get it sorted?"

"Yeah, I think so. Had to have the remains cremated, I think. You talked to Palmese?"

"Not since I got released, no."

"He doesn't know you're meeting with Vinetti?"

He glanced at the screen, his image still unmoving. Unwilling to hear the lecture he knew who follow about not keeping Gino Palmese in the loop, he shook his head but quickly changed the subject.

"Do you know who killed him?"

"Coppell?" Sonny shrugged. "A dozen people are claiming it. He wasn't known for making friends. But none I'd believe have the balls to do it. Everyone assumed they'd hit you at the same time. I've had my men just start spreading the word you're alive. Got damn tired of playing your answering service."

"You the one who told Ashli I'd hit the lock up?"

"Not me. Hell, you were out before I knew they'd picked you up," he chuckled and clicked off the television. "I give you run of the casino and take a quick weekend trip to Vegas. Next thing I know I come back to hear you've been arrested, bailed out and are in bed with the Vinettis." He shrugged. "Probably one of Ashli's many bedmates told her the news."

"Bedmates?"

Sonny's eyes narrowed. "You really have secluded yourself, haven't you? Do you have any clue what's going on with east coast anymore?"

"Keeping tabs on Ashli Vinetti has never been a priority."

"Well, you're the only one not paying attention. The entire family is watching her like a hawk. It seems she has a proclivity for badges."

Mitch's ears perked up. "You're kidding."

"Bedding feds...her latest indulgence. She goes through them faster than Jimmie can keep up."

Mitch hid his frown. Why wouldn't Mike have told him that? Wasn't that something that even the IOC would consider important information? "What's Jimmie doing about it?"

"He offed a few that she was idiotic enough to bring on Vinetti property. Since then she keeps her conjugal visits limited to distant cities."

"And he just lets her have her fun?"

"Jimmie always has a plan, kid. Don't underestimate him. But I think he learned quickly that he couldn't off every fed she took to bed."

"I can't believe the families are so easily persuaded to leave her be," Mitch shook his head. "Can't she find someone else more willing than a badge?"

"What do you think you're around for?"

Mitch laughed. "She's out of my league, buddy, and I'll be the first to admit it."

"So is this a long term gig or what?"

"I haven't even decided to work with them. They're a bit disorganized for my tastes. But, no. They just need a security revamp, I think."

"Are you kidding? Vinetti's the most organized guy on the east coast. He's managed to get his hands in every kitty. His legitimate businesses alone put us all to shame."

He grinned. "Do I detect some jealousy there, Sonny?"

"Hell yeah. Last year we were trying to get Senate approval on an insurance deal worth billions. We had everything perfect and then, at the last minute, the bill got tabled. The next day a new bill appears. Identical to ours but naming Diamond Insurance as the provider for government employees. It passed in less than twenty minutes."

Mitch chuckled at the audacity of it all. "Vinetti owns Diamond Insurance?" he guessed.

"And apparently over half the trade commission," Sonny fumed. "Pulled the carpet out from four families all with one phone call."

"Four?" Mitch raised an eyebrow. "You all were trying to edge out Vinetti?"

"Hell, yes. He's got enough already."

Sonny grimaced as Mitch fell into deep laughter. "What's so damn funny?"

"I would've done the same thing."

"You would've taken food out of our mouths-"

"Christ, you're not starving, Sonny. You just wanted to be king of the castle. Vinetti saw it and put you back in your place. Hell, how much would anyone respect him if he'd let you get away with it?"

"He aims too high," Sonny grumbled.

"He aims for Sicily, then? To head the commission?"

"Gino keeps him at arm's length. But, yeah, if Palmese ever retires Jimmie probably wants that too."

"As do many," Mitch sighed and leaned back into the cushions. "So are you going to keep trying to undermine him if I go to work there?"

"Of course," he chuckled. "Nothing like a challenge to keep things lively."

"Cat and mouse," he murmured. "It's a game to everyone."

Sonny pushed a beer across the table to him. "Coppell wasn't a game, Mitch. I would never let my men-"

"I didn't accuse you."

"But I need to say it," he interrupted. "I wouldn't do that to you. To put you through this? I know the guilt you carry around. You've done it since we were kids. Hell, for the last year you've been walking around like you're just waiting for someone to shoot you and end it all. You're tired; I know it. Coppell's murder was detestable. Unforgivable. But, for you, maybe it's the turning point you need to stop acting like a hired hand for everyone else."

"Vinetti's not a turning point. It puts on opposite sides of an impending war."

"A paper war," Sonny shrugged. "We don't solve things with the violence that took Coppell. Honor is the one thing we still manage to hang on to."

Mitch nodded. This was what he'd missed about the east coast- family. Even if it was a feuding one. Of course, it was also the reason he'd spend so many years in Canada- to try and drown the depths of the familial ties he'd been unintentionally building.

"We both know Jeffrey was a raging asshole 90% of the time, but I'm sorry for your loss, Mitchell."

He nodded, sitting up to clink bottles with him.

Sonny grinned. "But I'm glad his death brought you home."

CHAPTER SIX

Mitch knew better than to believe in coincidences. In his world, they just didn't happen. Most coincidences, he planned or orchestrated – that was part of both his government job and his undercover one. A rare aberration was usually the result of something he'd put into play months earlier and had just somehow forgotten. And then there were moments like this one...ones that defied logic or intuition or any other human rationale he could think of.

Sprinting across the narrow passageway between two wooden crates marked "esplosivi" in bright neon orange letters, he gritted his teeth wishing Ashli would kick off her spiked heels and run before one of the gunmen aiming for them realized he could kill them instantly with one shot to the pallets of gunpowder he was trying to maze his way through. Either they didn't read Italian (although he assumed anyone could figure out the meaning of the big mushroom cloud pictured on the nearby barrels) or they weren't really trying to kill them. Or...something more bewildering tugged at the recesses of his mind, a thread of intangible desperation that he couldn't seem to process while being shot at.

He frowned again, liking none of the options jumbling through his brain, and crouched down to check his pistol clip to see how many bullets he had remaining. Grabbing Ashli's arm, he yanked her the rest of the way through the hazardous maze and pulled her into the one defensible corner he'd been able to locate. He pressed back further into the cover of darkness, wincing as razor sharp nails bit through his dress shirt and buried in his flesh.

"We get out of this, and you've got to be declawed," he grumbled.

"Oh, sorry!" Ashli whispered, extracting her nails from his back and sliding her hands down to rest on his waist.

"Under other circumstances-"

"Oh, shut up, will you?" she hissed. "We're going to die here. They'll likely just drop our bodies off the wharf across the street. We'll float up in the spring; our bodies chewed down to nubs by whatever lives in that water."

He chuckled, readjusting his position to get a better look at their adversaries who had concealed themselves among the crates 100 feet away. "You underestimate my abilities. I have no intention of dying here." He squeezed her hand, more to try and get her to loosen her grip than to comfort her. "Or being eaten by fish. Relax."

"I hate you," she mumbled.

"Is that why you invited me out to dinner tonight?" he asked, raising his gun and firing off a shot. He listened closely to hear if it made its target and when the sound of a gun clattering to the floor met his ears, he smiled with satisfaction. Only four more to go. Unless they called for backup.

"No, I liked you then. Now that I'm being shot at? Not so much."

"Hey, they're aiming for you, sugar. I'm just getting stuck in the crossfire. You want me to leave?" He wasn't certain what derogatory term she was now throwing at him under her breath and didn't really care but talking seemed to be keeping her from falling into hysterics. "Nice way to compliment the guy saving your ass," he answered frostily as he fired another perfect shot through the darkness. "You got a cell phone on you?"

"The police?" she queried, dropping to her knees to dig through her purse. She tossed half of the contents on the ground... a snakeskin wallet, cranberry red lipstick, a glittery gold compact, a tiny vial of what he assumed was cocaine, a handful of condoms in violet purple packaging, a fistful of tampons.

Mitch had to look away. This was what happened to the average American when they were looking for their car keys in a mini-mall parking lot. Watching a woman he barely knew digging through her purse, her personal life strewn before him like a photograph, hiding in a pitch black warehouse while a couple of unknown goons tried to whack the shopping queen-these were not the things that happened to him.

"I don't think the Atlantic City police will be coming to *my* assistance any time soon, Ashli," he reminded.

"Oh, right." She hopped up, and he had to forcibly push her back down, so her head didn't get shot off. "Here."

"Stay down," he grumbled and dialed a number quickly, dropping his voice to a mere murmur. "Salvatore, it's Mitch. Do you still have a place down on the east end of the wharf? Can you get your guys down to warehouse seventeen, it's a few blocks away, and I need a way out fast?"

He waited for only a second, laughed so loudly that it caused the men to stop shooting and then sent a crooked smile Ashli's direction. "Yeah, she is turning out to be a handful already, isn't she? Thanks, Sonny."

He turned on his knees to face her and, under the dim safety lights he couldn't be sure but thought he could see a blush rising on her cheeks. She was tossing items back in her purse without bothering to look at them, the silvery sequins edging her purse trembling with either her haste or her fear. Reaching out, he picked some of the things up and crammed them into her purse as a peace offering. "It'll just be a few minutes. We just need to stay out of the crossfire."

It didn't seem to shake her mood, and he sank his back against the wall to sit beside her. "Jimmie really does keep you out of this type of thing doesn't he?"

She glanced his way, trying to see if he was making fun of her again but his eyes were the piercing blue she remembered from their meeting in her office the week before. She dropped back toward him with a huff, clutching her purse to her chest. "I haven't been shot at since I was," she hesitated and a crinkle formed over her brow as she tried to recall the last time, "since I was nineteen."

"And how old are you now?"

"Twenty-eight," she gave him a half smile, "or thereabouts. But, I'm sure you already know that. You seem to know everything about me already. Why is that?"

He flashed her a wide grin. "Security?"

"Likely story," she said but offered him a tiny smile. "Jimmie's really good about it. I wish he took his safety as seriously as he does mine but you men are pretty gregarious that way, aren't you?" She offered a genuine smile this time. "Don't answer that."

"I didn't intend to."

She jerked closer to him as the screech of tires sounded somewhere outside. He lifted his arm, letting her drop into his chest and tucked her head into his chest. His voice was low, not quite a whisper, but soft in her ear. "That's the cavalry, just keep your head low, okay?"

She didn't bother to nod; her face buried deep in his chest as the sounds began to crowd around them. Her ear pressed deep into his sternum, the sound of his even heartbeat and steady breathing making her feel safer than his touch. He wasn't frightened. No. He wasn't even the least bit alarmed. It was as if he was doing nothing out of the ordinary – like he was sitting in front of the television watching one of those disinteresting documentaries that never even caused a person to blink fast. What kind of person wasn't terrified to be sitting inches away from a gun battle so loud it was deafening? Chancing a look up, her eyes met his clouded, worried ones. The look matched ones she had seen in Jimmie for decades. He was worrying about her. Perfect.

His hand reached to touch her head, tilting her chin upwards to survey her more directly. "Are you all right? Are you hurt?"

Ashli shook her head, and this caused him to look even more worried. In his arms, she could feel his heart speed up a beat.

"Are you certain?"

"Yes."

He frowned. "Then why are you smiling like that?"

"Mitch!" a voice bellowed somewhere nearby, "stop hiding for God's sake and get up. We've cleaned up your mess."

Mitch helped Ashli to stand and waved, keeping one hand looped around her waist. "Over here. Ashli, do you know Sonny Markesi?"

Ashli nodded but failed to extend a hand in greeting. Instead, Sonny stepped forward and kissed her cheek and then Mitch's.

"Look," he turned in a circle extending the edges of his tuxedo jacket for them to appraise, "I even dressed for the occasion. Vinetti would be so proud."

"You look phenomenal," Mitch groused. "I need a fucking drink. Get us outta here."

Ashli hesitated as he led them to the car waiting just beyond the blinking exit sign, placing her arm on Sonny's. "Sonny, you didn't-"

"No," he laughed. "I didn't call your brother. I'm not about to be the one to tell him Mitch was letting you get shot by some dock hoods in my town."

"Your town," Mitch interrupted as they sank into the car, "isn't safe for anybody these days."

"Hey, I asked you to come here and clean things up but no," he glanced in the rear view mirror at Ashli, "you wanted to spend time with the Gucci princess."

"Screw you, Sonny," Ashli slugged his shoulder as she began to relax. "Wait until Jimmie finds out it was your territory where I got ambushed. Better start making your excuses now."

Mitch glanced from one to the other, looking for any signs of tension between the two but could decipher nothing. They both wore smiles on their faces, their words seeming more like childhood ribbing than anything deeper. He tilted his head Sonny's direction and, in response, Sonny laughed.

"She didn't tell you?" he managed through continued chuckles. "Jimmie and I don't get along too well. Stems from a few years back when Ashli and I disappeared at a party together one night. Too many drinks, romantic music-"

"Romantic, my ass," she grumbled. "He was groping me on the balcony at the Fontana Club when Jimmie appeared, scared shitless that I had been kidnapped. Which," she shrugged, "I kind of had been."

"I didn't hear you complaining at the time," Sonny winked, and she smiled in return.

"Yes, well, there's no accounting for taste when you're three sheets to the wind. Can we stop at your hotel so I can get cleaned up, Sonny?"

"Anything, princess."

Mitch fell into silence for the remainder of the ride, following them into Sonny's suite with a distracted frown upon his face. He had decided days ago not to go after Vinetti. More than the worry over Jimmie's business deals, it had been a much more personal decision for him. He and Sonny Markesi had been friends since childhood. They, along with perhaps two others, had been the only ones to make it out of the neighborhood still in one piece, and that had kept their friendship strong. As teenagers, they had fought over girls, popularity, and status in the local gang but as they'd grown up and everyone else disappeared everything had been forgotten, and

Sonny had become one of Mitch's closest friends. After Coppell's death, it had been here, in Sonny's suite, where Mitch had chosen to take refuge.

When he'd heard that Sonny and Vinetti were at odds, Mitch just couldn't do it. There was no badge, no government commitment that could convince him to pit himself against Sonny. Believing that a war between the two was inevitable, it had been easy for him to walk away from the Vinetti case. It was one of the reasons he had agreed to this ridiculous dinner in the first place- so he could tell Ashli he wasn't interested.

But if that's all it was – rumors gone amok just because of Jimmie's crazy over protection of Ashli, Mitch had no other excuse handy. He could think of no legitimate reason that his superiors would believe to get himself out of this assignment.

"Need another bottle?" a quiet voice grabbed Mitch's attention, and he looked down to see that he had managed to drink the half bottle of whiskey that Sonny had put in front of him.

Dark black eyes focused on him, not exactly a look of worry but more one of increasing unease. Mitch knew he was confused- perhaps one of only two people on the planet that actually cared about Mitch's happiness. He knew Mitch's thoughts were elsewhere, knew that a gunfight wasn't going to cause him to drink so heavily, knew that, under normal circumstances, he would never have been out alone with someone like Ashli Vinetti as company. But Sonny also knew Mitch's thoughts were his own – until he was ready to talk there was no point in even asking what was traveling through his mind.

"Sorry," he murmured. "And no. Water's probably a better idea."

Sonny handed him a water glass then slipped off his jacket, his shoulders taut against the fabric of his shirt from the adventures of the evening. He dropped into a chair opposite Mitch, taking a few breaths to let his muscles relax into the cushions. "Are you joining Vinetti?"

"You advising against it?"

"No. Not if that's what you want."

"Oh, no," he shook his head. "None of your philosophical bullshit tonight, Sonny. I've been playing bodyguard for hours now-"

"Exactly!" His eyes narrowed as he sat forward. "Mitch, come on, you could do so much more. So much better than being a hired hand for-"

"Sonny," he cut him off with a sigh. "We've had this conversation a hundred times. I like what I do. I don't want permanence. I don't want to be in charge of something. Anything really. I like the freedom a hell of a lot more than a having a permanent address."

Sonny held his hands up and dropped back into the chair. It was an impossible discussion, and he knew it, but he figured if he kept hassling Mitch he might catch him in a weak moment. After ten years it had been a fruitless effort, but Sonny had never been one to give up easily... he just guessed that the right circumstances hadn't appeared yet for Mitch to change his mind and want less transitory life. He glanced toward the bedroom where Ashli had disappeared to take a shower.

"She really didn't tell you about us?"

The disappointment was obvious, and Mitch laughed. "Yeah, she really didn't tell me. I'm surprised you didn't, though."

"Vinetti nearly threw my ass off that balcony. It wasn't one of my most glorious moments."

"Tough guy is he?"

"Throws a better punch than you but," he grinned, "you've got a hell of a lot better aim."

"Who are we aiming at?" Ashli asked, sweeping into the room in one of the hotel robes and dropping onto the sofa beside Mitch.

"We are planning the assassination of your brother," Sonny said, pushing a drink her direction.

"Oh, fabulous!" she grinned. "Can we make sure I'm out of town first because that would really ruin my weekend plans, you know?" She moved away from them, unable to sit still, and went to turn on the radio. She switched on a hard rock station and turned it up several levels before beginning to twirl around the room.

Mitch watched her move then tossed a quizzical look Sonny's direction. He shrugged but tapped his nose, guessing Ashli had likely imbibed in her drug stash before joining them. Mitch grimaced, causing Sonny to move over and sit beside him. He draped an arm around Mitch, both watching her move about the room in random patterns.

"Don't judge her so harshly."

"Sonny-"

"I know," he nodded, "you don't believe in imported drugs. But, come on, she's had one fucked up night."

"Where'd she get the drugs? Jimmie?"

"No," he shook his head. "Jimmie won't deal drugs. Never has. But she's a connected gal, Mitch. She can get anything and anyone she wants. You might want to remember that."

Mitch shot another irritated look at no one in particular then dropped his head to the back of the sofa. "How the fuck am I supposed to explain this to Jimmie?"

CHAPTER SEVEN

P eace. It was what Mitch wanted more than anything in the world. Not the general statement that people across the globe spout with they attempt to be patriotic but true peace in his own life. He could even be more specific if required to quantify it: he wanted nothing to do with either the IOC or the mob. He wanted both organizations out of his life completely. To be at such diverse odds, Mitch sometimes wondered if the two ever realized how intimately similar they were.

Both were vying for more power – one in Congress and the other in Sicily; both wanted more money, neither caring too much where it came from; and both asked way too much from the people that joined. Giving your life to the mob was no different than giving your life to the IOC. He could be killed working for either and that, more than most things, are what caused the lines to blur for many new recruits to the agency. The IOC offered little in the way of perks to its employees while the mafia? Whatever your vice, the mob could deliver in spades. In the way of bad habits, Mitch had lucked out.

Alcohol was his vice. More than drugs, sex, or immeasurable power, Mitch had always found alcohol most persuasive. It could ease a tortured soul, lift depressed spirits and be a cause of jubilant celebration. He didn't have a great preference – whiskey was his first choice, but it was more by default than preference. It served its purpose quickly while wine was civilized, rum an instant drunk, and sambuca a guaranteed hangover. And he had repeatedly tried them all. If he wasn't required to be so clear headed all the time, he'd likely be a drunk. In that regard, he supposed he had to thank both the IOC and the mob for preventing his permanent membership in AA.

He swayed the bottle in his hand, watching the liquid move about in random patterns, wondering if Jimmie was as drunk as he. He hoped he was; then his aim would be off, and he could get away easily. But, if Jimmie was sober, it meant the end would come right here and now and be quick and likely painless thanks to the high dollar liquor Ashli stocked in her residence in the wilderness of northern New York state.

It wouldn't be a bad place to go. If there actually was a peaceful place on earth, this was probably it. With its impeccable formal gardens, cobblestone paths that led from one building to another, unruly wild blueberry bushes that Ashli claimed were taking over the entire property, and the twenty country miles to the nearest neighbor, this was the closest thing to seclusion Mitch had ever encountered in America.

"This is a beautiful place you've got here," he murmured, hearing the slur in his own words and avoiding the somber gray eyes that he knew were focused on him from across the wrought iron patio table.

"Our refuge," Jimmie returned. "We don't allow strangers here."

Mitch shifted his eyes to the pistol sitting on the table in front of them, something in the recesses of his mind telling him that he should grab it while Jimmie was pouring himself another drink. But another voice was telling him not to care. "Would you like me to leave?"

Jimmie frowned, hoping he looked some manner of sober to this man sitting across from him. He wasn't – he'd been drinking long before he reached the compound after hearing that Ashli had spent the last few hours being shot at in some rundown warehouse by punks that no one could seem to put a name to. But he knew it wasn't Mitch's fault. By Ashli's account, she would have perished if Mitch hadn't been there to cover her ass. He wanted to blame someone; he wanted to strangle the life out of the people that had done this but without any details his hands were tied. He emptied his glass and extended the bottle to Mitch, pouring him half a glass. "No."

"I had to call in Sonny Markesi to get us out. I hope that's not a problem."

"You're longtime friends with him, right?"

"Since childhood," Mitch nodded. "I didn't have a lot of options."

Sinking back onto the uncomfortable, rigid back chair, he shrugged with drunken non-committal. He tugged his white pleated shirt out of his dress pants, letting it hang loosely across his lap. He closed his eyes for a moment, letting the scent of cedar wash over him as he inhaled deeply to calm the tremble in his stomach. His baby sister. Nearly killed and for what? No one seemed to know. She was the reason he'd killed his right hand, his closest friend, his most trusted confidant two weeks earlier. Alex had threatened her life if he and his girlfriend were not allowed admittance into the witness protection program. He wanted to gamble with Jimmie: Ashli's life for his freedom. It was one of the few bets Jimmie was unwilling to make.

His eyes opened slowly, trying to focus on Mitch's form a few feet away. The flickering torches surrounding the patio area made it difficult any time but tonight, hours into his drinking binge, it made it impossible. He dropped his gaze, focusing on the buttons of his shirt, which were much closer and seemed not to be dancing with quite so much vigor. "You saved my sister's life. I don't give a damn how you accomplished it. Just that you did. You have my sincerest gratitude."

Mitch withheld the bitter, sarcastic retort that came to his mind. He hadn't saved her for Jimmie's benefit. He hadn't even saved her because the IOC would have expected him to. Protecting people had been ingrained in him since birth, the absence of suffering one of the idealistic causes his homemaker mother had long aspired to. She had dragged him on every mercy mission she went on no matter how small or boring to a child: pans of lasagna with mozzarella so thick it required spatulas to dip it out of the metal baking tin were dropped off at the old widow down the street that had lost her husband in a car bombing; boxes of homemade cannoli with tiny chocolate shavings decorating the ends were delivered to the orphanage each Saturday; and then there were the pastrami and pancetta sandwiches she handed out to the neighborhood kids in the evenings when their fathers, normally always prompt for dinner, didn't show up.

She knew, he knew...a late father meant he would not be coming at all. Sometimes it was simple – he had skipped town, either because he was fed up or because he was running from the law. Other times, the times his mother somehow always knew and prepared Mitch for in advance, the father had disappeared and would never be found. No body. No trace. No sign of him ever again. Like a vapor of smoke that was there and then suddenly gone, these were the men that dropped into obscurity and rarely, if ever, did anyone bother to ask where they had gone.

He wanted to hate Jimmie, knowing that he was the type of man who made these fathers disappear. But he couldn't. How many people had Mitch himself made disappear even under the close scrutiny of the IOC? Dozens. Hundreds. He'd lost count ages ago.

"Mitch?" Jimmie was eying him, apparently having expected some form of response.

"I don't usually drink with others," he managed with a crooked grin, "I become a philosophical fool and start evaluating my life. Makes me pretty shitty company, if truth be told."

"I don't get drunk with other people," Jimmie agreed even though it was clear to both that he couldn't stand now even if he wanted to. "Usually because that's the easiest way to get a bullet in the back of my skull or say something that should remain private. Guess that means I have to hire you so if I say something stupid you're at least on my payroll first."

"Better to shoot your own employees than a stranger's?"

Jimmie chuckled, his head dropping backward with his laughter. "Something like that, yeah."

"Who is after her?" Mitch asked in a low voice, glancing around to make certain no one was anywhere within hearing distance.

"Everyone thinks I'm going to shoot you for putting her in danger, Mitch," he said waving around. "They've all disappeared to keep from being called as witnesses."

"They don't know you very well."

"No," he shook his head. "Not at all. And to answer your question, I don't know any reason someone would be after her. We tightened security after Coppell, just like all the families and, of course, after Alex's death. But no one should want her."

"From the inside?" Mitch expected an immediate denial, but when his question received silence, he turned a quizzical look Jimmie's direction.

"It's possible," he murmured. "Not likely but entirely possible. We've done a lot of expanding recently. There could be people among us-"

"No need to explain further. I'll dig around for you. About the west coast-"

"Nicolai Terenari." Jimmie didn't miss the flicker of recognition that passed across Mitch's face. "You know him?"

"Intimately."

"Care to elaborate on that?"

"No."

Jimmie didn't bother to try and scrutinize him having learned that, unlike most men he came across, information was not likely to be persuaded from Mitch. Not that he particularly required additional information about Nicolai. Raised in the boroughs of New York, worked his way up through the street gangs to take over his own business, eventually branching out to the west coast where he had remained for the last decade...his story made him the generic poster child for a gang leader. He was universally heralded for his ability to make multi-million dollar deals but, unlike families in the east, Nicolai's death toll was notoriously high. Rather than striking deals and negotiating, he paved his corporate ladder with sprays of bullets, leaving no one left to oppose his impending takeover.

The pinched look on Mitch's face told him that some previous dealings with Nicolai must have soured him on the man. This, in Jimmie's mind, was only another credit to Mitch's ability to discern character. He sent him a lopsided grin and pulled himself to standing, wobbling a moment as he tried to find his footing. "Let's go find you a room before we both pass out, hm?"

Mitch nodded silently, his mind teeming with drunken memories and conflicting emotions regarding the man whose family he had just agreed to join. Jimmie seemed legitimate in his thought processes, sound in the manner in which he evaluated and discerned the problems that were facing him. Rather than jumping to conclusions, he gathered his information, listened to the words of those who were there and then came to his own conclusions. A rarity among the criminal minds he normally associated with. Even Sonny ran forward on rumors alone, his Italian temper always managing to get the best of him.

Stripping off the clothes he'd now been wearing for two days, he stepped into the glass shower in the room Jimmie had offered him. Hot water washed down his back, and he dropped his head against the mosaic tile, wishing that a shower would sober him since he was nowhere near being able to relax enough to sleep. He considered another drink but, as he glanced at himself in the mirror as he dried himself, his haggard appearance told him it was time to lay off some of the alcohol. His black hair was shining, and he inspected it closely as he usually did, every day expecting gray hairs to start popping up on his head. They hadn't yet, but somehow he guessed Jimmie or Ashli would be able to put some there for him. He was reaching for his razor, planning on getting rid of the stubble he'd failed to take care of over the last few days when he heard the soft click behind him.

"Mitch?" Ashli's voice was soft behind him, and he eyed her suspiciously from the mirror.

"Are you all right?"

"Your brother didn't kill me if that's what you mean," he said moving to the area behind the door so he could remove the towel around his waist and pull on some pants.

"I warned you he takes my safety very seriously," she murmured, sinking onto the bed as she waited for him to come out of the bathroom. "I try to get him to stop, but it's been that way since we were kids. Since Teresa-"

"Teresa?" he queried, taking a seat across from her.

"Our sister. A few years older than me, younger than Jimmie," she shrugged. "It's complicated and not at all the reason I came here tonight."

"Why did you come here tonight?"

"To thank you. To not be alone. To have someone to talk to," she shrugged with each statement. "Take your choice."

He chuckled, still intoxicated enough not to be able to contain it. "I doubt you are ever alone unless you chose to be, Ashli."

"Are you drunk?" she asked, her eyes narrowing as she stood up to walk around him. He gave a slow nod, and she laughed. "You and Jimmie were drinking together? Is he drunk too?"

"I'd imagine he has already passed out," he answered.

She sent him an appraising glance. "You lie. He gets drunk with no one."

"He made an exception."

She dropped down to sit in front of him, her hands resting lightly on his knees. "You have joined his family."

Even drunk, her words caught him off guard. They were spoken not with fear or respect but something that it took him a moment to place... relief. She was relieved that he had joined Jimmie's family. Not *their* family but Jimmie's family.

He stood up, skirting around her to pour himself a glass of icy water. The crystal clinked in his hands as he tried to isolate the muddled anecdotes floating through his brain. How she bailed him, a complete stranger, out of jail for no apparent reason. How she threw he and Jimmie together at every opportunity. How she hadn't been in danger her entire adult life until the one night, she happened to be out with him. And now, the relief she was exhibiting as if she had succeeded at something no one else was aware of. He tried to shake off the nagging theory, but the investigator side of him wouldn't let it go.

He lifted his eyes to the gilt-edged mirror, watching her intently. She was loosening the belt on her red silk robe, fanning herself as if the temperature in the room had suddenly jumped a hundred degrees. Her negligee was a matching color but entirely lace, the fabric leaving little to his imagination. He could easily be taken in, watching her hands trace lightly against the firm roundness of her breasts. Were he anyone else he might have been fooled that her moves were truly innocent, not meant to draw him to her side. But he was not anyone else and as captivating as the idea of having her body sliding against his was, he would not allow himself to be taken before knowing the truth.

"We were lucky last night," he managed, his voice husky as she moved closer to his side, her fingers trailing along his arm as she reached to take his glass and have a sip for herself.

"Oh, they wouldn't have hurt me," she murmured in his ear.

It was a matter of fact. A statement. Not a guess, not a conclusion or summary. She said it with the assuredness of someone saying the sun would rise again tomorrow.

"How would you know that?" he questioned, allowing himself to be pulled into her arms, allowing her hands to caress him with seductive moves he'd rarely been privy to. He wanted her to tell him something believable. Something that would allow him the freedom to ravage her in his bed without reservations as to her intent.

But she hesitated. Not long...but long enough for him to know that it was she, not Jimmie, that was the devil within the Vinetti family.

When she finally did reply, her answer was already rehearsed, her voice a low purr. "No one could ever get passed you." Her clothes were removed before he took a breath, her body pressed into his, locking him between her and the tapestry someone had hung at a crooked angle on the wall.

He studied the vines and Valencia oranges in his periphery, everything seeming to hit him at once. The alcohol, her tempting caresses, her betrayal of either he or Jimmie (he wasn't quite sure which) and the disengaging numbness that always set in when his decisions were finally made.

"You could take the breath right out of any man," he whispered. She took it as an invitation, he supposed, because she dropped to her knees, her lips searing a path down his chest as she moved to unzip his pants. Before she could get her mouth around him, he grasped her face in his hands, forcing her to lift her eyes to meet his. "But as flattered as I am, I make it a point not to fuck people who try and have me killed."

CHAPTER EIGHT

He's a cool customer; I'll give him that," Jimmie murmured, pushing the coffee pot across to Ashli. "He didn't even flinch when he told me about your evening."

"Not everyone is as terrified of you as you seem to think," she answered, pouring herself a cup of coffee before getting up and returning it to the counter.

"You look like shit. What's the matter with you?"

She popped the toast up, even though it wasn't nearly done, and tossed it on to a plate. She tried to come up with a snappy retort for him, but her mind was too mollified by the previous evening's events to be able to vocalize a creative response. Instead, she sank back down across from him and slid the plate his direction. "Brent Calhart's office in Washington ran a check on him for us."

"What came up?" he tilted the heavy wooden chair back on its legs, ignoring the toast. "Not that I count on our lawyers to know much of interest."

"He's done time."

"Can we clear it?"

"No."

"No?" His chair screeched across the floor as he moved back from the table causing Ashli to wince. His eyes met hers, challenging her to complain about noise in light of her self-inflicted hangover. But she remained silent, her nose deep in her mug as if the steam from the drink was somehow going to unfog her brain. "Since when can't we clear a record?"

"Since it's a federal charge."

"Federal? What kind of guy have you hooked up with here?"

"He's done his time and hasn't gotten even a speeding ticket since." She turned away from him, grabbing a dish towel and wiping off the slate counter nearest her, concentrating on the specially designed cracks that had been laid by an Italian craftsman she'd flown over when they bought the place. She had known this would be a sticking point with him – he wanted people with executive office access to have clear records. It was moronic, considering Jimmie's long and distinguished criminal career but he had made rare few exceptions over the years.

"Even under Coppell?"

"Even under Coppell," a deep voice acknowledged. "Ashli-"

She whirled, the presence of their west coast security advisor catching her off guard. It was unlike Jimmie to bring him in for routine business, and she felt the knot beginning to rise in her stomach. Trying to keep her nervousness in check, she moved to him quickly, pulling him into a welcoming embrace. Although he was several inches shorter than her, even without shoes on, he had to turn sideways even to get through the kitchen door. "Bernie! What brings you to New York?"

"A summons apparently," he tilted a comical look toward Jimmie, made even more comical by the scowl Jimmie sent him in return.

"Summons?" she raised an eyebrow and turned to Jimmie. "Jimmie-"

But, as usual, Jimmie was already dismissing her with a wave of his hand. "Not your new friend, don't worry. We'll meet you in an hour or so, all right? Go roundup Mitch so the two can meet, would you?" As soon as she was gone, Jimmie's voice lowered several notches. "Tell me."

He sank across from Jimmie, folding his hands in his lap, knowing the news he had wasn't going to appease his boss. "Not much of anything. He did time, as you know, worked for Linski."

"In Canada?"

"Quebec," he confirmed. "Some small organizations in L.A., Dallas and here on the coast. He's got strong ties to Atlantic City. He joined Coppell a couple of years ago."

"As security chief?"

"Wrong. As his right."

Jimmie's eyes narrowed. This was definitely news. He had done several deals with Coppell and knew of Mitch but had never had the opportunity to meet him. Why would Mitch lie about a low-level job like security if he was so high in Coppell's organization? And why would he have not been present at a single meeting that Jimmie had with Coppell?

Jimmie's frown deepened, trying to piece together the missing parts of Mitch's history that no one seemed to know about. There were a dozen different explanations – he and Coppell could be childhood friends, Coppell could have owed a favor to Mitch's family, Mitch could just be the killer shot people claim him to be, and everyone knew Coppell needed a damn good shot close by. This was why he hated international business. In his own backyard, he knew when people breathed. Expand across the globe and he didn't know who was sitting in the seat right next to him. "What about now?"

"Now he's yours. Or so the street says. A lot of guys are beginning to get nervous. It seems this Mitch guy pulls a lot of his own weight around the boroughs and Atlantic City."

"His own business?" he asked his brows now furrowed to the point they nearly met in the middle.

"Not certain but definitely enough connections to put your organization at a standstill."

"Then we want him on our side, I'd imagine."

"You gotta be careful, Jimmie. A lot of people are looking at this as a marriage. You're marrying into Atlantic, Bronx, and Brooklyn. Business wise it may be profitable..."

"It will be profitable," he corrected.

"Okay, but your organization may suffer here in New York."

Jimmie didn't really have to consider this although he knew Bernie meant well. Mitch's weapons knowledge made him employable, his own business made him desirable, and his connections made him imperative. Expanding business was the only way to keep the Vinetti empire moving forward, and Jimmie was determined that if Gino Palmese, the current head of *la familia*, decided to retire as rumor had it, the vacated captain's seat would be bequeathed to him. Anything less would be failure.

"They won't turn on family," he countered. "I want him."

"He's first generation," Bernie's voice was grave causing Jimmie to laugh.

"No one is first generation anymore, Bernie."

"Born in Sicily. I've got a copy of his passport if you don't believe me."

"So, what are you telling me? He's got the old world customs down? Come on, Bernie. All those mafia movies are going to your head. He seems American enough to me."

"Just thought you should know."

"Yeah, thanks," Jimmie managed through broken laughter, "I'll make sure to check my sheets before I go to bed each night. Don't want any fish or horse heads to sneak in there by mistake, you know?"

"Terenari."

Jimmie leaned back in his chair, his fingers tapping distractedly on the table. Nicolai Terenari had become a thorn in the sides of many families on the east coast. Having his own west coast contingent, Jimmie had never had the need or inclination to do business dealings with him. That he couldn't seem to get along with the east was troubling, but it still didn't make Jimmie overly wary – some of Vinetti Industries best deals had been made when other east coast families were too cowardly to step up to the table. But Terenari had offered him money and a lot of it, only to "talk." He was asking for nothing, making no deals, outsourcing none of his business. He only wanted information. On what, Jimmie hadn't a clue. "He contacted me yesterday. Wants to set up a meeting with Mitch present. Why would he want that?"

Bernie stood up, moving to lean against the counter Ashli had vacated. He was puzzled; Jimmie could read it across his face. He poured himself coffee, and Jimmie's eyes narrowed.

"I am not a patient man, Bernie."

"Terenari has gained a lot of power out west. He's been killing people left and right. There is a rumor, but it's only rumor, mind you. I wouldn't want-"

"Out with it."

"Word is he killed Coppell."

Jimmie shook his head. "No way. Hired someone perhaps but not himself."

"I can only tell you what I hear," Bernie shrugged. "I can look into Kerlin for you. See if there's a connection there I missed somewhere, but my guess is he wants information on the hit to see what Kerlin knows."

"It would make it difficult for him to kill Mitch since he's now on my payroll," Jimmie leveled a gaze at Bernie. "Or is he wanting Mitch on his payroll?"

"I think that was the intent of many, Jimmie."

"This kid have balls of gold or what?" he grumbled. "He's already caused me more grief than half the people working for me. I'm still trying to figure out if this was a mistake or not."

Bernie hesitated a nervous twitch that Jimmie had memorized over the years. It always meant he had news that he didn't really want to share but felt obligated to. "What else?"

"He was at Palmese's deportation hearings."

"What?" he was up now, pacing the floor next to Bernie. "He would've just been a kid. Why was he at something like that?"

"I haven't been able to find any connection between them. Nothing. But he was there. It's in the court documents."

"Did you talk to Gino?"

Bernie frowned. "Palmese isn't going to talk to me."

"Yes, yes, of course," Jimmie nodded. "I'll have to contact him myself."

"You could always just ask Mitch."

Jimmie glared at him as if he'd just sprouted antlers. "Stupid suggestions like that are exactly why Gino won't talk to you," he hissed. He was pacing again, his mind now on Gino – the capo di tutti capo. They had made an alliance years before, but it was tentative – everything with Gino was tentative. He could love you one moment and, without taking a breath, order your execution. Why Mitch, who could only have been fifteen or sixteen at the time Gino was deported, would have sat amid the weeks of boring, incessant hearings were a puzzle. Perhaps his family had forced him to go. Perhaps he had gone just to see the famous mobster be put away. He could understand if they had some relationship together but that was impossible – Jimmie and everyone in *la familia*, for that matter, would have known long ago if there was some bond between the two.

"About Terenari-"

"Set up the meet," Jimmie nodded, trying to get his mind back on his immediate concerns. "Somewhere neutral. Chicago, first thing next month. The quicker we get him dealt with, the better off all of us will be."

"Yes, sir."

CHAPTER NINE

It had taken him two hours to find this place. He could have easily asked someone directions but trolling the grounds of the massive estate had been able to calm the rage Ashli had evoked in him. It wasn't that he had some aversion to being shot at – that was part of his daily job description. It was that she had taken the time, the forethought, to actually plan something so devilishly clever. And she had done it methodically - making certain to hire people that would shoot but not kill either of them. He released a breath of exasperation, leaning his body against the cold, anise colored stones that had once been a stable for horses. He had underestimated her desperation.

He glanced down the field to where targets had been set up by some of Jimmie's bodyguards. It was a longer distance than he would normal fire at, 45 feet at least, but the length didn't concern him. He had learned to carry and fire a gun years before he'd had sex…killing someone at any distance was now as ingrained in him as walking. Reaching down he picked up his

Colt, a 45 ACP, its hand engraved blue steel barrel glimmering under the rising sunlight. He held it loosely, letting it settle into the creases of his hand until the familiar weight was balanced and he could no longer make a distinction between his hand and the weapon.

He fired quickly, glancing at the target only once. Rapid shots rang out, his ears immune to the sound, and when he'd emptied the clip he reached for another he had in tucked in his waistband. He shut his eyes, firing round after round as Ashli's face flittered through his psyche. First, her polished corporate image, then the fleeting anger at her brother, the sensual stares that made men melt, the childlike mortification when he'd thrown her out of his room after turning her down. Yes, he had underestimated her. But it wouldn't happen again.

"Mitch?" her voice was soft, wary even, and he didn't bother to turn. "Please, can't I talk to you?"

He glanced at her, taking note of the jeans and t-shirt, the way her hair was pulled back into a ponytail. Perhaps she had figured he would react better if she played a more vulnerable female. He looked away, aiming and firing again, wondering if he had enough bullets left to keep himself occupied long enough to avoid her. He doubted it.

"They weren't to kill anyone," she offered.

"I killed two of them, Ashli. Defending you when you needn't be defended. How does that sit on your conscious?"

"Obviously not as hard as it does on yours."

Tucking his gun back into his waistband, he pushed past her and began walking back to the compound. "I refuse to continue this discussion."

"You can't refuse," she grabbed his arm and pulled him back toward her. "You work here now, in case you've forgotten. Do you intend never to speak to me again?" The venom in his eyes told her that was exactly his plan. "Please," she dropped her voice, "at least give me the chance to explain. If for no other reason than you deserve to know what you've gotten yourself into."

Curiosity was apparently another of his downfalls because Mitch couldn't resist her baiting. Reaching his hand out, he beckoned for her to lead the way. He wasn't surprised when she led him away from the estate house and further into the back gardens. This was apparently going to be a conversation she didn't want Jimmie to overhear. That, in itself, was intriguing enough, but when she sank down on a stone bench edging the grounds, and her eyes brimmed with tears, Mitch's patience was finally gone.

"Tears, Ashli?" he asked, his voice thick with sarcasm. "Tell me I'm imagining your latest drama."

"I expected anger but not hate."

"Hate requires emotion. Try apathy."

"Do I deserve that?"

"Undoubtedly. I killed two people for you. Innocent people."

"Not so innocent. Otherwise, they wouldn't have taken the job," she tried to reason. "Besides, most people in your position don't think twice about shooting someone."

"I am *not* most people," he growled.

"I'm learning that. So you know, they were heroin dealers from the East Side. You did the world a service."

"Don't patronize me."

"My brother does the best he can to keep me from the dark side of our world. But I'm not an idiot, Mitch. Despite your current opinion of me, I did this for him."

"Really? How does that work exactly?"

"He doesn't realize it, Mitch. You said it yourself - our security is in shambles. But he's so fucking worried about me that he doesn't realize it. Business is suffering. I'm sure you know that from word on the street. Not enough it can't be absorbed, of course, but it's not changing. We're getting to be known as the trouble-makers."

"Can't imagine why."

"If it took something like this to open his eyes, to make him face up to what the hell is going on around us then so be it. I'd do it again if it means keeping him alive."

"So you want me to believe you did this to keep him safe?" Mitch queried. "To keep the business safe? That's it?"

"Yes."

"You lied to him, betrayed him, for his own good?" Mitch leaned forward, his eyes glinting. "Are you sure that's the story you want to stick with?"

The response caught in her throat. "Yes."

Mitch exhaled. Leaning back in the chair, he watched her. He was unnerving her, he could tell, but to her credit, she remained silent and accepting of the non-verbal rebuke he was giving her. "I'll do the security revamp. If only to protect him from you, Ashli."

"I can accept that. I deserve that."

"I don't kill for your amusement. I don't kill because someone pissed you off. But nor will I kill because you took some random guy to your bed and Jimmie wants him gone. Understood?"

She nodded.

"The whole point of what I do is that killing is no longer necessary. Jimmie's safety, and yours for that matter shouldn't be contingent on how well someone can aim. You should feel safe at all times. That's my job. Not anything else."

She nodded.

"I cannot stress this clearly enough. No more feds. Not one. Nodding doesn't work for this one." In a swift move, he pinned her into the chair, his grip tight on her legs. His eyes locked with hers and his voice was a low growl. "You will not ever bring a fed into your bed again. Promise it."

She nodded but Mitch didn't move. Instead, he tightened his hold on her. Her eyes brimmed with pain filled tears, but she met his gaze. "Yes. I promise I will not ever bring a fed into my bed."

"We are clear?"

"Crystal."

Mitch let her go, heard the thick exhale of air she'd been holding. He could see her body shaking and, for a moment, considered leaving her to stew in her fear. Instead, he stepped behind her, dropping his lips to her ear. "And for the record? Red lace? Not my style."

"I'll work on it."

"You do that."

CHAPTER TEN

Mitch insisted on interviewing all 412 employees in the executive building personally. It took weeks, but each one was scrutinized - their childhoods, their marriages, their rankings at the golf course or bowling alleys - all at issue. Complaining resulted in immediate dismissal (that was Jimmie's decision) and any failure to show was met with a guarded security escort at the employee's front door. The result meant only a skeleton crew was left and, as Mitch had anticipated, Jimmie soon knew each one by name. When it came time to start hiring new crew, Mitch demanded Jimmie make each decision personally - relegating Ashli to bystander status. Even worse (in her eyes), he'd saddled her with a trio of bodyguards that were old enough to be her grandfathers.

"Do you ever take a night off?"

"Do you?" Mitch countered, leaning back in the leather chair he'd called home for the past few weeks. Although they'd offered him an office beside their own, he had turned them down. Instead, he preferred the terrace level which had floor to ceiling windows that overlooked the main casino floor.

Jimmie shrugged and sank onto the sofa edging the windows. "Don't you get tired of being caged up in this glass house all day?"

Mitch laughed. "You've no idea. The new security system will be up and running tonight. You can run a test on it whenever you like."

"Like a drill?" Jimmie asked, his curiosity piqued.

He nodded and moved to the windows. "It has several different levels depending on the threat or concern. See that new silver metal trim along the outer drop ceiling?" he asked, pointing to the casino floor as Jimmie moved to stand beside him. "If the casino alarm is tripped either by an individual or by remote via the cash weight-"

"Cash weight?"

"Each cash drawer has a specific weight. You already had limits on withdrawals, so I just enhanced that policy. If too much cash, by weight, is removed at once from the drawer without a passcode the casino will go into lockdown. Gates drop from each of those metal trims...no one, staff or customer, is going anywhere."

"Fort Knox uses a similar tactic," Jimmie nodded appreciatively. "I watched a documentary once."

Mitch laughed. "Good to know. I wouldn't want to add robbing the federal bank reserve to my resume."

"What about unsavory characters?"

"By unsavory, I assume you mean those against the family? We've installed facial recognition software. It loads all known criminals that go through the Interpol and local booking systems. Those not arrested can be input manually, and you can install permanent overrides for specific persons."

"And why would I want to do that?"

"Well, the most obvious reason? I had to override the system to stop flagging you. It would go off and send alerts to the staff every time you did your daily walks on the floor. Damned annoying that I got woken up every time you took those 2 am strolls to find a girl for the night."

"Bit sensitive that."

"No. It's allowing you to control who you trust enough to have access where."

"Did you override for Ashli?"

"She doesn't have a record; it wasn't necessary."

"You? Did you override it for yourself?"

"No. That's your call to make, not mine."

"Bet that's annoying them even more. You never sleep."

"Yeah, it's a struggle," Mitch shrugged. "They are handling it, though. You can also red alert someone. I did take the liberty of adding Alex's brother's name to that list. If he enters at any point, the upper floors and all elevators go into lockdown. It leaves him stuck on the public floor and security has protocols on how to approach from each direction."

"And Ashli?"

"Both suites are on a rotating passcode system that changes every two hours and overlaps the staff shift changes. There are fingerprint scans on both the access elevators and the office doors. I've assigned a man to her door permanently plus three additional bodyguards that will travel with her."

"The man assigned to her-"

"A non-issue. He's a kid, really. Ex-military, no family, left a sizable inheritance so not motivated by money, and, as long as you treat him right, he'll undoubtedly be your most loyal employee."

"Can you get him in here?"

Mitch nodded and sank onto the edge of his desk as he made the call. When the kid arrived, with the most formal of stance, he couldn't help but smile.

"Jimmie, this is Teddy."

Teddy reached out his hand, but Jimmie hesitated. "Don't I know you?"

"Yes, sir. I've worked here for two years."

Jimmie surveyed him, trying to put any memory with the face before him. "You are the kid who agreed our security was in shambles, aren't you?"

"Yes, sir."

"Still of that same opinion?"

"No, sir. Mitch has this place more secure than the White House."

"I didn't pay him to say that," Mitch laughed. "Relax, Teddy. You've got the job already. He's just making sure you aren't going to sleep with his baby sister."

Teddy's face flushed a deep crimson. "No, sir. She's, well, a bit forward for me. I'm a pretty simple guy."

"And if that changes?"

Teddy stood straighter. "Then I'd be the first to step away. You gotta understand, Mr. Vinetti, I watched my brothers die on the battlefield beside me. There are moments in your life when you try and fail and, well, others when you know ahead of time it's a stupid situation, to begin with. I watched twenty-two men die beside me because someone in charge sent us into a stupid situation. I don't do stupid situations and, no offense,

but getting involved with your sister would be a monumental-
ly stupid situation."

Jimmie sent a grin Mitch's direction. "Yep, I like him."

"Thought you might."

"Do you drink, Teddy?"

"Not on duty."

Jimmie laughed. "I'm not testing you. I was inviting you out
for a drink. If Mitch doesn't show his face in public soon people are going to think I've knocked him off. And *that* is a stupid
situation I won't get in."

CHAPTER ELEVEN

Jimmie sipped his drink from the corner of the room, watching as Mitch went from table to table shaking hands. It had been this way since they pulled into the neighborhood-people calling him out by name and catching up as if they were old friends. He leaned forward to get Teddy's attention.

"Is he from this neighborhood? Do you know?"

Teddy shook his head. "No, he's a Brooklyn boy like me. He stayed here for a while, though. It was being overtaken by some Russians. They'd turned the abandoned buildings into heroin dens or something. People were afraid to leave their homes and cops were getting shot every night. It was like a mini Detroit."

"So, he shows up, and everything's clean somehow? How does that work?"

"Clean is a relative term," Mitch interrupted, sinking into a chair. "It's safe."

Jimmie poured him a drink from the bottle and clinked glasses. "Well, whatever you did it worked."

"I just put pieces into play, nothing more. Bought some buildings, had them demolished or refurbed by union guys and then sold them back to the local bankers."

"And the Russians?"

Mitch grinned. "Let's just say we came to an understanding rather quickly and they moved on."

"You still have businesses here?"

Mitch shrugged. "Money flows but nothing permanent, no. Why?"

"I tried to buy a few properties here recently. One of the reasons I chose this place tonight actually. Money didn't motivate anyone."

"Not surprising," Teddy offered. "Mitch just got them cleaned up and the last couple of years your dramas have given you a rep for trouble."

Jimmie glared at him. "Did you mean to say that out loud?"

Teddy looked from one man to the other. "No?" he asked uncertainly, causing both men to laugh.

Mitch waved to a nearby table. "Bobby, come here for a second, will you?"

"You having a good evening, Mr. Kerlin?"

"Yeah, I want you to meet someone. This is James Vinetti, and he's looking to do some investing on this side of town. You think you can help him out?"

"Sure. Any specific properties or just in general?"

"This one actually and the two nightclubs at the other end of the strip."

"Well, this one is family owned and operated and has been since the 1910's. It's an institution. But I can guarantee you a table any time you like. The two nightclubs, though, that I can arrange. What are you looking at?"

"Two-thirds?"

Bobby stretched out his hand. "Done. I can have the contracts sent over tomorrow morning."

"Don't you want to know what I'm willing to pay?"

Bobby smiled. "Can't imagine it's something we will argue over, no. Night, gentlemen." He tipped his hat to them, squeezed Mitch's shoulder and then was gone.

Jimmie looked to Mitch. "What just happened here?"

"Seems like you just became a majority owner in a couple of nightclubs," Teddy answered.

Jimmie ignored him, his eyes boring into Mitch's.

"They are grateful it's a clean place now, Jimmie. They don't believe I'd steer them wrong."

"And?"

"And," Mitch drew out the word, hating to have to say the words, "they fear what could happen if they were left on their own again."

Jimmie sat back, considering. Mitch was either lying or obfuscating the entire truth. But, Jimmie knew, it wasn't any of his business to begin with. He'd just made a deal that would bring Vinetti Industries millions of dollars in a completely legal revenue. Over a single shot of whiskey. He shook his head and then smiled. "You, Vincenzo, are turning into one complicated man."

"Come on, let's get Teddy back before he passes out."

Jimmie nodded, taking Teddy's other arm as they struggled to get him up and into the car. "He is a good kid; you know it?"

"I think so."

"Hope you're right. It's really going to suck if I have to kill him."

CHAPTER TWELVE

He didn't have the energy even to wave at the guards lounging outside the executive floor entrance, barely managing to enter the passcode to Ashli's office correctly. He began pulling off his jacket as soon as he entered the suite, sinking onto the corner of her desk without preamble.

"Twelve deals in fourteen days," she mused, rising from her chair and moving to help him loosen the knot in his tie. "When he cut you loose, you didn't mess around, hm?"

"Just earning my keep," he offered, taking the tie she offered him and stuffed it in his pocket.

Her fingers traced the dark circles under his eyes. "You look exhausted." Broken, she wanted to say. Physically and mentally broken – Jimmie's pace was already beginning to wear through Mitch's calm facade. "Are you just getting in?"

"Chicago yesterday morning, Philly last night and I drove back this morning."

"You drove?"

"Wasn't a flight until this afternoon," he explained. "Jimmie said we have plans tonight. Know anything about that?"

Her eyes twinkled. "The real answer or the one I'm supposed to give?"

He chuckled and brushed away a lock of her hair. "Troublesome that you may be, I've missed you, Ash."

She might have considered it an opening to come on to him – if he hadn't called her Ash. She hadn't been called that in years – not since she and Jimmie's relationship had become strained. She reached a tentative hand to him, asking for permission, and he touched her waist, pulling her into a hug.

"How are you faring?" he asked quietly in her ear.

She sent him a genuine smile when he released her. "Better than you it seems. You really do look like the walking dead."

"Ever so kind," he grumbled and moved to sink into her chair. He stretched lazily, stifling a yawn. "Tonight?"

"Birthday party for Sonny."

Mitch glanced at his watch, his eyes narrowing bemusedly. "It's not his birthday."

"I thought you might catch that," she laughed. "Have you seen the paper today?"

"No. I canceled the delivery to the Lexus."

Ignoring the sarcasm, she reached behind her to grab the folded paper and dropped it into his lap. It took only seconds for his exhaustion to lift. "Feds hit Sonny?"

She nodded. "Last night. Had the casino closed for nearly six hours."

"That must've pissed off the accountants," he murmured, still reading the article.

"You didn't know?" she asked, unable to hide her confusion. He was one of them – how could he not know? But his facial features were easily deciphered in his exhaustion – he didn't know and was worried.

"Sonny's fine. Cursing like a sailor but fine. He's coming in to meet with Jimmie and a few others at the hotel tonight. Strengthening security and all that."

Mitch nodded. "Did they find anything?"

"Not according to the paper and Sonny wasn't hauled in," she shrugged.

He tossed the paper back onto her desk. "How are the bodyguards?"

"You mean the goons you've got following me everywhere?" she asked, wrinkling her brow. "Tiresome and annoying."

"But?" he asked smiling.

"Good at their job," she conceded. "I haven't been able to shake them once."

"Excellent news," he nodded then closed his eyes, a smile still across his face. "You feel safe?"

She hesitated. "Yes."

His eyes were open again in an instant; worried blue eyes focused on her. "Ash-"

She waved him off. "Stop being so damn perceptive, will you? They're fine. I just-"

"What?"

"I just feel safer with you," she managed, knowing it would probably come off as a come on but meaning nothing of the sort.

He surveyed her a moment to decide if she was truthful. Certain that she wasn't trying to make another move on him, he let his eyes drift closed again. "That's idiotic."

She bristled, wanting to damn him to hell but then deciding against it. There was no point antagonizing him when they were getting along so well. She stepped away, busying herself straightening the conference room table a few feet away. She didn't notice when he arrived behind her, didn't hear him until his breath was on her neck. His arms slipped to either side of her, locking her in place between him and the table.

"I didn't mean to say that out loud. I'm tired, but that's no excuse. My apologies." She attempted to turn, but his body locked her tighter against him, his hands closing in around her waist. "I only meant," he whispered, "the father apart we are the safer we'll both be."

Her breath caught in her throat, realizing that he was being honest – brutally honest – with her. She couldn't recall the last time someone had trusted her with the truth. And, of course, he was right. As friends, things were safe enough, but anything closer could blow up in their faces. What did she want? She wanted a life of her own. To do that, she needed Mitch at Jimmie's side – not hers. Knowing his lips were so unbelievably close to her neck, she couldn't imagine a higher price to pay.

"I've missed you, too." She managed in a more even, polished tone. She hoped that was good enough for him. She knew he would understand that she intended to behave.

With a swift jerk, he had her turned around, his arm resting lightly around her shoulders. In the same instant, Jimmie burst into the room. His eyes focused on them, glinting dangerously and Ashli attempted to move away. Mitch's arm dug into her shoulder, keeping her in place. She could feel his muscles tensing beside her, but his face retained its relaxed composure.

"Did you know," he asked Jimmie, "that Ashli has not been able to shake her bodyguards in my absence?"

Jimmie was still on alert, his eyes drifting at the close familiarity of their position but he gave a single nod.

Mitch chuckled. Not a tension-filled chuckled like she might manage but a chuckle she remember from when he was drinking – relaxed, calm, fearless. How could he be so stupid?

"She's not happy with me," he grinned, "which should make you ecstatic."

"Good men, I'd guess," Jimmie nodded, relaxing as he walked toward them. "Mitch, have you seen this?" He held out a paper in his hand, no longer even bothering to glance Ashli's direction.

"Yeah. You need me to take back security tonight?"

"No, no." Jimmie shook his head. "I just want you at my side. Get cleaned up and get some rest. You look like shit."

"Can't catch a break with you two, can I?"

CHAPTER THIRTEEN

Y ou smell like a brewery."

"Distillery," Mitch corrected.

"Is this still about Coppell?" Mike asked, sinking into one of the metal chairs lining the warehouse hallway. "Because he wasn't worth it, you know. He killed-"

"Yeah, yeah, hundreds of people. I've got it, Mike. No need to relay the history of the mafia for me."

"Is it Vinetti?"

Mitch frowned. "Surprisingly, Jimmie's a pretty level guy. Haven't had a real problem with him yet. Most of that's Ashli's doing, I think. She's throwing us together at every turn. She's not giving him an opportunity not to trust me. Helped, of course, that I kept her alive during that ambush in Atlantic. He's got some pretty big deals in the works. He's been expanding everywhere, but the capital funds are all legit. We're supposed to be meeting with Terenari, but it keeps getting shuffled between the other deals we've got going."

"Nicolai Terenari?" Mike leaned forward, resting his elbows on his knees. "We've been trying to pin him down for years. He moved out west and left all our undercover men behind. We haven't been able to get anyone in since then."

"Terenari's a smart guy. He keeps a tight knit group beside him. They've been with him since he was still blackhanding neighborhood merchants."

"You know him then?"

"Knew him. Past tense. I haven't spoken with him or any of his family since I was a kid."

"Maybe-"

"One mobster at a time, all right?" He shook his head at the audacity of the suggestion. "What do you know about a Teresa Vinetti?"

"Never heard of her."

"She's Jimmie's sister. No contact with the family it seems. At least, not in the time I've been around them. I get the impression she and Jimmie had a falling out when they were younger, and she's stayed in the periphery since then."

"I'll see if I can find out anything," he nodded. "Now, off the record," he dropped his voice, "what's going on, Mitch? I haven't seen you this out of sorts since, well, never."

Mitch considered the many things he wanted to ask...most notably what other moves the IOC was planning behind his back. But he knew that line of questioning would only put Mike's guard up. Instead, he offered him a friendly smile. "Want to tell me why you gave up a cushy job in D.C. to become my field officer again?"

"Nine to five didn't suit me."

Mitch cocked his head, the unease in Mike's voice obvious. Surely he knew that was a pathetic answer. Mike hadn't been his field officer in over three years. It hadn't been until the month before Coppell's death that he'd returned to the minefield of daily operations. Even with his freelance status, Mitch was smart enough to know no one would choose such a demotion. The more Mike paced along the edges of the room, the more the hairs on the back of Mitch's neck began to rise.

"Vinetti?" Mitch guessed. "Is he the reason you're back?"

"I advised you not to take this case, remember? Don't try and throw this shit back at me now."

"So the IOC wants Vinetti and doesn't trust the freelancer to get it done," Mitch surmised. "Good to know."

"Mitch-"

Mitch waved off the denial. This was the reason he stayed at arm's reach from the IOC – just like any other government entity they cared more about rules and regulations than real life scenarios. "For the record, I'm not drunk," he countered. "I just haven't been able to change my fucking clothes. I haven't seen a bed in two days and have spent the last two weeks flying all over the damn country. Your little escapade with Sonny has put everyone on edge, so I don't see any rest in my near future either. So, stop dispensing the bureaucratic bullshit and just let me do my job."

Mike knew better than to argue. It would only add fuel to Mitch's simmering fire. He didn't blame him for the anger – in his better days, he could remember the life and death situations that Mitch faced. Mitch had been straddling this line longer than any agent in the history of the bureau. That he continued to bring in collars without getting himself killed was a testament to the 24-hour wall he kept built around himself. But Mike knew a single crack in that armor could destroy everything.

"Mitch?" he softened his voice, counting on it to make Mitch turn. "Steer clear of the girl, all right?"

Mitch stopped mid-stride, whirling to face him. In all their years together, Mike had never once given him suggestions on how to handle himself. And yet it was a warning he knew better than to dismiss. "Ashli," he nodded solemnly. "Yeah, I don't need the bureaucrats to tell me that."

"That was from me, Mitch, not the home office," Mike admitted.

Of course, it was. The IOC didn't want Mitch to know Ashli had been bedding feds, but Mike didn't want to be caught in the crossfire either. Mitch clapped his shoulder as he walked past. "Yeah. I know that, too."

CHAPTER FOURTEEN

The lack of sleep and adrenaline rush from his meeting with Mike was difficult to shake. Standing in the doorway of the Verona Ballroom, he watched the party goers warily, the unfamiliar faces doing nothing to settle his stomach. He was thankful he at least looked the part. Someone- Ashli, he assumed- had the forethought to lay out a tuxedo for him and he'd managed to pull it on and hustle downstairs before he was missed.

"Going to block the doorway all night?" Sonny asked, slipping an arm around his shoulder. He patted the stubble on Mitch's chin. "Geez, kid, when was the last time you slept?"

Mitch tilted his head to the dance floor where a hundred couples were swirling about, flashy sequined dresses and black ties decorating the bare wood floor. "Quite a turnout for your birthday," he chuckled.

"Got some good presents, too," he laughed, taking Mitch's arm and pulling him toward the bar. "Ashli's got me shacked up in some room on the 19th floor. The place is smaller than my bathroom back in Atlantic. What's up with that?"

"Punishment for the Gucci princess comment?" he guessed, knowing how conniving Ashli could be when she wanted.

Sonny frowned- he'd obviously not considered this. "Speaking of unpleasant things-"

"I heard," Mitch grimaced, stepping behind the bar to pour himself a glass of whiskey since the bartender was taking too long. "Feds?"

"No," he cut him off. "I had another unexpected visitor yesterday."

"More unexpected than the IOC?" he laughed and followed Sonny to a table on the fringes of all the activity.

"Nicolai," he said in a hushed, almost ominous voice. "That son-of-a-bitch showed up at the casino demanding to talk to you."

"He knows I'm working for Vinetti."

"Didn't seem to give a damn. He is one lunatic, man. He nearly strangled two of my guys."

"Nicolai? Our Nicolai?" Mitch asked, disbelieving.

"I'm telling you; he's been reading too many Al Capone biographies or some shit. He just stormed in and started trying to take people out all by himself. He's gone off the deep end," Sonny managed in a hoarse whisper.

Mitch contemplated as he sipped his drink, wondering why Nicolai didn't just speak with Jimmie if the meeting was that urgent. "Is he trying to offload something on the east coast?"

"Didn't mention it to me," he answered, shaking his head. He dropped his head by a fraction, causing Mitch to lean closer to hear. "Antoinette was with him."

Mitch couldn't control the sputter in his usual calm. His glass dipped precariously close to the floor, Sonny catching it as if he had anticipated the move. "W-what?"

Sonny nodded, leaning back into his chair to avoid the gazes he knew were now focused their direction. "I know," he whispered, in an attempt to commiserate with Mitch.

Hostile and disquieting thoughts rushed through Mitch's mind, and his blue eyes flashed to Sonny with grief-stricken aggravation. "No. You don't."

"Mitch, where were you all afternoon? I thought you'd be sleeping," Ashli's sing-song voice cut through their tension, both men offering her false smiles. She glanced from one to the other, her eyes appraising them with a steady gaze. "Have I interrupted again?"

Mitch didn't bother to respond but lurched from his seat and pulled her toward the dance floor. Ignoring Sonny's penetrating gaze, Mitch moved them further into the crowd, enveloping them within a hundred scents of expensive perfume. His throat constricted, and he stopped, sucking in several gulps of air before pulling her into his arms.

"You're shaking," she said, her eyes widening in alarm.

He nodded, allowing her the observation without denial and tugged her body closer to his.

"Talk about something, anything, just for a few minutes, all right?"

She raised an eyebrow in confusion but he was paying her no mind, his head already thousands of miles away. "I did want to talk to you about earlier, in my office."

He managed a weak smile at her nervousness- it was so patently unlike her. "I'd rather we not talk about that. Blame the honesty on my exhaustion, if you would."

"I actually didn't mean *that*," she frowned. "I was curious about something else entirely."

"That's unlike you," he said, giving her sidelong glance of disbelief.

"I can have multiple pursuits at one time," she grumbled. "I was just curious if you no longer value your life or if angering Jimmie is just an amusing pastime for you."

He couldn't help but laugh, and she pulled away from him, instantly offended.

"I'm serious."

"Oh, I know you are," he managed through continued laughter. He sent her an apologetic smile and opened his arms, waiting for her to forgive him. With an exasperated sigh, she slid back into his arms, his hands pulling her closer than before. She dropped her head onto his shoulder, the hard, drawn muscles not surprising her. "You aren't going to answer, are you?"

"An hour ago I would have said I don't give a damn if anyone, including Jimmie, shot a round through my skull."

"And now?" she asked, puzzled. "Has something changed so drastically in the past hour?"

"Perhaps," he murmured, giving her a lopsided grin, "perhaps not."

"You are maddeningly confusing at times, do you know that?"

Hours later, once the party was in full swing, a handful had secluded themselves in one of the private conferences. Although the banter was convivial, a nervous undertone put everyone on edge. Except Mitch. For him, Vinetti's turmoil was no longer even on his radar.

Mitch balanced his arm on the back of Ashli's chair, his fingers threading through the loose tendrils of her hair absently. She tried to send him a look of warning, but his eyes were focused somewhere far beyond the table, his eyes darker than she'd ever witnessed. Jimmie's gaze drifted to her in between breaks in the conversation but rather than the furious reproach she'd expected; he tilted his head questioningly. She offered him a quick shrug, and his face broke into a deep scowl, his brows furrowing in bewilderment.

"Mitch, what do you think?" Sonny was the one to finally grab his attention.

His eyes roamed the table, a handful of men and Ashli, something telling him he had missed something important.

"About the federal intervention?" Sonny supplied, and Mitch offered him a half smile in thanks.

"I'd only worry when they stop searching."

"Because that means they already have something. Yeah," Sonny nodded, "that's what Jimmie said, too."

"I'll make a few phone calls, see what I can dig up," one offered.

"Until then, just clean house and keep everyone in check, right?"

"No need to ramp down I don't think. Mitch? Jimmie?"

Jimmie looked to Mitch, but he was once again miles away. "Nah, I think we're good. But if anyone hears anything-"

"No problem."

When the men started saying their goodbyes and letting Ashli led them to the gaming floors, it was Mitch who was the first to disappear. Jimmie was only steps behind.

"Feds hitting Sonny bothered you?" Jimmie asked, moving to stand beside Mitch at the edge of the terrace balcony.

"Hm?"

"Feds and Sonny?" he pressed.

Mitch shook his head. "Sonny keeps a clean house. Federal intervention doesn't worry me."

"You and Ashli looked pretty cozy on the dance floor tonight."

"You want to discuss your sister and me?" Mitch asked, raising an eyebrow.

"Is there something to discuss?"

Mitch laughed at the seriousness in Jimmie's voice. "Not if I can help it. Damn you're overprotective, aren't you?"

"She doesn't make the wisest choices for herself," Jimmie shrugged. "Or the family sometimes."

"Then trust that I will," Mitch sighed. "You shoot people. She sleeps with them. Everyone needs a hobby."

Jimmie opened his mouth to argue and then closed it. Mitch had a way of stating that obvious in such a matter of fact manner that it made it impossible to be angry at him for it. Instead, he clinked his glass with him in accession. "And you? What's your hobby?"

"Knowing everyone else's."

Jimmie smiled. "Knowing everyone's darkest secrets, hm? That makes you invaluable to a lot of people then."

"You mean dangerous," he corrected. "I'm dangerous to a lot of people. That doesn't make me invaluable."

"So I'm walking around with a guy with a big target on his head. Good to know."

"Not any bigger than yours," Mitch countered. "But isn't that my job? Making sure they miss and hit me instead of you?"

Jimmie shrugged rather than respond. No, that wasn't why he wanted Mitch around, but it wouldn't do him any good to say that out loud. The truth was, he was finding Mitch increasingly entertaining as the weeks wore on and it felt good to have someone that knew how to handle himself rather than having to worry if they were going to screw him over all the time. And, until tonight, he'd never seen a single break in the calm demeanor Mitch projected to the world. "You know my resources are available to you whenever you want. If you ever need anything, don't bother to ask. Just send the boys wherever you need them to be."

Mitch tilted his head Jimmie's direction, filled with curiosity. Even Sonny expected answers when Mitch called in a favor. He couldn't imagine Jimmie would be different, especially considering the short time they had known one another. Even more bewildering was that Jimmie had somehow picked up in the atmosphere that something was wrong. He could deny it, of course, but there seemed no point. So, instead, he nodded his thanks. "Appreciated but this isn't something that requires an army of hired hands."

Jimmie hesitated but only for a brief second. "Then how about mine? Whatever you need, we'll take care of it together."

"Thank you, again, but really I just need a few days off for some personal business. Considering the current circumstances that's impossible so it will just have to hold."

"You sure?"

Mitch swallowed the drink in his hand and gave Jimmie a brief smile. "It's held for a decade. Another few months won't make a damn bit of difference."

CHAPTER FIFTEEN

Mitch's eyes roamed over the guests, his unconscious noting something out of place that he couldn't quite register. Beside him, a blonde chattered mindlessly to Jimmie, but a quick glance told him Jimmie was as preoccupied as he was.

"Where's Ashli?" he murmured, and Jimmie nodded toward the edge of the room where she was leading a man down toward the private elevators.

He surveyed him, taking in any potential dangers in her latest conquest. He seemed harmless, nondescript even. He was dressed in a suit albeit not a high dollar one. A tie just a touch beneath obviousness so he wouldn't stand out in a crowd where he obviously felt uncomfortable. But it was the beads of sweat, the way the man repeated glanced over his shoulder and toward the front door that told Mitch something wasn't right. No family would be stupid enough to try a hit here in the Vinettis own hotel; they'd never make it out alive. Which meant there was only one thing he could be, and Mitch's stomach burned with fury as he realized what was about to happen.

He waved to Teddy just as he began a quick pace toward Ashli. He could feel Jimmie stepping in line beside him. Jimmie had felt it too...the edge in the air indicating something wasn't right. He just didn't have the knowledge that Mitch had to be able to figure it out.

"Teddy, get to the front door. Accept the warrant; we've got nothing to hide." He stopped mid-stride, realizing he was ordering around one of Jimmie's employees. "Sorry-"

But Jimmie waved him off. "Go."

When they reached Ashli, she was giggling like a teenager, draping herself against the guy. Mitch didn't hesitate before wrenching her away. "Get in the elevator."

"Mitch-" she looked torn between anger and fear.

It was impossible to control his fury. He wasn't so much angry with her as he was the IOC. That they would drop in on Vinetti without giving him a heads up. Hell, he'd met with Mike mere hours ago. They'd had plenty of time to pass the word but had chosen not to. Sure, the search of Sonny's place meant they were next – everyone knew that – but he didn't like being blind-sided by anyone. Unable to control the rage, his fist plowed into the nondescript guy she was with. Before he could lift him off the floor to hit him again, a flurry of Vinetti security was surrounding them and taking him on themselves. He whirled on Ashli, his eyes daring her to argue as he punched the elevator back open again and, placing his hand on her waist, shoved her into the car. Jimmie, one hand in his pocket, leaned against the car as the doors slid shut, waiting for answers. Instead, Mitch towered above Ashli, making her back into a corner as far away from him as possible.

"I told you never again. Never."

"Mitch, no, I-"

"Do you think I'm an idiot? Teddy's down accepting the warrants as we speak."

Ashli shook her head, realization dawning. "No, no. I had no idea-"

"Fuck whoever you want, Ashli, but I told you not to ever bring a fed into this building again. I will not be a part-"

"Mitch, I swear! God, I swear! He asked me to dance. That's it! Other than you and Jimmie he was the only guy willing to dance with me all night."

"And that wasn't enough to give you pause?" Jimmie asked, eyeing them both. "Who else would be stupid enough to try and make a move on you with both of us present?"

"Have you ever considered that someone might not give a shit and might actually find me attractive?" she hissed. "I'm not a damn doll you can put up in a display case, Jimmie."

Mitch growled. "This isn't about you! For chrissakes, Ashli, you sit behind a fucking desk all day and deal with accounts. It's not you who's in jeopardy by bringing feds in here, and you damn well know it. Probation for doctoring accounts isn't shit."

"Mitch, please-"

He stormed off the elevator as soon as the doors slid open, not caring if either of them followed. He couldn't deal with this. He'd been straddling these two worlds for years now. Giving the IOC only the needed information and no details about how he went about getting them was what had kept him above reproach. If the IOC didn't know what he engaged in then, they could hold nothing over his head. It was what made him different than every other agent they had. There was no way he was going to let his own life be put in jeopardy because she let his actions slip in the bedroom and the news got back to the IOC. He wouldn't allow them to have some illegal deed hanging over his head so they could order him around like a damn puppet.

She reached for him, but he was faster...his hands locking her in place against the wall, a vase crashing to the floor and shattering beside them. But he only held her there long enough to get attention before setting her loose. His voice, when he finally spoke, was a low, bitter, command. "Start acting like a Vinetti or get the fuck out."

CHAPTER SIXTEEN

Y ou told her not to bring feds here?" Jimmie asked, offering Mitch a glass of water as he sank onto the couch.

"I can fight outside forces," Mitch murmured. "I don't stand a chance fighting inside ones."

Jimmie nodded. "So that's it, then. What sets you off. I've wondered. Being unable to control a situation."

Mitch winced. It was a direct hit. He prided himself on hiding his emotions from everyone – IOC and mafia alike. It kept him alive. That he'd allowed Jimmie an opening as large as this one was hard to swallow. Maybe he was getting too old for this, too complacent after years of safety. He dragged a hand through his hair. "I need outta here."

"Sounds wonderful," Jimmie grinned. "But have you forgotten there are a hundred feds going through every room of this place?"

"Yeah and until they have something they can't arrest us." He stood up and grabbed his jacket. He wanted to be alone, but figured Jimmie needed an escape as much as he did right now. "You coming?"

"Where to?"

"We'll figure it out when we get there."

Less than a half hour later, the two men were several glasses down when Teddy stormed into the aging Italian eatery with his hand perched on his gun.

"Twenty minutes? Fall asleep on the job or something?" Mitch asked.

"The GPS server on the car when down," Teddy said, waving at the crew he'd brought with him to fan out around the restaurant.

"We disabled it," Jimmie offered and then tipped a bottle of whiskey Teddy's direction. "Join us?"

"No, sir, I can't-"

"If I know you, you brought no less than nine guys with you. I think we're safe."

"Eleven," Teddy nodded and took a seat at their table.

"How'd you find us?" Jimmie asked as he poured him a drink.

"That guy in the corner?" Teddy nodded to a shaky looking thug who kept glancing their way. "He owes you money. He called in to swear he was going to pay next week. You two must've scared the guy shitless showing up here."

"Ashli?" Mitch asked. Now that his anger had been tempered by liquor he could risk worrying for her safety.

"Locked in her suite. I put two guys on her room, but the feds are still swarming so no one's coming near the place."

"Markesi?"

"Also locked in his suite. Grabbed a handful of the old goombahs from the party and they've got a poker game going. Last I checked he was winning."

"What was the warrant for anyway?" Mitch asked and accepted the trademark yellow paper that Teddy pulled out of his pocket. He hesitated before reading it, raising it to Jimmie.

"My business is now yours. Let's hear it."

"Death of Jeffrey Coppell." Mitch raised an eyebrow expectantly. "Why would they think you have anything to do with that?"

"They arrested you for it," Jimmie laughed. "Seems like you brought the warrants down this time around."

"Nah, he was cleared," Teddy interrupted. He nodded toward Jimmie. "You off Coppell and get Mitch on your payroll and now business is booming. Seems a logical train of thought to me."

"Then they're idiots," Jimmie murmured.

Mitch sank back in his chair. The IOC knew Jimmie had nothing to do with it which meant they were searching for something else. The question was what. "What'd they harass Sonny for?"

"Trafficking narcotics," Jimmie offered snickering. "You'd think they could come up with something better than that, wouldn't you?"

"Pardon my question but isn't this why you had the security meeting tonight? To figure out what the feds are up to?" Teddy asked, looking from one man to the other.

"Yeah, well, *la familia* doesn't need to know everything, do they?" Jimmie shook his head.

"And they're probably thinking the same thing," Mitch grumbled. "Gino will be calling everyone to the table over this. Mark my words."

"Palmese?" Teddy shook his head. "No way. He's all the way in Sicily. He won't care what happens on this side of the pond."

Mitch didn't respond and dropped his eyes away from the piercing gaze Jimmie aimed his direction. He waved for another bottle and began pouring glasses for everyone as soon as it arrived.

It was Jimmie who finally broke the uneasy silence. "I figure Mitch is right. Palmese won't abide by dissension among the family. I'm surprised Coppell's death didn't spur a council meeting, to begin with. Coppell's holdings just got absorbed into Terenari's without much protest."

"Nicolai got Coppell's territory?" Mitch nearly choked. "No way in hell Gino approved that."

"He must have–"

"No. No fucking way." Mitch shook his head. "Gino wouldn't allow him an inch."

Jimmie didn't ask what made Mitch so certain but shrugged instead. "Then he's taken it upon himself to claim it."

"Nobody would be stupid enough to cross Palmese."

"Nicolai would," Mitch nodded solemnly. "He plays by a completely different set of rules, and he was in Atlantic last night. If the feds know, he's claiming Coppell's territory and then he appears on the east coast to solidify their opinion further–"

"Then the warrants on both Markesi and us make sense," Jimmie nodded. "But how would they know..."

"Ashli," Teddy offered, dropping his eyes from both men.

"Don't you dare–"

"Lay off, Jimmie," Mitch interrupted. "He's not calling her a traitor. He's saying what we all already know. She can't keep her mouth shut when she's in the sack, and we are getting to play cleanup for the aftermath. If we can't be honest at this table, there's no point in being here."

Although he continued to glare at Teddy, Jimmie nodded.

"Where's she getting the drugs?" Mitch glanced from one to the other.

"What?"

Mitch hesitated at the look on Jimmie's face. He didn't know...he really had no idea. "Are you fucking kidding me?" he hissed. "The moment she leaves the office, she's high as a kite, and you've never fucking noticed?"

Jimmie looked to Teddy for confirmation. It took several minutes before Teddy gathered the courage to respond.

"It's true. It's been going on for as long as I've worked here. Just alcohol at first then stronger stuff."

"Are there any other grand epiphanies about my organization you two need to launch at me tonight? Because, well, fuck you. Fuck both of you."

Mitch couldn't help but laugh. He could feel the anger rushing over Jimmie, but the hysterical nature of it all was just too much for him to contain. "Yeah, because we're the ones who've driven her to drown her life away, right? Come on, Jimmie, man up here so we can deal with this shit."

"You are an asshole," Jimmie grumbled and grabbed the bottle away from him to take a long swig.

"Okay." It was Teddy who tried to bring more decorum to the table. "We have the federal issue which seems like it will resolve itself if we can keep the feds out of her bed."

"That's been handled. She didn't know he was a fed, and I believe her. She wouldn't lie about that," Mitch answered and gave a soft laugh. "Not to me anyway."

"We have the issue of a fed getting in the damn building, to begin with," Jimmie said. "How exactly did that happen?"

"He didn't look like a fed!" Teddy defended.

"Mitch picked up on him instantly."

Mitch pulled the bottle back away from Jimmie and took a drink while forming his response. "We can tighten up the facial recognition software. Get one of the MIT guys to try and get us an updated database of federal employees."

"Or you know just have people watch for random strangers appearing at a private party," Jimmie grumbled.

"Stop deflecting," Mitch returned. "Teddy, you find out where her drugs are coming from. If you can't cut off the supply, tell me, and I'll do it. Jimmie, you lay off the big brother routine and give the girl some breathing space. She's as safe as she's going to be right now. If you don't trust her, then trust us to keep her safe. We need you to help us do our job, okay?"

"Assholes," he mumbled. "Both of you."

Mitch laughed. "Call the car, Teddy. It's time to go home."

CHAPTER SEVENTEEN

Y ou can't be here. Not now, not tonight."

"You do seem a little tense tonight," she said, moving to the bar to fix herself a glass of water. "Did something else happen? Or is this just left over from whatever Sonny said that tilted your whole world?"

He moved toward her, taking pleasure in the way she began to back up slowly. "*That* is none of your fucking business."

"You look...dangerous," she managed as he closed in on her, pinning her against the wall.

"Tell me you didn't know he was a fed. Tell me you didn't lie straight to my fucking face and betray me by bringing a fed into this building."

He could feel her hands shaking, hear the tinkle of the ice as her trembling hand caused the cubes to clink in the glass. But her eyes were as steady as he'd ever seen. She was fearful but not about to lie to him. "I promise you, I did not know he was a federal agent."

His body pressed her hips against the wall, his hands knocking the glass out of her hand and pushing her arms above her head. His lips were rough on hers, foregoing all gentleness with the adrenaline coursing through him. His teeth sunk into her neck, the yelp elicited from the back of her throat causing him to press even harder into her. He let her arms drop, grasping her thighs and pulling them to wrap around him as her moans became deeper. It was her nails digging into his shoulders that made reality rush back at him. He let her legs drop to the floor, his fists pummeling the door even as his lips continued to sear a path along her neck.

His voice, when he finally found it, was a hoarse growl. "I need you to leave."

◆ ◆ ◆

Mitch brushed the edge of her blouse to the side, the bruises his mouth had left behind glowing under the bright office lights. "I'm sorry for that," he whispered.

"I wasn't complaining," she smiled but made no attempt to move toward him.

"Still, it was uncalled for."

"Mitch, you warned me to leave. Stop acting as if you abused me or took advantage."

"I scared you. That's enough."

"You terrify me on a regular basis. In a million different ways." She let her fingers travel through his messy hair. "Don't apologize for that."

He leaned forward, brushing his lips gently across the marks before straightening her blouse to its proper place. "Thank you for leaving."

"I can be responsible, you know. I even went to bed alone."

Mitch shook his head. "I didn't."

"I know. And that's okay, too. If you're going to use some-one to ease your adrenaline rush or anger or hurt or whatever the hell that was, I'd rather it not be me."

"You are growing up, aren't you?" Mitch smiled and kissed her quickly on the forehead.

"Don't give me too much credit," Ashli frowned. "I fired her ass before you even had breakfast."

Mitch threw his head back in laughter. Still laughing, he cupped her face in his hands, giving her a gentle, lingering kiss. "That's my Ash, all right."

CHAPTER EIGHTEEN

M r. Kerlin?"

"Yeah?" He lifted himself from the bed, rubbing his face to try and wake up. When his eyes adjusted, a slender, strawberry blonde still dressed in her costume from the casino floor was watching him. He frowned. "What is it?"

"I'm sorry to wake you, but there is a man demanding to see you."

He looked at the clock flashing four am. "Demanding?" he asked, tossing the covers off and struggling into the pants he'd hung over the chair before collapsing into bed less than two hours earlier.

"Yes, sir." Her voice was quiet, her eyes dropping away from him as if she had somehow failed him. "He's armed, Mr. Kerlin."

Tucking his gun into his waistband, he stepped toward her, lifting her chin. He moved it from side to side, checking her for any damage. "Did he hurt you?"

"No, just frightened a lot of us."

"Did security flag him?"

"No, sir."

"He got a name?" he asked, pulling on a shirt and buttoning half the buttons.

"He announced himself as Daniel Rizetti," she said.

He straightened, the name familiar from somewhere he couldn't quite place. His brow furrowed as he tried to sift through the people he'd come across and, more specifically, one who would be so idiotic as to show up armed at the Vinetti building in the middle of the night. "Inform Jimmie for me, would you?"

"Yes, sir." She nodded obediently and then hesitated. "Would you like me to call additional guards, sir?"

He smiled. "No. I'll be fine but thank you for the concern. You sure you are all right?"

She nodded, a brief smile flashing over her face before taking off down the hallway.

He strode into the interior of his suite where Teddy was leaning against the bar, glaring furiously at the invader. Mitch chuckled and poured himself of a cup of the coffee that was already brewing. He took a sip and grimaced. "Teddy, your coffee sucks."

"I'll work on it, sir."

He leaned against the bar, eying the twenty-something kid sitting on the sofa across the room. The kid had turned his back to them and was sitting with his hands folded in his lap. Even from a distance, though, Mitch could see his body twitching. It was the gaudy brass colored ring on his pinky finger that finally caused Mitch's sleep deprived head to clear: Rizetti was one of Terenari's boys.

"You heavy?" he asked Teddy.

"Of course, sir," he answered, tapping the bulge under his left arm.

Mitch raised his voice, tipping the pot toward Rizetti. "Coffee, drink, Danny?"

"Coffee," Danny nodded, " I apologize for the late intrusion."

"Then you should have waited for breakfast," he countered, placing the cup on the table between them and sinking into a chair. "What can I do for you?"

He sent Mitch a quick flash of indignation as if Mitch had committed some unwritten rule by getting straight to the point. "Terenari is getting antsy, Mitch. You didn't call after Coppell, and now he hears you're with Vinetti. Now Vinetti's putting off a meeting for damn near five months-"

Mitch glanced at his watch to check the date. Five months. Had he really been with Vinetti that long? He grimaced, blaming his lack of knowledge on his recent travel schedule. "I have never made any commitment to Nicolai."

"But your history-"

"He didn't send you here to talk about old times," Mitch lowered his voice. "He wouldn't tell *you* of old times. I don't even know you so why the hell are you here?"

"Mr. Terenari wants to confirm the meet in Chicago. And," he hesitated, looking back toward where Teddy was still glowering, "he wanted to pass along some information as a measure of goodwill."

"Which is?"

Mitch could feel the air of superiority wash over the kid, his body even straightening to sit higher on the sofa. His eyes glinted, his voice dropping for only Mitch's ears. "Ashli's been marked."

Mitch hesitated, his fingers touching his gun in reflex. "Are we talking about the same Ashli here?" he asked. "Who by?"

"Your very own."

"Have you lost your goddamn mind?" his voice now a threatening, dangerous hiss.

"It could be a rumor," Danny interjected, seeing the break in Mitch's calm.

"Rumors that make it all the way to Nicolai usually have some more concrete basis," he snapped. "Get him on the phone."

"Mr. Kerlin, please, the time-"

"Now."

Danny nodded, his hands shaking as he picked up Mitch's phone and dialed the number. Groggy voices echoed from the other end as the phone was passed around.

"Mitch!" the voice sounded wide awake as if he'd been waiting for the call.

"Why the hell are you sending a guy to my place before dawn?" he growled, watching as Teddy moved to Danny, gripping his shoulder to lock him in place. "Have you lost all sense of decency in your old age?"

"Mitch, come now. Be civilized. It's been too long. I've missed that fiery temper of yours. I thought you would have come to me after Coppell, yes, but I'm not trying to give you an ultimatum."

Mitch hesitated. He'd never considered that was occurring, but now that it had been mentioned, he was livid. "You didn't send this kid over to tell me you regret who signs my paychecks, Nicolai. I want answers."

"I just want to meet. To catch up on old times and start anew with the east. Jimmie's being difficult, and I had hoped with our history-"

"I'm not starting a war here, Nicolai," Mitch warned.

"No war, Mitchell. Just conversation, you have my word on it."

"Trust is not my strong suit. As you well know."

"Of course but speak with Jimmie? I'm optimistic that the return will be positive."

"And Ashli?" he asked, almost as an afterthought.

Terenari let out a sympathetic sigh. "Terrible situation but I trust in your abilities far too much to think any outside intervention would ever be necessary for someone like her."

Mitch clicked off the phone, tossing it to the table. He was up and pacing now, silent as he contemplated Nicolai's guarded and all too accommodating statements. He knew Jimmie wasn't purposefully delaying the meeting. Jimmie had wanted to do it months earlier, but their schedule just hadn't allowed it. Why Nicolai would try and use Ashli as bait was beyond him. Unless he had some reason to believe that Ashli being in danger would be an irresistible taunt for Mitch.

He raised his eyes to Teddy. "Did you hear that?"

"Sir, I wasn't eavesdropping." Teddy straightened up, his nervousness obvious. Mitch couldn't blame him. Who would want to be a part of one mafia boss threatening another?

"If I asked you to remember key phrases, could you?" he asked.

Teddy's eyes flashed as he tried to decide what his answer was supposed to be and then he gave a single nod. "I think my amnesia could clear, yes sir."

"Good." Mitch turned to Danny, his eyes narrowing. "Your boss is persistent."

"That he is."

"Explain about Ashli."

"I can't, Mr. Kerlin. Really-"

"Did that sound like a request? I apologize. Let me be more precise: tell me about Ashli."

Danny's voice raised a few octaves, and his words came in a rush. "She's dangerous. Everyone knows that. Some kid in Atlantic is saying she's been talking too much. Complaining too much."

"She's a woman, of course, she complains," he snorted. "But she's not dangerous. Just scared. She's a little kid that's suddenly got bullets flying at her."

"Exactly. When you get scared, you either get stupid or very talkative. No one figures Ashli Vinetti for being stupid. She's going to give, and everyone has just been waiting for it. You coming just gave her an excuse."

"You know," he growled, "it sounds like you're trying to lay a lot of shit at my feet."

"No, no." He was backing up, moving toward the glass windows and away from Mitch and Teddy.

"Ashli has not copped a plea with anybody. And until you have proof otherwise, keep your fucking mouth shut, do you understand me?" Mitch had his hands around Danny's throat in a flash, pinning him against the wall. "If she does, it's something we'll handle within the family."

"If she rats, it is not just a family problem," Danny choked. "Other people are becoming leery of Vinetti's ability to handle his own family problems. You know that. We all know that. And if he can't handle her, someone else will."

Mitch's fingers tightened around Danny's throat, bouncing him hard against the glass. "You come into my home and threaten me? Threaten the Vinettis?" he spat. "Get outta here before I choke the life out of you on fucking principle."

Mitch was thundering away, his fury uncontrollable, when he heard the click. It was followed immediately by another. He stopped, knowing what he was going to see before he even bothered to turn around. He made a slow pivot, calm washing back over him. Finally...something that was in his control.

"Fuck you!" Danny was trembling, his fear making him unable to keep consistent aim.

Mitch's eyes traveled over Danny, deciphering the threat. He was truly just a kid. A kid sent on a simple errand who unwittingly got caught in a lifelong feud. Mitch raised his hand and lowered it, directing Teddy to lower his gun.

"Is this what it has come to for Nicolai?" he probed. "Sending children out to do his dirty work?"

"You piece of shit; I don't know why Terenari bothers with you."

"You don't come into someone's home and pull a gun on them. It's not how things are done. Has Nicolai taught you nothing?"

"If it wasn't for that whoring daughter of his-"

Mitch advanced on him, ignoring the gun pointing at his chest. He heard the click of Teddy's gun as he cocked it; heard the alarm go off as someone entered the suite without the correct key code. Taking advantage of the distraction, he lunged for Danny, knocking the gun out of his hand and dropping him to the ground with two well-placed shots in the jaw. His voice was low, furious. "Don't you ever, ever, put a fucking gun in my face."

A soft whistle sounded from somewhere behind him. "Things getting a little out of hand in here or what?"

Mitch didn't bother to look up but continued pummeling Danny, blood now staining his knuckles. When Danny finally stopped moving, Mitch sank to the floor, leaning his back against the sofa as he tried to catch his breath. Jimmie's hand reached across his vision, placing a glass of orange juice in his hand.

Jimmie sipped his own glass of orange juice as he nudged Danny with his foot, tilting his unconscious bloodied face to the ceiling. "Was he this ugly when he got here?"

"Not quite," Mitch breathed, his temper returning to normal under Jimmie's calming nonchalance.

"You," Jimmie waved to Teddy, "take the trash out, will you? And get that alarm shut off."

"Yes, sir." Teddy nodded and moved to Danny's prostrate form.

Offering Mitch a hand, he pulled him up from the floor and moved to the counter. "I come up for a normal breakfast-" Jimmie joked as Mitch began washing off the blood in the bar sink.

"Sheila called," he explained. "The strawberry blonde? She was worried about you."

"Nice to know."

"Well, you are nothing if not consistently attractive to the ladies," he murmured, surveying Mitch and shaking his head. "Although one wonders why when you always end up bleeding all over my furniture."

Mitch grinned. "Not my blood. Makes me the hero."

"Do you read literature, Vincenzo?" he asked, opening a bottle of vodka and tipping some into both their glasses.

"Too passive an activity for me."

"Heroes only appear in tragedies."

"And your point, scholar?" he asked his voice muffled as his used his teeth to tie the dish towel around his knuckles.

"Heroes always die."

Mitch groaned. "I've got a half dead guy in my living room, could you get to the fucking point here, Jimmie?"

Teddy couldn't withhold his snicker, and he immediately dropped his head, dragging Danny quickly out of the suite.

"Don't be the hero. I kinda like having you around," Jimmie said and then nodded toward the towel wrapped around Mitch's hand. "You want to tell me what the hell happened here?"

"Terenari sending his reminder about the meeting."

Jimmie frowned. "You're holding out on me."

"And you me," he countered.

"Why is Terenari coming to you instead of me?"

"Why didn't you tell me people are after Ashli?"

Jimmie jerked up, his back straightening and his eyes wide. It took a moment for him to regain his composure. "I shouldn't be surprised, I suppose. From everything I've heard about you-" he trailed off, moving to windows in avoidance.

Mitch followed, tipping more vodka into his glass. Nodding his thanks, Jimmie sank to sit beside Mitch on the sofa and lowered his voice. "She's scared, I know. It makes people talk."

"Jimmie," Mitch was quiet, "I can't protect her if I don't know the truth. Rumors fly all the time that people are copping pleas. It's a given in this life. But if people believe it, if they are willing to try and kill her because they believe it to be true, I have to have answers."

"It's not true. She's under guard 24/7, Mitch. She couldn't even if she wanted to. My men would catch her in an instant."

"Then she is in danger. Not a simple tightening of security for Coppell's death. There are people making attempts on her life."

"Threats," Jimmie corrected. "We've had no attempts. Except for that night at the warehouse with you which was just-"

Bizarre? Ridiculous? Bogusly planned by Jimmie's own sister, so there was no actual danger? Mitch shook his head. There was no way to try and assimilate that fabricated evening into the reality they were now facing. "Dismissive," he supplied, and Jimmie nodded.

"She was rebelling for a while. No constantly, before you came along. She'd tried everything in her power to shake my guys."

"She's over that?"

"Seems to be," he shrugged. "Was that your doing?"

"I tried to convince her that you were only trying to protect her," he admitted. "But I sincerely doubt that has anything to do with her decision to accept the new security measures."

"Probably has a fling with one of them going now," Jimmie grumbled.

Mitch chuckled. "So, what now? We going to keep hiding out or is it time to take the offensive?"

A slow, dark smile spread across Jimmie's face. "What do you have in mind?"

CHAPTER NINETEEN

In the end, it was Jimmie's plan that made headlines. Once the decision was made, everything fell into place quickly. The east coast families were invited to the casino, a lavish private party allowed everyone peace and security and, with as much fanfare as possible, Mitch was given shares in Vinetti holdings. It was a statement, a promise, and a threat all wrapped in one. Mitch warned the IOC of the intention and warned them to stay away or be deemed an immediate threat to all the families. Mike didn't like it...he groused for nearly an hour but finally relented. The IOC would not intervene. They agreed, just like Jimmie had, that Terenari was the more pressing issue and nothing was more likely to rouse his attention than a party to which he was ceremoniously not invited.

Now, as the party raged on below, Mitch was keeping silent vigil in his office several floors above. As with daily observations, he could see everything going on but manage to stay removed from it.

"Permanence, then?" Sonny asked, stepping into the office with a single knock.

"That's your biggest concern in this whole affair?"

"Well, yeah." Sonny frowned. "It's a different world for you, and I'm just-"

Mitch smiled. Worried. Sonny was worried. "It's political, Sonny. Nothing more."

"But-"

"I've already signed them back," Mitch said. "It's in a locked vault to be pulled out as needed."

"Vinetti demanded that?"

"No. He and Ashli both were pretty put out by it actually. That was my condition."

"I should've known. You aren't going to tie yourself to anything ever, are you?"

"You sound disappointed."

"Well, yeah, I kind of am. I mean, I wasn't crazy about the idea of it being Vinetti but, yeah, I'd love for you to stop this drifting shit."

"Your dislike of Vinetti is so perplexing to me. You know that right? The Ashli story doesn't fly anymore."

Sonny shrugged. "He endangers you, brother. What more reason do I need?"

Mitch laughed. "And you don't? Hell, most of the time I manage to find my own trouble."

"He-"

"What?"

"Nothing. Nevermind."

"Damn, Sonny, just say it. Whatever it is."

"I see what you don't, Mitch. It's what Palmese sees, too. The two of you are a damn formidable force."

"Is that what this is about? We aren't moving to take Atlantic City from you. I wouldn't be a part of something like that. You shouldn't even entertain-"

"No, no," Sonny sighed. "I only meant, there's few people you would willingly lay down your life for, right? And I see it. Palmese sees it. Vinetti is becoming one of those people."

"Bullshit." His denial was quick and unthinking, but Mitch felt a tug deep in the pit of his stomach. If it were true, if he had somehow bound himself to Jimmie - things had to change. Fast.

Sonny shrugged. "Whatever you say. But I'll tell you something...whether you see it or not, no man working for Vinetti has ever been trusted to spend two minutes alone with his little sister. Think about that the next time she's in your arms, okay?"

"So he trusts me with-" Mitch trailed off, refusing to admit the words aloud. For Jimmie, there was probably no deeper level of trust than that. "Fuck."

Sonny chuckled. "Yeah, fuck." He nodded toward the floor, where Teddy and Jimmie were striding toward them. "Heads up."

Tension etched into Mitch's muscles, unable to shake the curve Sonny had thrown him. He tried to bury it as they approached but when they mentioned Ashli's name, he finally broke.

"This is bullshit," Mitch growled. "We have more important things to be discussing than who your little sister is bedding tonight."

Jimmie surveyed him, picking up on the tension immediately. "What's happened? What's the matter with you?"

"Half of *la familia* is here," Teddy pointed out. "The wrong pick and-"

"War ensues. Yeah, I know it matters but for chrissakes, it doesn't require a meeting."

Stepping away from the men, he took the stairs two at a time. Ignoring the men surrounding her, Mitch grabbed Ashli's hand and pulled her onto the dance floor.

"What are you doing?" she hissed.

"Dancing with you. Is that a problem?"

"An unexpected occurrence. Are you drunk?"

"I imagine you've downed enough for both of us. Would you like another?" Rather than wait for an answer he motioned to a waiter and grabbed a glass of champagne off the tray.

"Are you angry? Have I done something wrong?"

Mitch hesitated, suddenly unsure. How she could transform from an independent, self-assured diva to an insecure child so instantly was beyond him. Normally he would chalk it up as an act to gain an emotional advantage over him, but the glazed look on her face told him she was too intoxicated to think that clearly. Taking the now empty champagne glass away and handing it to a nearby stranger, he looked at her more seriously.

"Did you take something other than alcohol tonight, Ash?"

"It breaks my heart when you call me that," she whispered. "Jimmie called me that when we were kids. Until my dad was killed. He hasn't called me that since."

"Hey," he tipped her chin upward. "What did you take? Can you tell me?"

"I'm not going to pass out on you and make a fool of Vinetti Industries. I do have some scruples."

"I worry about you so much more than I should," he mumbled.

"Did you mean to say that out loud?"

"Not at all," he admitted. He tugged her body into his, feeling her react instantly to the change in his touch. He left his hand drift gently over her bare shoulder, exhaling a breath to let it follow his fingertips.

"Everyone is watching us," she mumbled.

"That's what I'm counting on." One hand reached to cup her head, his fingers entwining in her hair. His lips drifted across hers, gently at first, slowly and deliberately tracing around the edges. She was already breathless before he finally pressed his lips into hers. Making a scene was what he wanted, he wanted all eyes on them...where every man in the building took notice. What he didn't count on was his body's reaction to her and the moment his lips touched hers the electrifying need that washed over him. They had been playing with fire for months, and now, he had been stupid enough to light the fuse. When he finally pulled away, her eyes were already open and looking at him.

"You were laying claim," she accused. "Making sure no other man in here would come within 100 feet of me."

"Yes."

"At least you don't deny it. Was this my brother's idea?"

"Your brother may try to murder me in my sleep."

"That gives me some vindication."

He couldn't help himself and pulled her into him again. His lips harder, more possessive. His hands grazed up the center of her back, feeling her flesh shiver with his touch.

"You know what makes this so dangerous?" she asked, her lips hovering near his ear. "Everyone fears Jimmie, but you don't."

No, Mitch thought. What makes it dangerous is that Jimmie was even allowing it in the first place. Sonny had been right. Jimmie would never tolerate his actions from someone else. "Is that what you like about me, Ash?" he hissed. "Because, I've got to be honest, continually hearing his name out of your mouth when I've got you in my arms is becoming insulting."

"No, that's not it."

His voice was husky, his grip tightening on her waist. "Then tell me, honestly. For once tell me the goddamn truth."

Her fingers slipped to his cheek, tracing a line up to his eyes. Even drugged, her eyes were clear enough to let him know she was telling the truth.

"Because you call me Ash."

It was more honest that he expected and it took him off guard. As simple as the words were, he knew exactly what she meant. He took her for who she was - the ugly, the broken parts, the parts that were responsible for murder combined with the calm, independent princess. Tears had started to trickle down her cheeks, and he placed his palms over them, hiding them before the world could see.

"I have business."

She nodded, accepting, and he could see her trying to get her emotions back in check.

"I'll be upstairs as soon as I can."

"Mitch, Jimmie will-"

"He's my problem now," Mitch assured her.

CHAPTER TWENTY

Y ou came." Ashli frowned.

"You doubt me quite a lot, don't you?"

"The opposite actually. But, after that scene, I did figure that Jimmie would make a point of keeping you away."

Mitch pulled off his jacket and tossed it to the chair beside her bed. Loosening his shirt, he dropped to stretch out onto the covers before accepting the glass of Scotch she offered.

"Everyone seems on edge," Ashli said. "Since your late night visit a few weeks ago. I get the impression I didn't hear the full story of that night."

"That would be an excellent assumption."

"Are we in danger then?"

"Yes."

"From whom?"

Mitch was silent, fingering the glass in his hand. He wished he had an answer, but the truth was, he just didn't know. Sensing his hesitation, Ashli slid to sit beside him, her hand resting on his waist.

"You've made this place better than Fort Knox. If something happens, it's not on your shoulders, Mitch."

"Thank you, Ms. Vinetti."

"I only meant-"

"I know what you meant," he said, waving her off. "None of it makes sense. I feel like I'm missing some vital piece of information, but Jimmie assures me that's not the case."

"Jimmie has no reason to hide anything from you."

"And you?" Mitch questioned, threading his fingers through hers. "What else are you hiding from us, Ashli?"

"Us," she whispered.

Setting his glass aside, he pulled her hand toward him. Without meeting her eyes, he pressed his lips into her palm and started tracing the pale blue veins in her wrist. "It bothers you, doesn't it? My relationship with your brother."

"No. Yes."

He raised an eyebrow as he continued to pepper her skin with kisses. "But it's not the jealousy everyone suspects, is it?"

She shook her head but didn't vocalize a response.

"No, you never did strike me as the jealous type," he murmured. He shuffled, moving her onto the bed completely, his palm brushing from the curve of her shoulders down the length of her body.

He let his fingers run gently through her hair, feeling her defenses lessen with each stroke. He could feel the dampness of her tears as they slid down his arm and he knew, whatever had been plaguing her had finally reached its tipping point.

"Has your guilt surfaced yet?" he asked.

She nodded. "I love him. I do. He's my brother."

"But it would make things so much less complicated without him around?" Mitch guessed.

"No. It would be so much easier if I weren't around," she corrected. "So much of his life, so much of the danger he faces is my fault. My responsibility. Our whole life it's been that way."

Mitch stopped moving, his eyes focusing on her. "Dramatics don't suit you."

"You think I'm being dramatic?"

He watched her again, trying to decide if he'd misjudged. But she had veiled her emotions with indignation. He exhaled and moved off the bed.

"Mitch, for chrissakes, I'm trying, to be honest!"

"Then stop trying and just be honest. It's not that damn hard."

"Mitch, please-" she was at his side, tears still streaming. "Don't tell me you haven't gotten in so far with something, so desperately deep, that you couldn't even see a way out. I know you have."

"You're drowning." He gave her a gentle smile. "Ash, I've known that from the second I met you."

"Then you do understand."

"This ends where it began, Ash. That's the way it always works." His whispered voice caused her to tip her face toward him, and it was impossible for him not to see the child she tried to keep buried. "Tell me where this started. Tell me and let me end it."

It would be his way out - if she told him the truth, he could stop whatever had brought this danger into their lives.

Whether it required IOC intervention or a rougher, darker hand, he could fix it and then get the hell out.

"You could do that, couldn't you?" she asked. "You could make us safe again."

Mitch didn't hesitate. "Without a doubt."

"And you could move on with your own life?"

"Yes."

His finger slid across her jawline, his forehead touching hers. "The truth, Ashli. That's all I'm asking for."

"I can't." It was quiet, barely a whisper but with a determination he hadn't expected. The strong-willed business Ashli was back.

He sighed. "Then you are not the Vinetti I'll have at my side." He dug his hands into his pockets, his eyes darkening. "Get out."

He was still standing in the same position when Jimmie entered his suite moments later. They eyed each other, neither saying anything, neither moving. Mitch was prepared for a battle, an argument or even a gunshot but none came.

"Terenari has invited us out to his place for a meeting. If you think it's safe, then we can leave tonight."

"Ask me, Jimmie." Mitch waved off the denial he knew coming. He was only half dressed, the bed was a disaster, and there was no way he had missed Ashli leaving the room totally disheveled. "Just fucking ask me."

"Did you sleep with my sister?"

"No." Mitch shook his head. "But if I had-"

"I'd be justifiably incensed." Jimmie let out a long, drawn breath. "But, she could make a far more dangerous choice."

"Then never, ever, ask me again."

CHAPTER TWENTY-ONE

Shares of Vinetti Industries and you are on the front page of every newspaper from here to California. What the hell, Mitch? What the fucking hell?"

"I told you it was coming."

"Not at this level of publicity! Do you know how far we have to bury your record? By the time this is over, only the freaking President is going to have access."

"Good."

"Good? Mitch, you cannot have a personal stake in his business."

"I have a personal stake in every case I've ever been a part of, Mike. Jimmie's just happens to be a financial one. I've already signed it back anyway."

"Truth?"

"Yes, that's the truth. I'll have a copy sent to you to prove it if you like."

He scowled. "Don't send me anything."

"The President then? Maybe he'd like a copy?"

"Fuck you, Mitch."

Mitch snickered. "Anything else?"

"The publicity?"

"That I could do without it," Mitch agreed. "We needed Terenari's notice but, yeah, they won't seem to let the story go."

"They say you and he are a force that could take on Palermo. How am I supposed to explain that?"

"Who's asking for an explanation?"

"Everyone!"

Mitch frowned at the non-response. If possible, Mike was even more put out than he was. He offered a half smile. "I'll try and keep out of the papers."

"Thank you. That would be just a grand help."

Mitch nodded.

"And Terenari?"

"Heading to the plane once I leave you."

"He's not...he's dangerous, Mitch."

"They all are."

"Just watch yourself, okay? I don't want the papers reporting on your death either."

"Duly noted," Mitch grinned and squeezed his shoulder. "And thanks."

CHAPTER TWENTY-TWO

Mitch froze, his mind unwilling to believe what his eyes were telling him were true. But there was she was, standing paces behind one of Nicolai's security guards, her piercing carbon black eyes watching him with the mischievous glint that transported him back to his childhood. Tendrils of coffee colored hair were piled haphazardly on her head, at odds with the rest of her polished look, her one act of defiance at having to dress up for her father's business associates. His eyes left hers momentarily, long enough to let them roam across the curves that she had acquired in the decade since he'd last seen her. Had she not spoken, he could have easily believed her to be a drunken mirage.

"Mr. Kerlin," she gave him a curtsy and offered her hand in greeting since he seemed unable to pull himself together. "Welcome, we're honored with your visit."

Mitch kissed her hand, his eyes still not breaking the gaze. "Antoinette-" his voice broke in disbelief, and he tried to shake himself, but too many memories were flooding through him for him to regain his composure.

Conscious of the men around them, Toni pulled him into a warm embrace, her lips grazing his ear. "Don't let my presence distract you," she murmured, "that's what he wants."

She broke away from him and sent him a winning smile. "It's been awhile, hasn't it? Life seems to have treated you well." She fingered his suit, her slender hands traveling down the lapels and tugging gently on his Italian leather belt. "Is it Brioni?"

"Haven't a clue," he returned, managing a shrug. "Some guy fits me; I wear what appears in my closet."

Her words had their intended effect- he had shaken clear of the shock of seeing her. Why she would choose to betray her father's intentions was a mystery to him, and he slid his arm around her waist as they moved down the hallway as the guards closed at their feet.

"You look quite phenomenal yourself," he appraised hoping his voice was returning to its normal steady state. "How is boarding school treating you?"

She narrowed her eyes at him. "Exactly how fucking old do you think I am?" she growled under her breath, causing him to laugh.

"Yeah, you're not a mirage," he chuckled again.

She hesitated at a doorway, turning face him. "We allow no weapons beyond this point. Safety, of course. Are you packing, Mr. Kerlin?"

"No."

"No?" she queried, eying him with disbelief.

"No," he chuckled, smiling down at her. He undid the button on his jacket and opened it wide. "However, it would be my pleasure if you feel the need to check."

"You are still such an ass," she managed under her breath, watching as he stepped into the room and the door closed behind him.

"You've come alone?" Terenari asked, hugging Mitch as he stepped into the conference room. "I thought Jimmie was to chaperone us."

"He is arriving later," Mitch nodded. "I just needed a few minutes alone with you."

"Of course, of course!" Terenari's white teeth flashed a grin, his arms waving to the men around the room. "Please, leave us, won't you? My old friend," Terenari hugged him again, leading him to chairs in the corner as the men filtered out of the room.

One remained, standing with his hand perched on his gun. Mitch inclined his head toward him.

"You do not trust me, Nicolai? Have we come to this already?"

"Certainly not, my boy." He shook a pudgy finger at the man. "I said leave us, must I say it twice?"

"Sir-"

"Go or I'll shoot you myself!" he roared, and the man disappeared immediately.

"You rule with an iron fist."

"Is there any other way?"

"There used to be," Mitch shrugged. "I was surprised to see Antoinette."

"Yes, I thought you might be. She's turned into a beautiful woman, hasn't she?"

"Indeed. Looks just like her mother."

Nicolai chuckled at the implied insult. "We can all thank God for that, can't we? Hopefully, she'll age with grace."

"Grace is an interesting description of your daughter."

"Oh, you'll see. She has calmed herself since the old days. She'll make a fine, loyal wife. Knows how to mind her own business too, if you know what I mean. But loyal. Loyal above everything."

"As any daughter should be," Mitch nodded. "Nicolai..."

"You want to warn me about Jimmie? He's a hot head, I know. It warms me to know you still care enough to take the time for me, Mitchell. Vinetti's no good for you. He has no vision. Not like you and I-"

"I didn't come here to warn you about Jimmie," Mitch corrected. "I came to let you know; you'll receive no loyalty from me should you make a move against Vinetti."

Nicolai raised his hands, laughing. "No, no. Of course not. He will not make you happy, but I wouldn't interfere in your decisions. Vinetti will be safe. It was you I wanted to see anyway." He took hold of Mitch's hand, grasping it tightly in his own. His voice dropped several octaves. "You have not told him, then, about our history?"

"I didn't feel it necessary."

"And if I should?"

"Then so be it," Mitch shrugged and stood up. "Your choice is your own."

"You mistake my words for a threat, Mitch. I mean no such disrespect. I merely wanted to make certain you are comfortable with whatever may slip out of this old, addled brain." He waved a hand across his forehead dismissively, a crooked grin on his face.

"Addled will never be an apt description for you, Nicolai. And tell him what you wish. I care little what Jimmie knows of our relationship."

"You know, we are celebrating tonight," he said, clapping Mitch on the shoulder. "Yesterday was my daughter's birthday. You and your friends are welcome to join in the merriment. Then, tomorrow, we shall meet, hm? Pleasure before business?"

"Nicolai-"

"Come, we mustn't disappoint Antoinette. How long has it been for you two?"

"I'm certain she wants nothing to do with me, Nicolai. Surely you remember-"

"She has grown up, Mitchell. Seen the error of her ways. She is at my side. She could easily be at yours-"

"I doubt she is nearly so forgiving of me as she is to her father," Mitch smiled. "But nonetheless, I shall make sure to save her a dance."

CHAPTER TWENTY-THREE

Something had changed in Ashli and Mitch couldn't decide if he quite trusted it or not. The party had been in full swing for hours, but she had remained on the sidelines, quietly sipping the same glass of wine all evening. She chatted with those that approached, danced a few times with Jimmie and Sonny but had otherwise remained a quiet, dutiful Vinetti. It unnerved him.

"You are ever the wallflower tonight." He sank into a chair beside her. "Should I be wary?"

"Always." She offered him a brief smile. "I'm pretending to be you tonight. Watching, observing, evaluating."

"How's that going for you?"

"Honestly? It's no wonder your brain is always functioning at, like, some higher level. It's exhausting trying to keep track of the goings on."

"Was that a compliment or an olive branch?"

She shrugged. "Both. I think."

"Then I accept. Both, I think." He leaned forward and clinked glasses with her. "So what have you surmised?"

"You know Antoinette. And Terenari, for that matter."

"You've been surveilling me?" He laughed. "Okay, I'll bite. Yes, I know them both."

"How well?"

He frowned. That was the question, wasn't it? He knew the people they used to be. Who they had turned into? That still plagued him.

"That wasn't meant to be a hard question."

"It's a complicated one nonetheless. How well do I really know you, Ashli?"

But she was not to be diverted. "You look at her differently."

"Pardon?"

"Antoinette Terenari," Ashli explained. "You look at her differently than you do everyone else. Like she has broken your heart."

"You are observant tonight."

"Is it true?"

"No," he shook his head, offering her a false smile. "I broke hers."

"You were lovers?"

"No. I was a big brother. Her superman, I suppose, in the world in which we grew up."

"As you are mine now," she offered.

"I failed her," he warned, his voice emotionless.

Ashli softened, her hand reaching out to touch his. "You won't fail again," she whispered. "It's no longer in you to fail."

"You trust in me far too deeply," he replied, uncomfortable with her sudden possessiveness. "If you'll excuse me."

She was standing in a group of men; the smile plastered across her face seemingly an opening for any of them. They were chattering, offering her birthday wishes or some other nonsense. She was adjusting her dress, a long burnt orange velvet that contrasted with her dark hair when her eyes lifted to meet his. He stepped through the crowd, offering her his hand. She hesitated, and he half expected her to reject it completely but, with a glance around her, she took it and let him lead her onto the edge of the dance floor. He stood without moving, one hand sliding to her waist, and the other drifting across her cheek as if he was still afraid she was a mirage.

"We're being watched," she murmured, her eyes meeting his. "Dance with me?"

He nodded, pulling her into his arms, keeping her body inches from his in an awkward formal stance.

"You certainly know how to make a grand entrance."

"After this long, any entrance would be a grand one. Tell me, do you always surprise so easily or was it just for me?"

"Only you."

"At least that's something," she grumbled. "You haven't lost your ability to charm the ladies, I see."

"And you haven't lost that venomous tongue of yours," he laughed.

"Is she your latest conquest?" she asked, nodding towards Ashli who was now spinning around the floor with Jimmie.

"Wouldn't you love to know?"

"Looked more like you were conversing with the devil," she countered.

"Feels a bit like that when I'm around Ashli," he admitted. "But she's completely different when you get her out of public view."

"I can relate to the two different worlds syndrome," she laughed. "Vinetti seems like a pretty decent guy."

"Haven't been with him too long," he hedged.

"Do you stay anywhere very long?"

"Not if I can help it. What about you? What happened to those college dreams and getting far removed from all of this?" he made a sweeping motion with one hand before pulling her back into his arms.

"Do we really want to relive how our choices over the past decade had led either of us to this spot right now?" she asked, inclining her head to one side. "You, Gino's gifted one, being courted by my father? Me, the former anti-mafia girl, being bounced around the room as if I'm up for show?"

"Are you saying we're both making mistakes?"

"I'm asking if it really fucking matters," she grumbled and dropped her head back to his shoulder. "We're here, and there's not a damn thing either of us can do about it now."

"Damn, you have become one bitter broad, haven't you?" he laughed and pinched her waist playfully. He slipped his hand into hers, entwining their fingers. "Come, let's get some air."

"They're watching us," she hissed, trying to hold him back.

He chuckled, dropping his lips next to her ear. "They'd be fools not to."

She stood a pace behind him as they stepped onto the balcony, his hand still holding tight to hers as if afraid she might leave his side. Several men lounging against the railing straightened with their appearance nodded a silent greeting and then moved passed them and back inside. She smiled, knowing even her father could not clear an area so easily. He turned without warning, and her hands went instinctively to his chest, blocking a collision. But once they were there, she seemed unable to move them.

This was the body that had once laid beside her in the backyard, hoping for stars but seeing only citron glows from the street lights overhead. The chest was wider, definitely more muscular but the curves and angles all still felt the same. She had memorized them in the days following her mother's death when she curled into his protective arms and shut the world away even when a dozen mourners were in the same room offering their condolences. Her couch had forever smelled like him- smoky, from his family's wood fire, with a hint of menthol from the crème he'd been using since he started shaving a few months earlier. He was the only one that she ever really considered her friend.

And yet, he was the one who had left her. Deserted her to join this family of lawbreakers and murderers that she had once abhorred with a passion deeper than any lust she'd ever experienced. She'd spent weeks curled up in that same spot on the sofa, worrying about the terrible things that might be happening to him in jail but, at the same time, cursing him into oblivion for being so stupid to have involved himself in this world in the first place. By the time he'd gotten released, Nicolai had shipped her away to boarding school in France. She'd never heard from him again and never had the courage to try and contact him.

"I hated you," she whispered, her head dropping into him, his arms tightening around her shoulders in the hug he couldn't offer her in public.

"Have you grown out of that yet?" he questioned, his voice equally soft with no trace of sarcasm. "Because I've missed you, girl."

She didn't respond immediately, moving a few paces away from him so she could think clearly. Memories flooded through her, as she knew they were Mitch, and she needed time to quiet them. She had forgiven him. Years ago, in fact. And the moment she had returned to Nicolai's side she knew they would meet again- the circle they ran in was much too small to believe otherwise. But this was not the way she had anticipated. She had envisioned a wedding or perhaps a funeral where she could be aloof and cold and treat him as if he was nothing more than a hired hand while she was the daughter of the man Mitch feared.

But Mitch feared no one- his easy stride into the meeting with her father had proven that. Whether it was because he had become so self-assured over the years or just because he no longer gave a damn about anything, she couldn't hazard a guess. He should fear her father. He was not the honorable man he had been when they were kids. She had been with him, stood beside him, as he strangled a rival boss in their living room. If Mitch believed Nicolai would offer Mitch some sort of reprieve because their families had once been neighbors, he was deluding himself. He retained no such ties of loyalty.

"You have become quite the commodity it seems," she murmured, refusing to face him. "Is that what you wanted? Is this what you've worked so hard to achieve all these years-having men make fools of themselves to have you at their side?"

"I am not a piece of meat that can be bought at the local market," he growled, sliding his hands in his pockets to prevent her from seeing the fists that were drawing tighter. She of anyone should know him better than that. "My loyalty is not for sale. Feel free to take that back to your dearest father."

He was leaving her. Storming out. His blue eyes flashing daggers, hatred, and fury she hadn't witnessed since Gino had cornered him into staying in the States after the deportation fiasco when they were teenagers. She had cornered him now, even though she knew better, and she immediately regretted it.

Her hand reached to his arm, yanking him hard back toward her before he could escape. "I am not my father's errand girl," she murmured. "And I had no idea. I'm sorry."

"No idea what?"

The bitter voice told her she was still not forgiven, so she pulled him closer, ignoring the tense muscles and the fists still clenched in his trousers. "I had no idea what this must be like for you. Everyone wanting something from you. Every hour of every day someone gambling for a piece of who you are."

She tugged gently, and he let her pull one hand out so she could hold it tightly in hers. She stretched to her tiptoes but only when he leaned toward her could her lips reach his ear. "Please, I meant no offense."

"Are you always so apologetic to everyone? Or just the men your father wants on his payroll?" he asked icily, jerking away from her.

"And what is that supposed to mean?" she hissed.

"One minute you are insulting me and the next apologizing? Go find another sucker, Toni."

"Fuck you," she spat, her anger now matching his. "Do you think I want you working with my father? I'd do everything in my power to keep that from happening whether you are treating me like shit or not. I certainly wouldn't do anything to help him achieve his goals. Not without a gun to my head anyway."

Mitch tried to process her words. Even in her anger, there was a warning in there for him somewhere. He wasn't sure why it was obvious to him; perhaps she hadn't changed nearly as much as he thought she had. He'd never met a woman that didn't have some latent fury towards her father, but this was deeper, something she was expecting him to understand. Something he should understand but ten years away from her side had made it difficult to read between the lines. He used to know her every move, could utter her words before she spoke them, and knew which direction she would run when a street gang ambushed them on the way home from school.

But the bony kneed, scrawny, headstrong girl he knew was now a curvaceous, obstinate, woman that caused men and women alike to run in fear. She wasn't the attention seeking debutante of Ashli fame but drew people to her with a quiet, obscure need that was unexplainable. He'd seen it happening all evening- a man would take the time to walk across the room to her hushed corner only to face her with a dumbfounded look as if he'd forgotten why he had approached her in the first place. She'd fire back with a smart ass comment about what the hell he wanted only to have him scurry off in terror that he had now offended Nicolai Terenari's only daughter. He'd found it immensely entertaining throughout the evening. But now that her fiery temper was directed at him, it wasn't quite so amusing.

He tried to remember why he was angry with her but couldn't. She was protecting him. Or, at least in some measure of her mind thought she was. That made him worry for her sanity. No one, absolutely no one, worried about his safety. That was like worrying about the rain- death would come to him and likely in a very violent way just like the rain would fall whether you prayed for it or not. Both required the right set of circumstances but, with patience, the outcomes were both inevitable. He opened his mouth to speak and then closed it again, feeling utterly bewildered for the first time in over a decade.

"You-"

"I what?" she growled, her eyes narrowing even more in his direction, her hands moving to perch on her hips.

"You believe I'm worth saving," he whispered with incredulity.

CHAPTER TWENTY-FOUR

Mitch slipped off his shirt and stepped onto the balcony, letting the bitterly cold air assault his skin. If the meeting with Terenari hadn't been bad enough, the fighting between Ashli and Jimmie had sent his every remaining nerve on edge. Before leaving their suite down the hall, he threatened to throw them both off the 20th story if they didn't grow up. A soft knock at the door caught his attention, but he had no intention of answering it. Only Jimmie or Ashli could be visiting him at this hour, and he had no desire to see either. Jimmie would want to bitch about Ashli, and she would be seeking refuge. He didn't have the emotional balance for either.

"Mr. Kerlin-"

The soft voice caused him to whirl, his gun drawn in reflex. He lowered it immediately as Toni skittered back toward the glass door.

"Fuck," he slid it back into his waistband and shook his head. "Don't do that shit to me, Toni."

"My apologies," she murmured. "My father asked that I see if there is anything else you need before you depart."

Mitch turned, the unnatural cadence of her voice making his eyes narrow. He watched her attentively as she moved closer to him now that the gun had been safely tucked away. Her brilliant fuchsia slip shimmered under the hotel lights; her hair tussled in odd waves with the wind. He could see the shivers along her neck and arms, her clothing providing little protection from the frigid weather.

When she reached a hand out to graze along his bare chest, he jumped back as if she was on fire.

"Get inside before you freeze," he grumbled and, placing his hand on the small of her back, pressed her into the room and shut the sliding door. Grabbing a blanket off the bed, he wrapped it tightly around her shoulders and pushed her into a chair in the corner of the room.

"And what," he asked quietly, "could I possibly need at this hour?"

She didn't respond but remained sitting quietly in the chair, her eyes not meeting his. Her teeth were still chattering, her legs now folded up beneath her. Mitch moved to the phone and picked it up.

"No-"

He eyed her outburst with curiosity but kept the phone to his ear. "Can you send up a pot of coffee, please? Thanks." He hung up and paced only a moment before the coffee arrived.

"Mr. Kerlin, I apologize. We only have house blend available at this hour. If you'd like, we can send someone..."

"House is fine," Mitch waved him off and shut the door behind him. He poured two cups and took one to Toni, who still wasn't looking at him. "Take it," he ordered, and she undid her hands enough to do so. She sipped silently and, when half the cup was gone, he approached her again.

"Better?"

She nodded.

"Now, tell me what the hell you are doing coming to my room half naked at four in the morning."

"I believe you know why I'm here."

"If you were a whore, I suppose I might could fathom a guess," he said, dropping onto the edge of the bed nearest her. "But, as it is you, I am utterly perplexed."

Her eyes flashed. The angry, furious flash that he knew was a warning from childhood. It was the look that told him she was about to start throwing dishes or rocks or whatever else happened to be at hand. He slipped the cup away from her, but her eyes had returned to a dull, disinterested, black.

Her silence was answering him. It just took a moment before he understood. He looked at her with dumbfounded comprehension. "You have got to be kidding me."

"Nice to know you find me so amusing," she returned, her temper now flaring.

"Oh, come on, Toni. You show up in my room to seduce me, and you didn't anticipate that I would be at least a little amused? Do you think I'm that fucking hard up?"

"Pardon me?" she was on her feet now, the blanket falling to the floor, her fingers tightening into fists at her side. "What am I? Rabbit fodder?"

"No, no," he chuckled. "You are quite enchanting; I assure you. I just meant-"

"Yes, what did you mean?"

"Geez, Toni, you're like family. Come on." He grabbed the hotel robe from the bed and tried to help her pull it on, but she jerked away from him and thrust her arms into it by herself.

"It's not as if this was my idea, you know. The least you could do is be a bit of a gentleman here or did that get thrown out when you replaced everything else with the fancy Christophe Claret and diamond cuff links?" she spat, wrenching the robe tight around her waist.

Mitch sat the cup down slowly, his back turning away from her. She had been talking quickly, anger flooding through her, but it hadn't been directed at him. Her venom spewed, yes, but he had done nothing to warrant it. He replayed the words slowly in his head, but it was her touch- her hand sliding up his bare back- that brought things into focus for him. He turned slowly, her fingers moving with him as they traveled over his stomach and up his chest. He watched her intently, knowing her movements were purposeful, but her eyes were terrified. He reached his hands to her face, his hands holding her still to look at him. What had she said? A gun to her head...that's the only way she would be willing to help her father.

"Nicolai sent you to my bed?" He didn't expect her to respond, knew that she couldn't without betraying her father, but he knew her eyes could never lie to him. They hadn't been able to since she was eight and she had tried to steal his hotel during a marathon Monopoly session. When he received the unspoken answer, he pulled her into his chest, her head dropping heavily into him with an endless exhaustion. "Oh, girl," he murmured as her body began to shudder in his arms.

"Mitch-" Jimmie's abrupt voice called from the doorway and Mitch had no opportunity to move to a more appropriate stance before he rushed into the room. "Oh, I..." he took a step back.

"Don't you ever fucking knock?"

"How the hell was I-" Jimmie started but then stopped as Toni turned around and nodded his direction. Jimmie's gaze flew from one to the other, his body straightening with unanswered questions. "The plane's ready. Ashli took a commercial flight, and I'm heading out in a few minutes on the charter. If you need to take a later flight-"

"No." Toni's voice was strong, a smile plastered across her face. "That won't be necessary. Mr. Kerlin," she offered him a kiss and then offered Jimmie one as well. "Mr. Vinnetti, it was a pleasure having you both here. I look forward to seeing you again."

"Jimmie," he grumbled, his eyes refusing to look at either of them. "Call me Jimmie."

"Jimmie, then," she responded and kissed his cheek again. "Take care of him, won't you?"

"Toni-" Mitch began, but she was already gone.

"Do I-"

"Not now, Jimmie. I can't deal with your shit right now." Mitch leveled a furious gaze at him as he grabbed the nearest shirt and yanked it on.

"What the hell did I do?"

CHAPTER TWENTY-FIVE

Going to try and sway you to his side by letting you bed his daughter now, is he?" Jimmie chuckled, but his eyes were watching Mitch with a steady, penetrating gaze.

"Antoinette's not for sale," he grumbled, downing another swig of the whiskey Jimmie had offered him. He moved to the stereo system lining one wall, clasping the glass tightly in his hand. He knew Jimmie was right. Nicolai had made it clear he had no problem sending Toni to his bed.

Nicolai knew their history- he knew they had been best friends in childhood before he started racking up convictions and she was sent away to boarding school. They had never been romantically involved. Instead, she was more the irritating little girl next door that wouldn't leave him and his buddies alone. She drove him insane with the holier than thou attitude that she wore on her sleeve. She treated him like a common hood and now, years later, her own father was attempting to prostitute her to him in hopes of some long-lost neighborhood connection would get him an alliance with Vinetti Industries.

Before Mitch could control his fury, his glass splintered into a dozen pieces, falling softly onto the plush gray carpet of the Vinetti jet.

Jimmie was at his side, a heavy hand on his shoulder. Ignoring the broken glass, he slipped another into Mitch's hand. "Tell me."

Mitch dropped his eyes to the glass, watching the amber liquid swish against the crystal with the plane's gentle movements. He knew Jimmie was concerned - from the moment he'd appeared in the hotel room he had been full of unasked questions. He'd remained quiet, offering Mitch the benefit of the doubt, but Mitch knew it was burning inside him that he might be having an affair with Terenari's daughter.

He took another sip, pushed past Jimmie and sank down on the sofa. "Got another bottle?" he asked, offering him a lopsided smile.

"A dozen. Meant for a client but they are yours if you need them." Jimmie shrugged, grabbing two bottles of Woodford Reserve out of a box and placing them on the table in front of Mitch. He dropped onto a chair. "Long lost love?" he prodded.

"Lord, no." Mitch struggled to contain his laughter. "More like a guardian angel I never asked for. She was the righteous girl next door that destroyed all my mother's dishes when she found out I'd been arrested the first time. She was the one who tagged along and always got herself in trouble. Then we ended up having to protect her stupid ass from getting attacked by some hood on the street corner. Nicolai ended up carting her off to boarding school at Gino's recommendation."

"Gino Palmese?" Jimmie asked, his eyes now lifting. His voice was guarded, but he figured Mitch was too drunk to notice. "You two know each other?"

"Known him since the day I was born," Mitch nodded. "My father was a drunk, a pretty useless one at that. My mom went into labor at three in the morning, and he was nowhere to be found. Gino scooped her up and carried her the four miles to the midwife in Valderice. Or so the local legend goes."

"Go figure," Jimmie murmured.

Mitch waved him off as if the revelation was inconsequential. "We distanced ourselves when he got deported. It was better for his business to keep me stateside to look over his interests. Then I ended up in the penn."

To look over his interests. Jimmie let the words roll over his tongue as he remembered the cryptic intel about Mitch being at Palmese's hearings. So everyone was wrong - there was a connection there. One that had somehow been hidden for decades. And were it not for his current turmoil, Jimmie knew he would never have even learned this tiny tidbit.

"Lucky you weren't deported, too," he commented.

"Hm," Mitch nodded without further explanation. "Toni was the jewel of the neighborhood, you know? The one everyone expected to be a lawyer or at least the wife of a lawyer-politician."

"And now her father is whoring her around for his own interests." Jimmie gave a low whistle. "And you didn't know?"

"No," he shook his head, downing his glass in one swallow. "And she didn't either, I don't think."

"You mean you're the first he's tried this with? He must really want you. To give his only daughter to you."

"What a fucked up way to look at it. She's not a piece of meat to be-"

"I didn't mean it like that, Mitch." Jimmie shook his head and poured them both another drink. "I just was thinking if you're this fucked up over the ordeal, think what she must be going through. Daddy's pride and joy turned into a whore-"

"Stop calling her that," Mitch asked, his voice pleading, "please."

Jimmie nodded in apology. He was quiet, watching Mitch as he downed drink after drink until he finally forewent the glass and began on the bottle. "She's family to you, isn't she?"

It took Mitch a moment to let Jimmie's question filter through the drunken haze. She had been...years ago. But what was she now? More than a stranger, not exactly a friend- she existed somewhere between the netherworld of old sepia photographs in his closet and the $1,500 ties that evidenced the world to which he currently belonged. He gave a slow, thoughtful nod before starting to drink again.

"I've been blind about my sister in the past. I know that. But my vision is finally clearing." Jimmie glanced to Mitch. "You protected her. From me, from herself, from the families. With a single fucking dance, you claimed her and assured her safety from everyone. It took until now for me to understand that but you did. And I'm indebted."

Jimmie leaned forward, grabbing the bottle to take a drink for himself. He hesitated before handing it back, his eyes locking with Mitch's. "Tell me to go back and we will."

"You have-"

"An unimportant meeting. I can make 2 million in a phone call," he shrugged. "Just say the word."

Mitch nodded, unsure of what the right thing to do was but knowing he couldn't leave things with Toni as unsettled as they were. "They are headed to Sacramento."

◆ ◆ ◆

"Antoinette, you look stunning as always," Mitch kissed her cheek, feeling the blush rise on them.

"Decided to stop preying on the wildlife long enough to come dance with me, did you?"

"Who said I came to dance with you?" he countered laughing but was already tugging her towards the center dance floor. "You don't seem surprised to see me."

"My father is very persuasive."

Mitch smiled. That explained her hostility- she thought he was here to join Terenari's ranks.

"You do have some interesting house guests, I must say."

"Crotchety old men and their twenty-something wives with their outrageously expensive and recently remodeled bodies," she spat. "Thrilling company, I assure you."

"Oh, come now, surely you've been paying more attention than that," he scolded. "Take Guiseppe over there," Mitch nodded his head toward a man in the corner. "He's trying to get in bed with your old man's latest fling."

"I wish someone would," she chuckled then sent a gaze to a couple behind her. "And what about them?"

"That would be Senator Davenport, head of the joint committee on genome research. He's hoping for campaign contributions, of course. The blonde 22-year-old is his daughter. Whom he's happy to offer up to anyone in the room willing to cough up a certain amount of cash. Not that she would mind.

She finds Italian men, powerful Italian men, as some sort of temporary plaything."

"Know that from experience do you?" she asked lightly, but Mitch could feel her tense in his arms.

"Certainly not." He eyed her for a moment, the plastered smile on her face not matching the furrow on her brow. He knew mentioning the ordeal in his hotel room would cause her to run away, but he had to get answers. He pulled her closer into his arms. "Do you need to talk to me?"

"I need nothing."

Mitch didn't miss the exact pronunciation of her words, and his lips dropped to her ear, his breath warm against her cheek. "Do you want to talk to me privately?"

"I don't see that as something my father would allow," she pushed away from him slightly and offered him a tiny bow. "Thank you for the dance, Mr. Kerlin."

She was issuing him a challenge- he knew it just as if he'd issued it himself. He touched her arm before she could depart, offering her the smallest wink. "You underestimate me, girl."

He gave her a few moments to regain her position beside Nicolai, his eyes surveying the growing line of guests waiting to bestow their gratitude on Terenari. Near the front of the growing group, Sonny Markesi's tall head was moving above the rest, ignoring the masses. Mitch followed suit, moving easily between the drunken crowd and directly to Nicolai.

"Mitch!" Nicolai's arms reached out, just as Mitch had expected, and pulled him forward. "I didn't expect you to join us here this evening. I thought you were headed home."

"You know me, Nicolai. I never do the expected."

"Surely I'd have been made aware if Vinetti crossed the threshold of my new home. Are you out without parental supervision?"

"Jimmie is not with me," Mitch acknowledged. "I just thought I would offer you my well wishes for the vineyard opening."

"Please, let's go somewhere. We had no time yesterday. We should take the time to catch up."

Mitch broke the possessive grasp Nicholai had on his arm. "Perhaps tomorrow? Sonny and I are scheduled to have breakfast. I presume you'd be willing to join us?"

Sonny barely managed to hide the look of genuine surprise before Nicolai turned his way. "Seven? Or eight if that's better for you?"

"No, no," Nicolai smiled brightly. "Seven would be wonderful. You have plans for this evening then? With anyone I know?"

Mitch laughed off the question. "Actually, no plans. I've been trying to get your daughter alone for a while now, but her dance card seems quite full."

"Antoinette?" Nicolai glanced at Mitch for a moment then his eyes flew to Toni, who was standing a pace away. "My dear, certainly you aren't being disrespectful to Mr. Kerlin. I can't imagine you'd ignore such an important guest."

Mitch wondered what she had told him about the previous night. Did she tell him she had succeeded or that she had failed? Or had she said anything at all? That he might ask for a report on her activities caused Mitch's stomach to churn. Perhaps she had merely blamed it on Jimmie and his untimely interruption. He smiled to himself, knowing that's exactly what she would have done.

"No, I did manage one dance with her," Mitch interrupted before she could respond. "I was just hoping for something more-" he trailed off purposefully, causing both Nicolai and Sonny to glance at him in curiosity. "Just somewhere less conspicuous for a chat."

"Ah, certainly. One can never tell what gossip can spread by a mere conversation," he nodded as if they were all conspiring against Jimmie in his absence. Mitch wondered if he would find it nearly so amusing if he knew Jimmie had chauffeured him to the property himself.

"I'm sure she'd be happy to go anywhere with you, Mitch," he pulled her forward, nearly shoving her into Mitch's chest. "Wouldn't you?"

"Of course," Toni nodded, her hand sliding into the crook of Mitch's elbow. "Have you seen the new grapes that were planted? They were sent over direct from your hometown, I believe."

"Indeed." Nicolai beamed with satisfaction. "Feel free to take your time returning."

Mitch nodded, sliding his hand around her waist and drawing her closer as he led her through the crowd and toward the front door. "And we didn't even have to slip out of our bedroom windows in the dead of night," he chuckled.

"I think the man would screw you himself if he thought that would get you on his payroll." she grumbled as soon as they were out of earshot.

"Possibly," he shrugged as they stepped into the cool night air, "but I think he believes you would relish that activity much more than he."

She scoffed and distanced herself from him. "I'd relish nothing of the sort."

He smiled, stepping in line behind her and tucking his face into her neck. "Are you saying you don't find me appealing, Toni?"

"I find nothing appealing these days," she returned. "Especially those things that have come from the depraved ramblings of my father's mind."

"Hm," he fell quiet as they walked, allowing her to lead them deeper into the darkened paths of the vineyard. When she sank onto a wooden bench between a break in the rows, Mitch hesitated in joining her.

"If you'd like to be alone I'm certainly not going to run to your father and tell him I left you unescorted. I can walk around instead if you prefer-"

"Don't be absurd, sit down." She took hold of his hand and pulled him down beside her. She offered him a genuine smile, the one he remembered from years before. "I'm sorry if I offended you. I didn't mean to. I'm just a tad bitter these days."

"Is that what I am to you?" he asked, watching her intently. "An affiliation that exists only in the mind of your father? I suppose that would be fair. It's been so long."

"Oh, lord, stop being so dramatic. I expect that from Jimmie but not from you," she answered testily, but her eyes were sparkling with amusement. She leaned toward him, pausing long enough to get his undivided attention, then let her lips brush gently over his. It was so light, so nearly not there, that

Mitch couldn't decipher if it were a friendly gesture or something more. "Welcome to Carricante Vineyards."

"He's named it that? Really?"

"Anything to get him closer to Gino."

"Yeah, that'll do it." Mitch laughed. "Gino wouldn't even
send him a single grape for this endeavor; I'd bet."

Toni smiled. "And you win. He tried, but Gino shot him
down. Sent him a crate of raisins in response to the request. I
tried to warn him but..." She shrugged.

"But what?"

"My opinion isn't the most influential around here these
days." She tucked her arm into his. "But enough of that. Tell
me of you, a lifetime missed, and I'll tell you of my deviant mafia princess ways."

As if they had not lost a moment of time, once he had convinced her he had no intention of joining her father, he and
Toni picked up right where their friendship had left off. She
talked of Terenari's new inept recruits; Mitch shared stories of
his drinking binges with Jimmie. They swapped stories of
Markesi, Gino Palmese and the other men that tended to cross
their paths on a regular basis. Toni admitted to a drunken
night in Los Angeles that resulted in passing out backstage at a
rock concert only to have Terenari's bodyguards burst in and
carry her out. It would have been sheer humiliation, she said,
if she'd been sober enough to realize what was going on.

In the darkest moments before dawn, when a bitter rain
began to fall, she brought up his mother's death. Mitch
couldn't bear to do it himself, and she clutched his hand in
support as he relived the darkest parts of his life. They sat in
silence after, both lost in the memories that they had been liv-

ing to forget. As dawn finally began to break across their shadowed forms, they began the slow walk back to the main grounds.

"Here, let me." He stepped toward her as her trembling fingers tried to tighten the clasp on her dress, the shivering of her body causing him to rub her arms. "Have I given you pneumonia now?" he laughed and put his jacket over her shoulders. "It's not nearly as cold as the Atlantic winter. I remember when you and Paulie disappeared from-"

"You look like you've just come from a wrestling match," she interrupted quickly, nodding toward his soaked and rumpled dress shirt that still hung untucked from his trousers. She tried to help him tuck it in, but her hands were still shivering. She gave up and held tight to his shirt tail for a moment, her eyes drifting toward the horizon that was wavering between a hazy purple and a dusty peach. "He's is going to kick my ass. It's dawn."

Mitch held her as she tried to start walking back, knowing this was the one conversation they'd both purposefully avoided all night. His hands were silky on her skin; his fingers wrapped only tight enough to keep her from moving away. His voice was quiet, solemn. "Will he?"

She hesitated, his protective nature now seeming to seep from his entire body without so much as uttering a word in her defense. It worried her- his quick conclusions that were nearly always right but would definitely always get him into murderous trouble. It was like when they were kids, and he would tell her to run- she'd run as ordered and it never failed that he would come home nursing a dozen bloody scratches a few hours later. But she knew he was not that little boy anymore.

He was gossiped to be the deadliest shot in *la familia*, he was Vinetti's right hand, Gino's protégé...he was the one person who frightened her more than her father. He could destroy her or save her with a single swift glance, and she wasn't prepared for either option. She straightened to face him more directly. "I can handle him."

"You don't have to. You know that, right?" he asked, tucking a rain-soaked strand of hair behind her. "Without question?"

"I didn't," she whispered refusing to look at him, "but I suppose I do now."

"Toni," his voice dropped as he pulled her into his arms, his head dropping to place his cheek against hers. "If it ever gets to where you can't handle it, it only takes one call." He pulled away to check her eyes, to make sure she was comprehending the out he was offering her. "Anywhere, anytime. One call."

Mitch was unwilling to allow Toni to suffer for their evening out. He knew she would be plagued with questions no matter what but he knew his presence would prevent Terenari's anger...as long as he believed Toni had kept him happy.

She tried to pull away from him as they entered the breakfast hall but Mitch wouldn't allow it. Instead, he slipped his arm around her waist and began laughing as if she had told a hysterical joke. All eyes lifted from the table and Nicolai rose to meet them halfway.

"My apologies, Nicolai, for keeping her out so late," he smiled warmly. "I appreciate you letting me steal her away from all her admirers."

"I'm sure no admirer could ever hold a candle to you, Mitch," he returned. "You two have a history, unlike any others. Don't you, Antoinette?"

"Indeed," she smiled. "I do recall Mitch trying to steal my underwear and sell it on the street corner when I was ten. Do you remember that, Daddy? You nearly wore out his-"

"Ah, boys will be boys," he interrupted and silenced her with a sideways glance. "I do hope you had a good time."

"I'm sure I bored her to tears with my tales, but she was kind to listen to them." Mitch turned to her, his lips barely brushing over hers. "Get some sleep. I promise to call soon."

She nodded then leaned to give Nicolai a kiss on the cheek. "Goodnight, father. Please wake me should you need anything at all."

"No, my dear, sleep the day away. I'll have one of the men make sure you are kept undisturbed. You deserve your rest."

CHAPTER TWENTY-SIX

Mitch dropped down onto the leather sofa, the chill of the slick fabric immediately easing the aches and pains coursing through his body. His head fell to the arm, his eyes drifting closed.

"I could have shot you already," Jimmie's hoarse voice filtered to him from near the doorway. "That was nearly a mill out of my pocket that you just lost."

"Right now that would be a welcome improvement," he countered, struggling to sit up.

"Relax," Jimmie pushed him back down, pressing an ice pack to the darkening bruise on his cheek.

"What the hell happened to you, anyway? I thought you were just making a routine run up to Buffalo."

"Hell if I know. One minute I'm cruising along listening to piss poor radio stations and the next Ashli is scraping me up off the state highway."

Jimmie paused. "Ashli? What was she doing there?"

"Hey, man, she's your sister," Mitch struggled to sit, clasping the ice to his skin as the numbness began to wash through his nerves. "Didn't she tell you she was headed that way?"

"No," he sank opposite Mitch and slid him a glass of water. "She told me she was going to be in Philly this weekend."

"That's-" he trailed off, searching for the right word.

"Convenient?" Jimmie groused. "Her stories are beginning to wear thin with me."

"Give her a break. She's probably got some boyfriend stashed up there she doesn't want you to know about."

"She was in D.C. last week."

"Where'd you hear that?"

"You knew?"

"Of course not. You just aren't known for having the most reliable sources."

"Fuck you, Mitch."

"Oh, come on, Jimmie. We've been through this shit. Are You going to believe every bit of gossip you hear on the street now? Next thing you know, I'll be hold up in Quantico singing songs to the IOC."

"Are you?"

"Man, you are losing touch with reality," Mitch grumbled, stretching back out on the couch.

"You didn't answer."

"Yeah, well, some things are too ignorant to dignify with a response. Especially when they come out of your mouth."

Silence hung in the air, the clinking of Jimmie's carafe as he poured himself a glass of water the only sound in the office. Mitch waited, longer than he expected to, and finally forced his eyes open to stare at Jimmie. "What aren't you telling me?"

Jimmie was quiet, watching Mitch intently. "Why don't you get some rest? You've been going nonstop since San Fran."

"Jimmie, come on-"

"Really. It's been over a month now. Even you can't handle that pace."

Mitch's eyes narrowed, his senses now fully engaged. "Where's Ashli?"

"Safe. In her suite." Jimmie sank down opposite him. "Mitch, an attempt was made on Sonny's life."

"Who did he piss off?"

"He's in the hospital, Mitch," Jimmie said, cutting him off. "It was a professional hit. They blindsided all of his men."

"How bad?"

"He's in critical condition but expected to live."

"When?"

"During your run to Buffalo. When we couldn't reach you…"

Mitch nodded, waving off Jimmie's concern. "Has the hotel been locked down?"

"Teddy took care of that," Jimmie nodded. "You've found an extraordinary talent in him."

"I should go-"

Jimmie placed a comforting hand on his shoulder. "He's asked that you not come to Atlantic. He's afraid you'll put yourself in danger. All the families could be at risk."

"Of course," Mitch nodded, wondering why he hadn't recognized that immediately on his own. All the families…it took a moment for the words to register. His eyes flew to Jimmie, but he shook his head.

"Antoinette's fine. I made a courtesy call to Terenari to let him know of the troubles, and he confirmed her safety. She's not even in the states right now."

"Thank you," he managed when he was finally able to exhale. "I should-"

"Rest," Jimmie commanded. "You should rest. Then we'll make decisions. Okay?"

When Mitch awoke hours later, his wounds had been bandaged, and the once empty room had been become a bustle of conversation. Men were milling about, on alert, but none seemed worried. He locked eyes with Teddy who gave him a reassuring smile. So they were safe. At least for now.

Mitch accepted the coffee Jimmie offered him, trying to make sense of the things being thrown at him. Feds moving in on Vinetti without his knowledge, Terenari waging some clandestine war with the east coast, Sonny in the hospital at the hands of some unknown assassin?

He glanced to Jimmie who was asking him something about a meeting they had in Miami the following week and whether or not it should be postponed considering the security issues. Something about a weapons export to Cuba. The IOC would go nuts for information like this, he thought. Could Jimmie have picked a worse country to do business within the current political climate? Perhaps Sierra Leone but beyond that, Mitch could think of nowhere more volatile with which Jimmie could start building ties.

"I'll need to skip the meeting."

"Pardon?" Jimmie glanced up from his laptop, his eyes shuffling from one of his bodyguards to the other.

"I know it's bad timing," Mitch interjected, "but there's someone I need to visit. You're welcome to come, of course, but-"

Jimmie raised his eyebrows. He'd never had anyone desert him with such cavalier. That just didn't happen to him. "And just who is so damn important?"

Mitch's eyes moved to the guards behind him, and Jimmie waved them off. They stepped outside, shutting the door behind them.

"I need to see Gino," he said.

"I've been trying to get Palmese for months. Since before California even." Jimmie shook his head. "He's unavailable. When we get back from Miami, maybe-"

"He won't be unavailable for me."

It wasn't arrogance, Jimmie noted. It was simple, as if Jimmie should have realized it before the words were uttered-more of a tortured whisper as if it pained Mitch to actually have to admit such a thing out loud. And, of course, that was probably true. Their alliance or friendship or whatever it happened to be was known to no one. Jimmie had been trying since San Francisco to find out anything but it had all been a fruitless search. He had been contacting Gino since then hoping he would shed some light on the issue but he had refused to return any of Jimmie's calls. The idea of going to see him face to face when he wouldn't even talk to him on the phone sent chills up Jimmie's spine, afraid he had somehow managed to offend the man without realizing it.

"Jimmie?"

Mitch was eying him with confusion, undoubtedly wondering why it was taking him so long to form a coherent response. He would go without him- Jimmie was certain of it. And then he'd never learn anything. "Yeah, okay. I'll make the arrangements."

"Ashli must be hysterical," Mitch managed after several minutes of silence.

"She's safe," Jimmie returned, "I honestly haven't had enough patience to hear anything else from her right now."

"I'll check on her."

"Mitch-"

Mitch turned at the doorway. "Yeah?"

"She's not-"

"What?"

"Nothing. Just let me know how she is."

"Of course."

CHAPTER TWENTY-SEVEN

Sonny's dead." Ashli's voice was trembling from somewhere in her darkened room.

He grimaced at her pronouncement. "No."

"And Jimmie?"

"Safely upstairs lamenting your poor choice in men," he answered, sinking in the chair beside her bed and snapping on the lamp. He stared absently at the oversized t-shirt that she had pulled down over her knees, her disheveled hair giving an indication that she wasn't as calm as Jimmie expected. "No company this evening?"

"No."

"Is it a special occasion?"

"Are you done with the pleasant insults now?"

"Your witty banter exhausts me."

"Don't believe a girl can be both sexy and smart, do you?"

"Believe me when I say your intellectual capabilities have never been in question."

"What did you come here for anyway?"

"My apologies," he nodded. "I merely came to check on your safety considering the recent events."

"I heard the feds ransacked the Chicago office," she said offered.

Mitch raised an eyebrow. "Really? I hadn't heard that. But," he added more to alleviate his own worries than hers, "that office is clean. It always is. So you have no need to worry."

"Right. I never have to worry my pretty little head, right? You and Jimmie will take care of everything, and I'm just meant to play along and-"

"Not tonight, Ashli."

"Why because I'm some delicate flower that can't handle the truth? For chrissakes, Mitch. You know me far better than that, don't you?"

"I'm just trying to do my fucking job, all right? This hasn't been the easiest night for me either, you know."

He could feel her eyes on him, surveying him. Judging and surveilling, he thought. But, for once, he didn't care.

"I'd forgotten. You and Sonny are very close, aren't you?"

Mitch scowled rather than respond.

She moved to stand beside him, offering him a hesitant kiss on the top of his head. "I'm sorry, Mitch. For everything, but especially for this."

He couldn't let himself dissect it...why she would be apologizing at a time like this. His anger flared at her self-absorption, pondering if she really believed that she need only say a few kind words to get him in the sack. His voice was a low growl as he stood up and straightened his clothing. "I don't need apologies. I need the names of the people that would dare do such a thing."

"Stop." She lunged forward to hold him back as he tried to move to the door. "I'm not good at these things. I don't know the right things to say or the right motions I'm supposed to do to make this better for you. Please," her voice was gentler now, the tender voice from their meeting at the estate- the one he'd been waiting to hear again for over a year. "Just tell me what I can do for you."

Before he could rationalize against it, his mouth buried into the nape of her neck, a mixture of grief and adrenaline overtaking his common sense. He pressed into her, the curves of her hips seeming tiny and fragile compared to her gruff movements. He tore hungrily at her shirt, leaving it hanging in shreds against her arms as his mouth engulfed her chilled skin. He could feel the heat rising within her as his lips blazed a path across the curves of her stomach. His hand slipped up her bare thighs, the low moan that escaped her lips causing his fingers to tighten dangerously around her throat. Ignoring any gentleness he might have shown someone else, he yanked her hair to the side, lacing his fingers painfully into the water soaked strands. His teeth buried into her shoulder as she touched the flesh of his chest...her own violent touches making him want to punish her even more. His eyes fluttered open and then closed again as she moved, and then opened wider as if his unconscious had registered something he wouldn't allow himself to believe.

The mark was small...tiny enough not to be noticed under any of her normal clothing. It was still red and irritated, slight speckles of fresh blood still clinging to her flesh and it dawned in the back of his mind that this was where she had disappeared tonight...to find solace in cocaine or heroin or whatever she had been able to get her hands on this time. He felt his stomach turn as his body reacted to her urgent motions. She was attacking him now- he knew no other way to describe it. Hands; mouth; tongue; hips... all of her body viciously smothering him as her passion turned into a demand for ownership of him.

He tried to ignore the infinitesimal mark but couldn't seem to tear his gaze away. Her touches weren't electric anymore but distracting, the curves of her body seeming more destructive than alluring. He dropped his hands to his sides in distraction, but she didn't even notice. Like an animal released, she was clawing and tearing at him while he stood unmoving, his lack of responsive movements going unnoticed. She thought she owned him. No, she truly wanted him. He could tell by her desperation that she felt he could give her what she had been searching for all this time. All those men, all those nights, and it had come down to a lowlife hired hand that was best friends with her brother. That he was allowing her to use him infuriated him.

"No," he murmured, breaking away from her to sink into the chair. She advanced on him slowly, hesitantly, dropping to her knees and sliding forward to touch him. An earthy scent of rain and grass-nothing he had expected from the prima-donna image, she presented to the world- drifted to his senses. She smelled nothing of perfume or bath oils like any other woman he'd been with. Rather a mere trace of cologne mingled with an outdoorsy, almost masculine scent, of crushed pine needles and raw physical need. Like Jimmie, everything about her exuded power, arrogance and defiant manipulation. He knew he couldn't break free from her alone- too much had gone wrong too quickly for him to be able to turn away from the comfort she was offering him.

"Please, no," his voice was even softer, begging. He had been reduced to pleading with the devil- was this what he deserved?

But just as her fingers began to march against his legs, she was wrenched away. He didn't care. They could be killing her, ravaging her, strangling her within an inch of her life and he had nothing left in him to give a damn. He hadn't been able to protect Sonny, why should he ever believe he could protect her?

"Don't touch him," Jimmie's voice was hollow, sinister...the voice he reserved for those he intended to kill. He met Mitch's eyes only briefly, his muscles constricting in mutual despair. How had he been so oblivious to the pain he was in?

Yes, he'd learned Mitch could lie with the best of them when the need arose but to have not seen the guilt over Sonny's life being placed in danger? Jimmie cursed, furious at himself for compartmentalizing his feelings to the point he'd nearly buried them.

Taking Mitch's arm and steering him to the door, he didn't bother to glance at Ashli when he spoke. "Get packed. We're leaving for Valderice in an hour."

CHAPTER TWENTY-EIGHT

I let my guard down with her," he mumbled, not looking at Jimmie as he continued to stuff items into his suitcase. "I'm sorry. I knew better but was somehow unable to prevent it."

"No one can keep their guard up all the time, Mitch. Although you've been giving it a pretty damn good attempt lately."

"Apparently not good enough."

"She didn't realize how out of place her actions were. She doesn't comprehend these parts of this life. To know the grief, the worry, the emotional conflict you can experience when an attack is made. She just doesn't understand. I don't mean to excuse her behavior. It was inexcusable for her to-" he trailed off. "I'm just glad it was you and not some random jackass she picked up on the street this time."

"Her demons are her own."

"Yeah but sometimes she needs to pull her head out of her ass and realize it's not all about her," Jimmie grumbled. "I asked Teddy to come with us. I hope-"

"That's fine. He deserves the rest. He's been carrying too heavy a load in my absence, I'm sure."

Jimmie raised a questioning eye. "You haven't been absent."

"Well, I've obviously not been here," he responded, tapping the side of his head, "or shit like this would never have happened."

Jimmie didn't argue, knowing there was nothing he could say that would ease the burden Mitch had placed on himself. "We're putting a load on Gino without warning," he said instead. "I don't think he'll be too happy about that."

Mitch zipped his suitcase, his eyes shining with sudden clarity. "You fear Gino?"

"You don't?"

"No. I don't." He squeezed his shoulder as he strode past. "Relax, Jimmie. In my presence, you have absolutely nothing to worry about."

"Somehow that doesn't inspire my confidence."

"Guys?" Teddy stuck his head through the doorway. "Ashli's gone."

CHAPTER TWENTY-NINE

Jimmie braced himself, waiting for the shot to come. He was four inches away; it was impossible to think he might miss. His mind floundered, wondering why out of all the things he'd done wrong in his life, that he was now going to die because his dumb ass kid sister had run off and screwed some punk she picked up on the street. What a fucked up way to go. Two hours ago he had sent his men scurrying through the entire state assuming his sister was kidnapped. It was Mitch who had suggested the alternative that led them to the upstate house: that she had not been taken but, instead she had run. And now, here they were. Having walked in on the two of them drunk, high and naked. Anger had fueled him until the man had pulled the gun. After that, his brain stopped functioning. As his reverie continued, he realized he felt nothing. No searing pain, no needle point tearing into his skin, no heated trickle of blood.

A heavy hand dropped to his shoulder, Mitch's voice pulling at his senses. "Jimmie, sit down. Take a breath. You need a drink?"

Jimmie let himself be led to a chair, Ashli's screams from somewhere nearby reminding him vaguely of a strangled cat. Mitch's voice was powerful, authoritative, and even Jimmie had to admit a bit frightening in its calm delivery. It would shock anyone to their senses.

"Start acting like a Vinetti or get the fuck out."

Ashli's simpering stopped, her only sound a sharp intake of breath as Jimmie assumed she tried to get her more basic emotions in check. Jimmie glanced up in time to see some non-verbal exchange between the two of them that he couldn't decipher- a reminder of some previous conversation, perhaps- but Mitch had accomplished his goal. Ashli was standing still, her tears silent, her back straight and waiting for further instructions.

"Move away from him before you get blood all over yourself," Mitch murmured, sliding his gun back into his waistband. "There's a car at the gates. Get in it and get to New York. No stops, no cutesy diversions. Get to the hotel and lock yourself in the suite until you hear from us, understand?"

She nodded, but that wasn't enough for Mitch. He shook her shoulders. His voice was softer now, more forgiving. "Tell me you understand, Ashli."

"I understand."

"Go." He stepped out the door behind her, motioning to one of the bodyguards. "Find Teddy."

"Sir, I can-"

"Find him."

"Yes, sir."

It only took a half hour before Teddy stepped into the kitchen of the estate and then immediately took a step back.

His eyes danced to Jimmie who had his head in his hands, the dead body lying on the floor and then to Mitch, who was leaning against the counter, sipping a cup of coffee from a still brewing pot. Teddy gave a low, drawn-out whistle.

"Looks like you found her," he murmured and was glad to see Mitch smile. "Want me to clean this up?"

Mitch nodded, then stepped to him and dropped an arm around his shoulder. "My apologies but I called-"

"Because no one else can know," he nodded. "I understand."

"I thought you would," Mitch smiled. "We don't know who he is yet. They were both high as a kite when we got here. Get prints then make him disappear. Jimmie and I are going back to the city. Come to the hotel when you're done."

"Yes, sir."

"Straight to Jimmie and me, all right?"

"Of course. The plane?"

"Keep it on standby. We'll move as soon as everything is secured."

"Yes, sir."

CHAPTER THIRTY

V an Halen?" Jimmie asked, tapping Mitch's feet aside to give himself room to sit on the sofa.

"Calming influence," he answered, clicking off the stereo with the remote and dropping the room into silence. "Eddie is a God. You talk to Ashli?"

He nodded but didn't elaborate. "It's impossible sometimes- this life of ours, isn't it? Does she not think that I would prefer simplicity? That I could go about my business without having to carry a gun or be surrounded by bodyguards?"

"Perhaps she thinks you enjoy the adrenaline rush."

"Then she's a fool," he spat, but it only took a moment for him to soften. "And I'm a bigger fool for never explaining to her otherwise."

"That kid had enough coke in him to keep the air force fly- ing," Mitch offered, shaking his head. "He was going to kill you, Jimmie. Stop beating yourself up and move on."

Mitch pulled himself to sitting, yanking off the tie that hung loosely around his neck and tossing it to the table. Untucking the tail of his shirt, he pulled out his gun and laid it on the sofa between him and Jimmie. He took a heavy draft off his water, letting a hand run through his hair.

"May I?" Jimmie asked, his fingers hovering over the engraved blue steel of Mitch's gun. When he nodded his assent, Jimmie picked it up gingerly, his hands traveling the barrel, his eyes following the intricate detailing.

"No serial number," he observed. Not a filed down serial number. Just no serial number period. Not even an indention in the weapon where one would normally be placed. It wasn't a customized gun but a custom one. It had likely never even seen the inside of a manufacturing plant.

Mitch was watching him without reply, undoubtedly wondering what thoughts were going through his head.

"That was one hell of a shot," he offered. "One shot to the neck. He didn't even have a chance to pull the hammer." Jimmie nodded in admiration. "I've been in a lot of bad situations in my time. Nothing like that. In my own home. I can't explain the feeling that-"

"You don't need to," Mitch interrupted.

"I've heard stories the past year, you know. About your infamous aim. I've seen the guards at the estate talking over the targets they retrieve after you've been at the shooting range."

Mitch frowned without lifting his eyes.

"Didn't know that, did you?" Jimmie chuckled.

"I can't believe they don't have something better to do with their time."

Jimmie placed the gun back on the cushion then shifted to balance his elbows on his knees, his fingers threading together.

He rubbed his temples, pressing his eyes closed with his fingertips. "Ashli would have let him kill me," he murmured.

"Only out of fear."

"No, I know her. I love her. I've protected her to the point she hates me for it. She would have regretted it later, I know that, too," he said, shaking his head. "But I also know she stood aside, hoping you would miss."

Mitch refused to make eye contact, knowing Jimmie was right. It was exactly what she had done. He had raised his gun, leveled it without thought and fired before the piece of shit had a chance to take a shot at Jimmie. And all the while, Ashli had stood motionless, coming to the aid of neither him nor Jimmie.

Jimmie opened his mouth to speak, but Mitch placed a hand on his arm, silencing him. "Teddy, come on in."

He turned around aware, for the first time, that Teddy had entered the suite. He lifted an uncertain gaze to Mitch, wary of how long Teddy had been there. Listening to their conversation, evaluating Ashli's loyalty...witnessing Jimmie's own heartbreak. But Mitch gave him a single shake of his head, reassuring him without words.

"I've taken care of everything. Is there anything else that I can do for you or you, Mr. Vinetti?" Teddy asked, standing before them. "I'm sure you haven't eaten. If I can-"

"You're a good kid." Jimmie gave him a faint smile. "Thank you for your concern. Would you see to my sister, please?"

"Already done, sir. I have the best men standing guard at her door. With your permission, I'd prefer to stay close." He gave a solemn nod. "I'd rather not leave Mr. Kerlin, or you unguarded."

Jimmie chuckled and nodded to where the gun was still perched between them. "You think someone is going to get passed him?"

"No, sir." Teddy shook his head. "I'd just rather he not have to worry about such a thing after, well, after such an eventful night."

"Hm," Jimmie glanced to Mitch, noticing for the first time his haggard appearance. Although his eyes were bright, still filled with adrenaline, his body looked as if it was starting to fold in on itself. "Take up a spot outside the suite, okay?"

"Thank you, sir." He nodded then turned to Mitch. "Mr. Kerlin, Ashli asked that you phone her as soon as you get a moment."

"Not tonight," he mumbled, waving him off. "Tell her I'll see her at wheels up."

"What do you suppose she wants?" Jimmie asked as Teddy disappeared, leaving the two alone again.

"I don't know," he returned, his voice holding a trace of sarcasm, "perhaps to vilify me for murdering her damn lover? As if I can't handle that on my own."

A tortured expression crossed his face, but he washed it away quickly, replacing it with placid indifference. But it wasn't so fast that Jimmie missed it.

"You feel guilty for killing him," he surmised.

Mitch didn't bother to deny it.

"But not out of disloyalty," Jimmie continued, puzzling out Mitch's emotions. "Because taking a life, any life, actually means something far deeper to you." He looked to Mitch for confirmation but received no response. "You feel guilty for saving me, then. Is there a way for me to fix that for you? To make it easier for you to swallow?"

"No."

Jimmie's voice was even quieter, a murmur, so slight Mitch thought he was talking to himself. "Toni? Sonny? Could they erase your guilt?"

Mitch considered. Killing someone had become increasingly easier over the years; he'd learned to compartmentalize the actual physical act itself. But, in the aftermath, when the adrenaline had run dry when he was alone, safe with his defense mechanisms no longer on red alert, the guilt would envelope him. It was a stupid, childish response that he kept expecting to disappear, and yet it never seemed to.

The conflict of knowing he could kill with the same inhumanity as the criminals he was supposed to be fighting caused his stomach to churn, his heart to race and beads of sweat to trickle down his spine – he hated his own recognition at how much he had in common with the men he was trying to destroy.

Would he ever learn to kill without guilt? He shook his head, fiery eyes focusing on Jimmie's softer, more somber ones.

"I hope to God not."

CHAPTER THIRTY-ONE

The glowing lanterns strung across the oversized stone patio cast a surreal glow over the hundreds of party goers that had convened on Gino Palmese's Mediterranean villa. Villa was perhaps a disingenuous way to describe it: at over 15,000 square feet it was the largest single residence on the entire island. Dignitaries, ambassadors, and rival corporate stockholders had all been bartering for the property when Gino showed up in his characteristic style and provided the owner an unknown sum of money in cash – untraceable America bills. The property had been signed over in the middle of the night, the local magistrate presiding over the transaction while still in his bathrobe after being roused from sleep at three in the morning.

From his perch on the northernmost balcony of the property, Mitch could understand Gino's affection for the place. Defensible from every side due to its high elevation over the island, the palatial space would allow Gino to have numerous guests while still providing him enough room never to have to actually see them for the duration of their stay. Mitch's eyes roamed the crowd, wondering if Jimmie was finding this as relaxing as Mitch found it stressful. His eyes found him quickly, lounging on the plush pool chair as two women in matching white bikinis, gold bangles glittering from their wrists, danced around him in obvious drunkenness. Mitch knew Jimmie was in heaven.

"They will be gone by tomorrow, Mitch. Will you come out of hiding then?" Gino chuckled as he stepped up behind Mitch without so much as a footstep of warning.

"Perhaps," he answered, hugging him. "I know this couldn't have been your idea."

"No, no," he laughed, and Mitch was glad to see him in such good humor. "Marla wanted to welcome everyone. I suggested she invite a few friends over."

"Your latest stray. She defines her friends quite broadly."

"Dangerous, I know. But, she has me whipped as the Americans say."

"You seem quite happy this evening."

"What's not to be happy about? Aside from the crowd below? I have a beautiful new home, an amazing view of the stars over the open sea, a new shipping fleet to call my own and," he clapped his hand on Mitch's shoulder, "my closest allies at my side."

"I'm honored, Gino."

"Don't be honored. Those moronic twits below are honored," he spat. "Be you."

Mitch nodded and motioned for Gino to sit while he fixed the two drinks. "You heard about Sonny?"

"Yes. He's okay?"

"Several hours of surgery but yeah, he's coming back around."

"Good. I know what he means to you."

Mitch offered him a glass and then sank down into the chair opposite him. "And you? What's happening in your world?"

Gino laughed. "You've been nothing but phone calls for two years, and that's all I get? Is that Vinetti's influence?"

"No, it's my self-preservation being on overdrive."

"I hear, of course. I know you've had a rough time of it. First Coppell, then Ashli, and now Sonny?" Gino shook his head. "You should have called much sooner."

"Nothing I can't handle, Gino."

"I don't doubt you can handle it, Mitchell."

"Jimmie. You forgot Jimmie."

"An attempt was made on Jimmie? When?"

"Just before we got on the plane. I don't think it's related but," Mitch shook his head, "it's still there."

Gino's eyes narrowed. "Is it the Vinettis? Or is this something following you?"

"That's the question, isn't it? I just don't know."

"That's unlike you."

Mitch nodded. "I've lost perspective, I think. Let myself get distracted."

"Yes, I know that as well. She's here, you know." Gino gave a small smile. "Antoinette."

"No. I assure you I did not."

"Well, that eases some of my heartache, at least," he said with a frown. "And your safety?"

"I'm careful, Gino. Your lessons echo in my head always. That hasn't changed."

"You were acting like a loose cannon."

Mitch stood up, moving to pace the room. "Yes. I won't deny that. And then she resurfaced. It changed a lot of things for me."

"It changed a lot of things for everyone," Gino corrected. "We are family, you and I, aren't we?"

"Of course." Mitch nodded. "Gino, please-"

"My seriousness worries you, doesn't it?"

"Undoubtedly."

"I apologize. On such a happy night I should never do such a thing. Tomorrow, we shall talk tomorrow."

"Gino," Mitch grabbed his arm as he tried to move back inside, a stray thought finally flittering into his mind. "Are you in danger?"

He laughed as if Mitch had told a joke he'd never heard before. "Always, my friend. Always."

"Because of me?"

"Don't be so arrogant," Gino scowled but then hugged him. "Welcome home, Vincenzo."

CHAPTER THIRTY-TWO

Mitch turned back to his view of the party and, as if called, Jimmie was staring at him. He lifted his head in question and Mitch motioned to his watch then the horizon. Jimmie nodded understandingly. Whatever it was could wait until sunrise.

"Mitch!" a whirl of turquoise and citrus orange blurred onto the balcony and into his arms before he could get control of his senses again. But the smell of her was unmistakable, a blend of fresh ocean water with a hint of something summery sweet could only be one person.

"Been skinny dipping in the Tyrrhenian Sea tonight, have you?" he asked, pulling away from Toni gently as he surveyed her straggling hair. "Should I bother to ask if you were alone?"

"And a fine welcome to Sicily to you, too," she returned, but the smile remained stretched across her face. "Why are you up here all alone?"

"Who says I've been alone?"

"Ah," she nodded. "Gino was with you then. People were wondering."

"People?" Mitch circled her, his eyes moving uneasily over the darkness. "What people?"

"Pour me a drink?"

His response was distant, distracted, a vague mumble of something that he believed he should say even though her words weren't really registering in his thoughts. "You're too young to drink."

"Where have you been while I've been growing up?" she laughed. "I've been legal even in the States for some time now."

Her light tone was beginning to irritate, a knot rising in the pit of his stomach. As she twirled around him again, he gripped her shoulders tightly, forcing her to stop and face him. "What people, Toni?"

Her swinging ceased, the intelligence he knew so well finally breaking through her euphoria at being without parental supervision. Years of dark moments had prepared her well, and she deciphered his look in an instant. "I didn't know them," she answered quietly. "Nor did I respond."

"Were they asking for Gino or me?"

She hesitated. "Gino. I believe."

"You believe?"

She was quiet, a furrow forming on her forehead as she sifted through the many conversations she had encountered during the evening's festivities. "Gino," she confirmed.

Mitch pulled his cell phone out of his pocket and moved paces away from her – as far as the wrought iron balcony would possibly allow. He glanced over the railing as he spoke, his voice muffled but his eyes locking with a half drunken Teddy who was now standing at attention watching Mitch from the middle of the dance floor. Before Mitch had clicked off the phone, Teddy was on the move, his hand raised only slightly but enough for the guards to begin circling him for further orders.

"Mitch?" Toni's eyes stayed on Teddy far below; her voice filled with uncertainty.

"You worry too much," he admonished with a chuckle. "Come, tell me stories of your late night affair. Was he a local?" Mitch took her arm, leading her into the parlor and sinking into the soft, peach colored sofa that lined one wall.

"You are trying to distract me," she argued but sat down beside him anyway.

"Allow me that."

She nodded and moved to fix herself a drink, ignoring his penetrating gaze. "Would you like one?"

"Not tonight."

"That tells me more than you realize."

"When have I ever doubted your powers of perception?" he chuckled and pulled her down to sit beside him again. "Tomorrow, you and I, when all these people are gone, will sit alone on the beach and drink until the sun rises."

"Promise?"

"Well, Jimmie and Teddy will likely interrupt, but it will not be by my doing. I promise."

"Tomorrow then?"

"Tomorrow. Now tell me about the Greek god you enchanted."

"You are using me as a distraction," she laughed to ease his tension. "I am fabulous at distraction."

She wasn't lying. After nearly an hour and a half of regaling Mitch with stories of her recent escapades which ended not with a torrid romance with a Greek god but a skinny dipping session with a bunch of teenage boys who stayed paces away from her murmuring in Sicilian and thinking she couldn't understand their embarrassed comments, Mitch was in stitches. He was laughing uproariously by the time she got to the end where the boys' parents appeared and dragged them home while cursing the American girl for her harlot ways.

"Mitch?" Teddy's voice sobered him immediately, and he moved to the doorway in one swift movement that caught Toni off balance and almost caused her to topple to the floor.

"Tell me."

The news did not surprise him nor did it worry him. It would require tightening security for Gino, which Mitch and Jimmie would happily provide, but the unorganized Italian crew who were currently angry with Gino were small time crooks that didn't appreciate Gino cutting off their shipping contracts. Nothing related to the dangers they were facing back in the states. Simple business and certainly nothing that would have caused Gino's earlier seriousness. Mitch ordered Teddy to tighten security, place more guards around the perimeter and lock down the residence before the party ended to keep any drunks from attempting to stay the night.

"Has Jimmie been informed?"

"No, he was occupied."

"Occupied?" Mitch searched his memory. "Not the bikini twins?"

Teddy couldn't help the chuckle that escaped. He cleared his throat. "No, someone else caught his fancy. They are upstairs. Shall I inform him?"

"Better leave that to me. You two stay here and get acquainted."

"Of course," Teddy grinned. "So you're the infamous Antoinette. I didn't even know you were here."

"Isn't that your job?" she joked but took him by the arm. "I have been hidden up here with Mitch. He really is a downer at parties, did you know that?"

"He has his moments; I assure you."

"Gossip about me and find yourself unemployed," Mitch said with a wink to show he was joking. "Surely you two can find better things to talk about. Jimmie, for example. He's always good fodder for gossip."

"I prefer not to be shot, thank you very much," Toni retaliated and shoved Mitch toward the door.

CHAPTER THIRTY-THREE

J immie?" Mitch knocked once on the door.

"Go away," a female voice laughed from somewhere behind the oak door.

"It's Mitch."

The door opened immediately before the girl in the bed even had time to cover herself. Not that she seemed in any hurry to do so. Her eyes sparkled when she saw him and let the sheet fall to the bed again, her naked body stretching welcomingly across the bed.

"Can you at least cover yourself?" Mitch grimaced, looking away with as much distaste as he could manage. "Will she be staying the night?"

"Not if you need otherwise," Jimmie answered without bothering to lower his voice.

"I just need a few minutes privately."

"I'll be right down."

"Only a minute really. Balcony perhaps?"

"Of course," Jimmie nodded then glanced at the woman in his bed. "Cover yourself up, will you? I'll be back in a minute."

Mitch was quick in his report to Jimmie, letting him know why to anticipate the extra guards around the residence and in particular, within the house itself. After assuring him it had nothing to do with their own turmoil, he skirted out of the room before the girl could flaunt herself again.

When he returned to the parlor, the laughter could be heard from down the hallway. Another voice, Gino's, had joined their little group, and Mitch couldn't keep the uncertainty from rising in his stomach. Upon entering the laughing ceased and all eyes turned his direction. He leaned against the door frame, watching each one in turn.

"So you couldn't find something else to gossip about," he surmised, shaking his head.

"Bedtime for me," Toni chirped and moved to kiss his cheek. "He loves you, Mitch. He's only worried about your safety."

"I know that. Teddy, will you see Toni to her room and check on where Ashli disappeared to? I haven't seen her since we arrived."

"Yes, sir." Teddy nodded his goodbye to Gino. "Don Palmese."

Mitch moved to fix himself a glass of water, his eyes never leaving Gino's. "They told you about California."

"Yes."

"Because you asked?"

"Yes. Have no doubt they wouldn't have mentioned it without my prodding," he assured him.

"I wasn't doubting." He sank into a chair opposite Gino, sliding a glass of grappa his direction. "You were stalling this conversation to learn more information."

"Of course," he replied laughing. "Would you have done any different?"

"Probably not," he admitted. "And what did you learn?"

"That the devil is trying very hard to chain your soul."

"Gino," Mitch had quieted, his voice barely audible, "I need to know about Nicolai."

"No, you want to know," he corrected, exhaling. "And I can't blame you. But Mitch-"

"Don't patronize me. If these deaths are on my hands, if this is something following me around, I have a right to know."

"You think this is him?" Gino hissed. "I will kill him with my bare fucking hands."

"I don't know it. But it's a possibility, isn't it? Don't tell me it hasn't crossed your mind. You wouldn't be following my movements in such microscopic detail if it wasn't a possibility."

Gino hesitated. "Yes, it has. But-"

"You cannot shield me from him, Gino," Mitch argued. "Unless you are shielding him?"

Gino spat on the floor in response, his eyes flashing.

"Then tell me what I'm not seeing!"

"I can't."

"Can't or won't?"

"You have spent two years secluding yourself from everyone. Including me. How do you expect me to know the answers?"

Mitch stood, his calm starting to wear thin. He moved to refill his glass just to keep his hands occupied. "You had Nicolai send Antoinette away, didn't you?"

"Yes. You knew that."

"But not away from her father as you've led me to believe all these years. You," Mitch accused, "sent her away from me."

Gino was beside him now, his hand heavy on his shoulder. "Yes. That's true. And deep down you know why. So does she."

"I'd almost forgotten about her," he murmured, not bothering to look at Gino.

"Then you forget about her again!" he roared.

"He sent her to my bed, Gino," he said, his voice breaking as he whirled on him. "Like a common whore. Sent her into my room in the dead of night while he sat, two floors below, gorging himself on cannoli."

Gino lifted his eyes. "And did you-"

"Of course not! I didn't leave once for her safety only to take away her virtue a decade later."

"I doubt you would be-" Gino dropped off, knowing better than to finish the statement. "You must forget her again, Mitchell. She's made her choice, and she's chosen to stand beside her father."

"She chose nothing," he growled. "She was forced into this just like every other woman in *la familia* is forced to do the bidding of the men around her."

"You don't know-"

"I do know. I've seen her. I see it in her eyes, and they don't lie. I failed her once," he mumbled. "I won't do it again."

"Is this a private fight or can anyone join in?" Jimmie's voice was solemn as if waiting for Mitch and Gino to shoot him where he stood for the intrusion in their private affairs. Although Mitch's eyes flashed, he didn't protest, and Gino exhaled a heavy sigh, waving Jimmie permission to enter.

"Perhaps you can reason with him. I seem to be getting nowhere."

"I don't anticipate being able to change Mitch's mind on anything once he's set his course," Jimmie chuckled. "I doubt anyone has that ability. Did he learn that commitment from you, Gino?"

"Commitment? More like stubbornness," Gino scoffed but then his eyes narrowed, his voice lowering. "If you don't expect to change his mind then you presume to influence mine?"

Jimmie raised his hands as a peace offering. "I hope to only offer some objectivity."

"And you think yourself capable of that? You can't even keep your own family together. Are you objective where your sister is concerned, then? Have you changed so much in such a short time?"

Jimmie hesitated, Gino's words cutting into him. Mitch opened his mouth to intervene, but Jimmie raised his hand to silence him. "My family is here. Safe. Ashli, Mitch, Teddy," his voice dropped to a whisper, "Antoinette. And in some bizarre twist that I don't even pretend to understand you, Gino."

Mitch chuckled.

"You cannot claim Antoinette."

"I'm not claiming anything," Jimmie said, shaking his head. "She's free to do whatever she chooses. But we can offer her protection should she ever need it. She will be welcome at our side."

"And if she doesn't want to be there?"

"Then I would venture to guess I'm going to have many, many long nights babysitting an intoxicated Mitchell Kerlin."

"You act as if this is a choice that has to be made now," Mitch interrupted. "It's not. I only want her safe. She's a kid. She doesn't need to be making any life altering decisions at this point."

"We had this discussion two decades ago," Gino grumbled. "Being at your side is not safe. There are things even you can't protect her from. Did your mother's death teach you nothing?"

Jimmie glanced from Gino's fury to the heartbreak etched on Mitch's face, and his jumbled thoughts began to clear. Being at the hand of a mafioso was a death sentence - something you never did to someone you cared about. It was why they lived such solitary lives, why a true relationship was a weakness none of them could afford. From Mitch's broken look, Jimmie knew...it was this life that had taken hers.

"I know that," Mitch placed a hand on Gino's arm. "And I would never be so irresponsible as to fall in love with her. She's a friend. An extremely close one, yes, but a friend. But if she needs safe haven, I-"

"We," Jimmie corrected.

"We," he allowed," will never forsake her. I don't give a damn who her father is. I will protect her, Gino. No matter what it costs me. Or you."

Gino looked from one to the other, his emotions unreadable. After a few moments, his eyes closed and he squeezed Mitch's hand. "So be it."

CHAPTER THIRTY-FOUR

He's amazingly protective of her, almost like a daughter." Jimmie's voice held a note of question.

Mitch smiled. "Or a sister."

"Touché."

"He seems to accept dissension from you far more readily than anyone else."

"It's not dissension." Mitch shook his head. "He knows my loyalty to him can never be questioned. Disagreements are just that – differences of opinions and nothing more. Sometimes I win, sometimes he does."

Jimmie could stand it no longer and his eyes burned with curiosity. "And you came about this level of equality with Don Palmese how exactly?"

He hesitated, turning to face Jimmie. "It's nothing secretive, really. It's just easier if well if some ties remain quiet ones."

"That's actually the definition of secret, Mitch."

Mitch was thoughtful, his mind streaming with the extreme effort Jimmie had gone to for him. He had feared Gino, perhaps still did, and yet had swallowed that to help him try and explain about Toni. It cost Mitch nothing to fight with Gino, but it could have cost Jimmie everything, and yet he still did it – for Mitch's sake. Mitch lifted his eyes to Jimmie. "Grab us some breakfast and meet me down at the patio, all right? I need to check on Toni."

"She knows we've been fighting about her," he warned.

Mitch snickered. "Of course she does. She's Toni."

He was halfway through the hallways when Ashli materialized at his side, her arms flinging around him to stop him in his tracks.

"Are you still drunk?" he hissed, wrenching Ashli's arms from around his waist as he checked the corridors for any witnesses nearby.

"High as a kite, actually," she responded, her voice several octaves higher than normal.

Mitch grabbed her arm, shaking her. "Have you lost your mind completely now? You brought drugs into Gino Palmese's home?"

"No. It was that guy at the party." Her head tilted as if trying to determine what she'd done wrong. Her thoughts wouldn't clear though so she gave up and pressed her body closer to his. "It's so beautiful here, isn't it? Romantic?"

"Teddy!" Mitch roared, trying to hold her an arm's distance away without hurting her.

"Mitch, we could help each other. If you'd only listen..."

"Whatever you say, Ashli," he grumbled, his hand twitching impatiently as he waited for Teddy to appear.

Her body pressed into his, her lips crushing against his before he had the chance to push her away. It only took a second for him to gain his senses and his hands shoved her backward not caring if she knocked herself unconscious. His eyes blazed with fury, but a calming hand was on his shoulder instantly.

"I'll take care of her," Toni whispered. "Keep her away from Gino until she sobers."

"No, you won't."

"Afraid her bitter disposition and nymphomaniac tendencies will wear off on me?" she chuckled and kissed his cheek. "Teddy and I can handle her."

"No." His voice was strong, commanding. It was an order, and she shrank back.

"He's right," Teddy's voice was softer beside them, his arm looped around Ashli's waist. "You shouldn't be alone with her. People will talk."

"I care little-"

"I care," Mitch interjected, taking her arm. "Come, I need a drink."

Taking her hand in his, he dragged her back to the bar to grab a bottle of vodka before joining Jimmie on the patio. He planted her in a seat next to Jimmie then cracked open the vodka and tipped it in his orange juice.

"You were gone for five minutes. How the hell could something have gone wrong already?"

"Your sister," Toni spat. She opened her mouth to say more, but Mitch cut her off.

"Don't be judgmental. You were naked with three guys last night."

"Swimming," she clarified before spearing fruit from Jimmie's plate and popping it into her mouth.

Jimmie sighed. "I'll go."

"No." Mitch shook his head. "Stay."

"Pardon?"

"Even Gino's hospitality has its limits."

Jimmie's eyes narrowed at the carefully measured words. "What the hell did she do?"

"Drugs," Toni provided. "She was completely stoned and making moves on Mitch in the damn hallway where the whole world could-"

"Enough." Mitch silenced her. "Teddy is secluding her until she gets her act together."

"And Gino?"

Mitch shook his head. "He doesn't know."

"Thank you."

He nodded and tilted the bottle toward him. When Jimmie nodded, Mitch poured a heavy draft into his glass. They drank in silence, both their eyes focused on Toni as she continued to steal food from each of their plates. When she finally stopped for a breath, she looked up to meet their eyes.

"What? I'm starving."

Jimmie grinned. "Being naked with three guys will do that to you."

"You are such a smart ass."

"And you love that about me."

She flung a croissant at him, missing him by inches, but grinned. "Yeah, Jimmie, I kind of do."

Picking up his fork, Mitch took a bite of the nearly cold omelet Jimmie had brought for him. In between bites, he watched the two banter back and forth. As if they had known each other all their lives, he thought. He exhaled. "Jimmie is interested in our history. Yours, mine, Gino's."

"Really?"

"Actually," Jimmie shrugged, "I think I'm good. No need."

Toni leaned into him conspiratorially. "But if you don't know, how can we possibly hope to lure you to the dark side?"

"Don't worry, fiery little one," he promised kissing her cheek. "I'm already there."

CHAPTER THIRTY-FIVE

Mitch was near drunk by the time Toni found him on the beach. One bottle of whiskey lay discarded beside him and another was stuck in the sand, tilting at an odd angle as the fringes of the surf brushed against it. His white shirt had been rolled at the sleeves, his bare feet sticking out from underneath the overly long jeans he'd been wearing before his disappearance. He had missed dinner, missed the requisite cognac with the men, and none seemed worried about his absence. Even Teddy, who prided himself on knowing exactly where Mitch and Jimmie were at all times, seemed nonplussed by his absence. Of course, Teddy probably did know where he was but was choosing not to share it with anyone. That was why Mitch loved him so much.

"I was beginning to think you were going to stand me up," he grinned. "Tell me you brought food."

"You are drunk," she smiled and dropped down beside him. "Which means I have a lot of catching up to do."

Mitch laughed and took the sandwich she offered him while she slipped the whiskey bottle from the sand and took a long swig. "Good thing I drank so much at dinner, hm?"

"Did I miss an impromptu party?"

"No. I was just drowning out Ashli's indecipherable babble."

Mitch hesitated before taking a bite, his eyes not meeting Toni's. "I fear I'll be terrible company for you tonight."

"Jimmie hinted as much," she shrugged. "Want to tell me why?"

He considered and then shook his head. "Not really."

"Hm," she sank back on her elbows, watching him. "Because you don't trust me?" she ventured.

"No, not at all. It's just-" he trailed off, unsure of how to phrase it. "I'm not proud of myself," he managed finally.

"Nothing more?" Her voice was quiet, unsure of whether to believe him or not. He could lie so easily, to anyone at any time that she was uncertain of whether it was now being directed at her.

He tipped her chin to his, his half drunken eyes as serious as he could manage. "I have never, nor will I ever, have any reason to lie to you. I may not tell you things, but I will certainly never lie about them."

Rather than respond, she sipped the whiskey silently as he finished the sandwich she had brought down for him. When she heard him crumble the wrapper, she let her gaze drift toward him, a smile playing on the edges of her lips.

"Are you always so serious when you drink?"

"Unfortunately, yes," he chuckled. He dropped his head into her lap, stretching his legs out to avoid the rising surf. "I tend to become quite the self-absorbed philosopher when I drink. Judgment for my own actions and such. Sober, I rarely bother to take the time."

"So you intend on depressing me?" she asked, laughing. "What a fabulous evening this is going to be."

"Does my life depress you?" he queried, snaking the bottle out of her hand and taking a drink.

"Only when it makes you unhappy."

"Ah, the well learned voice of a woman taught to only appease the men in her life. The legacy of a mafia princess."

"I appease no one unless I choose to do so," she bristled and would not look at him, even though she could feel his eyes watching her. "Drinking with you is no fun," she breathed.

"I warned you."

"Tell me about Ashli. Do you love her, Mitch?"

"Ashli Vinetti?" his body shook in her lap as he laughed. "Lord, no."

"But she loves you?"

Mitch was quiet, the whiskey dulling the well-formed response he usually had at hand. He glanced away, his eyes attempting to focus on the pale orange glow of a ship's mast in the distance. "I don't presume to know how her mind works." He gave a half smile. "It's not me she's after really, so much as the safety I provide. Or she believes I provide," he dropped his voice. "She is terrified for Jimmie and feels I can bridge the link between them that's been lost."

"Instead, you've only made it wider," she deduced. "You've become the brother Jimmie never had. It makes her inconsequential to him."

"No." He shook his head. "To outsiders, perhaps that how it seems. But that is not the case."

"Do you miss having her more involved?"

"She balanced us, kept us grounded. Once, our base of operations was the east coast. Now we roam the entire globe. It's an exhausting prospect."

"Hm," she took another drink, letting the bottle rest on his chest. "You have business on the mind tonight, it seems. Either that or you are choosing not to discuss Ashli in personal detail."

Mitch smiled, understanding finally drifting through his mind – why Toni was so curious, why Nicolai had tried to use Ashli as bait so many months earlier. "You are under the misinformation that Ashli and I are lovers. Haven't I taught you not to listen to gossip?"

Rather than bother to deny it, she eyed him warily. "It's not true?"

"No. It's not true."

They were quiet for a moment, Mitch tearing at the label on the bottle still resting on his chest. He vaguely wondered how Toni had ended up here, at Gino's private residence without Nicolai, but then let the thought drift away. He wasn't sure he wanted to know how she managed to escape Terenari's guards or what might happen to her upon her return to him. He wondered if ignorance as to her plight excused him from not offering her safe haven.

"Do you need protection?"

"Pardon?" Toni was smiling, amused at his random speech. "Did you leave me out of a conversation you were having with yourself again?"

"Something like that. Do you?"

"No," she shook her head. "Nicolai is off with his latest girl-friend. I'll return home before he even notices my absence." She brushed back the hair blowing across his face. "But thank you for asking. And we've finished the last bottle."

"Jimmie's brought us another," he returned without moving or looking up.

"I hate it when he does that shit," Jimmie grumbled, dropping down beside them. "Eyes in the fucking back of his head, I tell you. I figured Mitch had depressed you enough, and it was time for me to liven up this party."

Mitch sat up, taking the bottle from Jimmie. "And what do you have in mind?"

Jimmie's eyes gleamed. "You two look awfully cozy down here. Care for the three of us to go inside and continue this?" He chuckled as he kissed Toni's cheek. "A proper welcome to Sicily, Antoinette."

She shoved him away laughing. "It seems you've had enough to drink already, Jimmie. Your insanity has reached new levels."

"One can always hope," he grinned. "And I've not had a drop, thank you very much."

"You aren't drinking?" she asked.

"Not tonight," his response echoed with Mitch's slower, more drunken reply.

Toni's eyes shifted from one man to the other, the hairs on the back of her neck beginning to rise.

"Teddy," Mitch called softly, and a shadow moved forward from somewhere behind them. "Please move Antoinette to an interior room on the third floor if you would."

"I have a room-" her voice trailed off with the strangling look Mitch sent her.

"Immediately, please."

"Yes, sir." Teddy took hold of her arm to help her off the ground. "Shall I-"

"I'll be up with further instructions shortly."

Jimmie watched them go before he let out an exasperated sigh. "You must stop doing this, you know. Thinking you are betraying the family by saying no. It's ridiculous. Even Gino agrees."

"You're going tonight?"

"Hell yes. You are going to miss all the fun. Stop hating yourself so damn much, Mitch, all right? We grow weary of your drunken introspection."

"Fuck you," he spat, allowing Jimmie to help him off the ground. He wobbled a moment then straightened. "Fuck you," he repeated, just for effect.

"You and Toni got a thing going I don't know about?"

Mitch narrowed his eyes. "What happened to the leggy blonde in your room?"

"She did have great legs, didn't she?" Jimmie exhaled. "She's off to who knows where. You'll be alone with the girls tonight."

"Gino's out?"

"Disappeared after dinner. Teddy-"

"Take him with you."

"You sure?"

"Please."

"I swear, you're the most paranoid guy I know."

"It keeps you alive, doesn't it?"

"So far," Jimmie grumbled. "Breakfast tomorrow? That little bistro down by the dock?"

"Bistro?" Mitch chortled. "How very European of you."

Jimmie paused. "Good point. We've been here way too fucking long. Breakfast on the plane. Wheels up at eight?"

"Make it nine. I can get Toni on a flight."

"See you then."

CHAPTER THIRTY-SIX

Teddy," Mitch took his arm as he entered the hallway to the third floor. "Go with Jimmie, all right? The girls will be fine with Gino's staff."

"But-"

"And so will I," he smiled. "Take care of Jimmie for me."

"Yes, sir."

Mitch tapped on the door across from where Teddy had been perched and opened it quietly. "Toni?"

"Should I be worried?" she asked, pulling the door open and then shutting it behind him.

"No."

He didn't elaborate but instead surveyed the room Teddy had chosen for her. With bright, nearly tropical décor, the walls were covered in a satiny tapestry that contrasted obscenely with the dark paneled wood. A small sitting area in the corner held two chairs, one covered in a pale blue and the other a soft coral. The bed was covered in a simple handmade quilt, and Toni's single overnight bag was still sitting open at the edge. "The room suits you."

"You took away my balcony view," she feigned a pout but waved off his explanation. "I do like this room. Very colorful. Are you still drunk?"

He nodded. "Unbelievably so." His eyes roamed over her, surprised that she had already changed for bed. She should have known he would be coming to check on her before he retired. Her jeans lie discarded on the bed, replaced now by a silken tangerine colored slip that could only have been picked up in the local market down near the wharf. A bit delayed, his thoughts came together.

"Were you expecting someone?"

"Only you."

His eyes narrowed, but she laughed and led him to one of the chairs. "Don't look so scandalized. I was headed to bed, Mitch. I didn't realize you weren't going with them to seek retribution at the docks. When you had Teddy stand guard, I assumed you had left."

He nodded, accepting the answer without bothering to question how she knew the evening's plans. He dropped into one of the chairs, dragging his fingers through his hair. She moved passed him, sinking into the other and curling her legs up underneath herself.

"You smell like-"

She looked appalled, taking a sniff of her own arm. "Like what?"

His eyes drifted, shaking his head as if he'd lost his train of thought. "Nothing. Never mind."

"Yes, you are still drunk."

He tugged her toward him, pulling her from her seat and into his lap. "How long have we known each other?"

"The years have blurred. I suppose, since back when you were still hiding dirty magazines from your parents."

"I never looked at dirty magazines," he corrected. "There were too many whores walking the neighborhood each evening to need to waste money on stupid things like that."

"Frequented them often, did you?"

"No," his voice dropped a notch as he slid his fingers into hers. "They thought it was funny. Flashing themselves to the young boys on the street. 'Future customers' they would chant at all of us. Free looks until you grow up then you pay." Mitch's drunken rendition of their voice made him laugh. "Horrible place, that neighborhood."

"I was whisked away to boarding school, remember? I missed out on all of that. And then we moved to California...." she trailed off.

"He's been hard on you since then, hasn't he?" Mitch murmured. "He's changed. He broke ties with the neighborhood, who he was. I can see it when I look at him. He's not the same person that played ball with us boys on Saturdays."

"He hated that neighborhood too, Mitch. I guess he thinks he rose above it."

"You can't rise above what you are," he countered then smiled. "Do you remember the first time I got arrested? I was what, seventeen and you were maybe six? Seven?" he laughed. "When I was released you showed up at my house and threw my mom's favorite dinner dishes at me until Gino came over and made you stop. Do you remember?"

"I remember," she nodded. "And then you went away. You hadn't come back by the time we moved to the west coast. I thought I'd never see you again. I was so furious at you for so long."

She touched his hair, letting her fingers slide across his cheek. "And then one day, a decade later, you appear. A new suit, a new brother, a new career – a new you."

"For better or worse?" he asked, taking her hand in his to keep her from touching his face, unwilling to accept the comfort she was trying to offer him.

"Both," she murmured, "always both."

"Bedtime for you," he whispered, moving her gently off his lap.

She crawled into bed without argument, letting him tuck her in as if she was a little kid again. "You'll stay until I'm asleep?"

He chuckled but lay down beside her anyway, offering her a kiss on the forehead before stretching out. "Just go to sleep quickly or I'm liable to pass out first." He was quiet for a moment, listening to her soft breaths beside him. "Toni?"

"Hm?"

"I was terrified they were coming for you next. After hearing about Sonny, I mean."

"You are much more of a target than I will ever be. Everyone knows that " she answered reasonably.

"What is that supposed to mean?"

A soft touch grazed against his face and then was gone. "If you were terrified, think how I felt."

"Night, girl."

It was during the wee hours of the morning when Mitch received his first hint that something wasn't right in Toni's world. More than the murmurs or the shivering or frightened tossing and turning that rumpled all the bed covers, it was the intensity of her dreams that nearly brought Mitch to his knees. That there was something so devastatingly poisonous in her life and that she would hide it from everyone – especially him, when she knew he could protect her – made his anger flare and his fury toward her grow with each passing breath. That she felt she could not trust him, or would not, washed away all the words of trust she had been telling him while awake. His anger had grown to the point of waking her when a soft muted voice, more of a whimper of helplessness, cut through him as if she had knifed him directly in the heart.

"Daddy, no."

It was neither a plea nor beg but a matter of fact statement. Whether Nicolai was doing something to her or someone else, Mitch had no idea but the effect was still the same – the dreams that were haunting her were about her father. And she knew, while Mitch could protect her from him, it would un-doubtedly put the families at war. By her silence, Toni was protecting Mitch, and that was more painful than anything.

When she came downstairs the next morning, it was im-possible for Mitch to look her in the eye. She swooped in, kiss-ing him, Teddy, Gino and Jimmie on the cheek before pouring herself a glass of juice.

"Must you always be so chipper?" Ashli grumbled.

"Must you always be so sour?" she returned, her smile nev-er fading. "Who is the lucky one to escort me to the airport this morning?"

"Mitch-"

"Gino, I believe," Mitch cut into Jimmie's response without bothering to look up. "The rest of us are headed back to the States this morning. We're actually running late as it is."

"Fabulous, can we stop by the market again, Gino? Would you mind terribly?"

"Of course not. For a ray of sunshine like you, anything, my dear."

Jimmie was downing his coffee quickly, keeping his face as placid as possible. "Are we ready then?"

Mitch nodded. "Hurry up, Teddy, finish your omelet and let's go."

"Yes, sir."

Toni moved among them, giving hugs and kisses as Teddy gulped the rest of his breakfast in one bite and washed it with a cup of coffee.

Mitch bent down to offer her a kiss on the cheek, hesitating a moment by her ear. "Be careful of your bedmates, girl," he whispered, causing her to give him a quizzical look. "You talk in your sleep." He moved away but not before noticing how her face blanched to icy whiteness.

CHAPTER THIRTY-SEVEN

Mitch stretched out as far as the tiny metal chair would allow, chains at his ankles clattering against the yellow seventies formica. When Mike entered a half hour later, Mitch was snoring softly.

"Get those off him and get some coffee in here."

"Yes, sir."

"Most people piss their pants when detained by Homeland Security."

"Have I offended their sensibilities by dozing? My apologies."

The door opened, and a man clad in all black bent down and unlocked the shackles attached to the floor grates. Another followed just behind, holding out an over-sized mug. Mitch accepted the lukewarm coffee with near glee, finishing it in two gulps.

"Bring us a fresh pot."

"Yes, sir."

When Mitch finished another cup, he finally frowned at Mike. "Customs? You pulled me in Customs? That's pretty low."

"Sonny shot, a midnight rendezvous with Nicolai Terenari's daughter and a mad flight to Sicily- what of that growing list of mischievous behavior precludes me from carting your ass off to Guantanamo for an extended vacation?"

Mitch sat in silence, accepting the rebuke. Mike was right. He'd been entirely lax in his reporting considering the pace he'd been keeping.

After a few more minutes of ranting, Mike finally grew quiet. "Do you have anything to say for yourself?"

"I deserve that."

"We thought you were dead, Mitch." Mike sank down on the table opposite him. "*I* thought you were dead."

"I apologize. Truly." Mitch shook his head. "I haven't been alone since it happened. I've had Jimmie or Ashli with me 24/7."

Mitch could feel him gauging him, trying to decipher his honesty. "You don't have to believe me but whoever told you your news should have told you that as well."

"Actually, they did. They said they couldn't even get near enough to pass a message."

"So this little dance was because…"

Mike's eyes narrowed. "Because you deserved it."

Mitch nodded, accepting. "You took the Chicago and Philly offices?"

"Yeah and didn't get a damn thing. They go back to business in fourteen days. Has Vinetti made a deal with Terenari?"

Mitch laughed. "Not a chance. There is no love loss there. From either side."

"War?"

He nodded. "It's coming. No denying it."

"Who will win?"

Me, Mitch thought. He leaned forward, his voice soft. "Who do we want to win?"

"Good question. I've no idea the answer."

"Let me know when you find out."

"What were you doing in Sicily?"

Mitch didn't hesitate. "Jimmie was meeting with Palmese."

"Shoring up his ties?"

"I don't think so," Mitch caged. "More like searching for safe haven if it's needed."

"And was it offered?"

"No. But I have no doubt it will be."

"The last thing we need is Palmese offering Vinetti protection."

Mitch straightened. "Why is that?"

"That's just not a relationship we care to foster."

"Interesting." Mitch sat in thought a moment then stood up. "Can I go back to work now or is there something else?"

"The Feast of San Gennaro is this week. Tourists have been pouring in for days."

"Mm-hm."

"Vinettis have a hand in that?"

"Every family has a hand in it. You know that."

"But he's never shown at that dinner Father Lorenzo hosts."

Mitch leaned against the door frame. "I've wondered about that myself. To my knowledge, he's never even sent a representative."

"Maybe you can-"

"I can't make him go, Mike. That's entrapment."

"But if you could-"

"No."

"What about you? You haven't made an appearance in three years."

"And you think now, after all, this time, when I'm standing beside a Vinetti who has no invitation, is the time to return?" Mitch huffed. "I'm too old for suicide missions."

"It wouldn't be," Mike assured him. "We have the place wired; you know that. They are taking bets on you appearing."

"Really? Now that's intriguing. Who's betting on what?"

"Nevermind that. Just know we have no reason to believe you are in danger."

"Well, that's an official order if I ever heard one."

"Probably," Mike nodded. "You seem to be your more clear-headed self these days. Placating Terenari, Palmese, Markesi, getting Vinetti a foothold in those night clubs."

"Legitimate funds."

"But whatever goes through the back door won't be. No mob controlled night club is going to be clean."

"I'd argue that no club on the eastern seaboard is clean."

"Point taken," Mike said nodding. "They're probably all dirty."

"How do you decide?"

"What?"

"They are all dirty, right? How do you decide to go after Vinetti rather than the one owned by some Hollywood celebrity or a real estate banker?"

"Mitch, James Vinetti is-"

He waved off the excuse he knew was coming. "Fine, don't answer."

"Mitch-"

"Whatever, Mike. Placate someone else. I know what the IOC wants. San Gennaro it is."

CHAPTER THIRTY-EIGHT

I've had men looking all over for you," Jimmie said, stepping into Mitch's suite.

"Who found me?"

"No one actually. How do you manage to disappear so completely like that?"

"Jealous?"

Jimmie moved to the bar, pouring himself a drink. "Like you wouldn't believe. You got a hot date in the middle of the afternoon?"

Mitch continued to button his shirt, looking at Jimmie from the mirror. "Don't I wish."

"You don't seem too happy for a guy dressed so impeccably. Please tell me you aren't running off to elope or something because that would really fuck up my week."

He laughed as he finished his tie and took the drink Jimmie offered. "I *am* heading to church."

Jimmie was silent for a minute, watching as Mitch pulled on his overcoat and a silvery scarf that perfectly matched his tie. Only when Mitch pulled a tri-color carnation out of his pocket did Jimmie finally understand. "Oh, shit," he choked. "San Gennaro."

Mitch froze. It was not the reaction he had expected. When Jimmie failed to say anything more, Mitch grabbed a bottle of water from the bar, trading it for the whiskey in Jimmie's hand. He let him take a few gulps before zeroing in on him. "What the hell was that?"

"Nothing. Just surprised is all. You haven't been stateside in years. I just didn't expect you to be a part of something like that."

"It's my heritage, Jimmie. The Sicilian passport pretty much makes it obligatory."

"Bullshit. There's probably not another native Sicilian in the bunch."

Mitch bristled at his tone. "I'm on my own time. But even if I wasn't-"

Jimmie shook his head. "That came out wrong. I'm not judging your attendance. It was just unexpected."

"You already said that."

"So I did." Jimmie nodded. "Have you been attending long?"

"I haven't been since before I left for Canada. But, yeah. I attended my first when I was nine."

"You are indeed a harpoon of mysterious revelations to-day."

Mitch sat down on a bar stool, trying to decipher Jimmie's cryptic comments. "And you look like death. Either explain or let me get to mass before Father Lorenzo has my hide."

"My father, when he died, was not in the good graces of those sitting at Lorenzo's table."

"Killed?"

"No. Not by them." He shook his head. "But they did not mourn his passing."

"From what I understand, neither did you."

"No. Neither did I."

"So you've spent decades living in his shadow? Is that what this is?"

"Avoiding more like."

"You should know, avoidance? Not really my thing."

Jimmie managed a half laugh. "That is the first non-surprising thing you've said all afternoon."

"Get dressed. Father Lorenzo has no tolerance for tardiness."

"Mitch-"

"No excuses." Mitch put a confidant hand on his shoulder. "It's time to make your own history."

CHAPTER THIRTY-NINE

Mitchell Vincenzo!" Father Lorenzo enveloped him a hug before he'd even entered the parish hall. "The prodigal boy returns!"

"It's only been a few years."

"One year is too many."

"It's just dinner, Father."

"Just dinner, pfft!" He glanced to Mitch's side. "And introduce me to your new friend."

"Father Lorenzo, this is James Vinetti."

His eyes darkened. "I knew your father."

"I-"

But Mitch was already interrupting. "Good thing you believe in all that forgiveness and no sins of the father thing then, isn't it? Because all of us know his father was an ass."

It took a moment, long enough for all eyes around the tables to turn their direction, but eventually Father Lorenzo enveloped Jimmie into a warm hug. "Welcome to my table, James."

When he left, Jimmie turned dark eyes to Mitch.

"Don't look at me like that. It wasn't some voodoo family respect thing. Cash is the only currency he deals in."

"Seriously?"

"Every seat at this table was bought. Who you are merely determines how much it costs you." Mitch grimaced. "You were fucking expensive, so that you know."

"Then I guess I should get off my ass and make us some deals, hm?"

Mitch clinked glasses with him before sinking into one of the smaller tables in the back of the hall. "You do that. I'm going to sit here and drink until I can stand to be around these people."

"I'm-" Jimmie stuttered. "I'm going to leave that one alone. For now."

It was hours before Mitch finally felt numb enough to mingle with the others. Jimmie had made friends fast and was swirling deals with just about everyone present. Mitch admired the way he worked the room. Despite his misgivings, despite the shadow of his father, Jimmie had made the table his own in a single evening. His presence was almost ethereal, power drawing men toward him and his innate charisma keeping them at his side.

Mitch was sitting with a crew from Queens, listening to them share battle stories when his phone vibrated an emergency message. By the time he read it and looked up, Jimmie was already heading his way.

"Ashli?"

"No, she's fine. You are observant tonight."

"I've not drunk as much as you. What is it?"

Mitch made his goodbyes then stepped in line beside Jimmie as they headed for the door. "Masseria's brother finally raised his head."

"I'll handle it. Where?"

"Jimmie-"

"I need to know my sister is safe, Mitch. Who would you trust that with?"

No one, Mitch thought. Absolutely no one. "I'll drive."

Two hours later, the two pulled the car onto a darkened street. Only one street light remained working, all the others having been shot out long before their arrival. Litter decorated every inch of the area, wind kicking it up in tiny tornadoes of trash.

"A Hoboken whorehouse?" Jimmie stared at the derelict building through the tinted windows. "He is some kind of classy."

"You ever met him?"

"Once or twice in passing. Do we know anyone here?"

"I can assure you that I know no one here," Mitch said and then offered him a dark smile. "But I make friends fast."

"Where's Teddy?"

"I had him take Ashli up the estate. No reason to have her in the city in case something goes wrong."

They sat in silence, their practiced eyes surveying the entire neighborhood. Waiting and planning but neither bothering to discuss it. After a half hour, Jimmie disappeared around the corner to get coffee. Sinking back in the car, he offered a cup to Mitch. "He show up?"

"Yeah, he's in there. One of the guys just texted me that he's still drinking at the bar, though."

"There's a bar in there?"

"Well, sofa and a dusty fifth of Jim Beam."

Jimmie rolled his eyes. "Want to tell me what happened between you and Toni that caused the sudden flight change?"

Mitch grimaced and shook his head rather than reply.

"Did you sleep with her?"

"Really? Did you pay no attention at all during that argument?" Mitch groused. "Can't believe you asked me that."

"Stop being so damn touchy. If you are putting me at war with Terenari, I have a right to know."

"This isn't your war."

"You are beside me. That makes it mine."

"I don't need your help," he said, bristling. "Let's go. He's found a room."

Mitch stepped out, straightening his suit and tossing the Gennaro carnation into the gutter.

"You misunderstand, Mitchell," Jimmie shook his head, resting his arms on the hood of the car to face him. "You have stood beside me through things that would have sent any other man in a dead run the opposite direction. A fight against you is a fight against me."

"You owe me nothing, Jimmie."

"I'm not so noble a creature as to repay debts with my own life, Mitch. We," he dropped his hand heavily on Mitch's shoulder as he joined him in the paces toward the building, "will keep each other alive."

CHAPTER FORTY

They went in together, talking only briefly with the man they had inside. Mitch gave him a stack of bills, orders to clear out the rooms as much as possible and to pay off the owner. By the time the two headed up the stairs, no one was asking any questions. They opened the door, not surprised to find him naked with a girl already bent over the bed. They stood in silence, waiting to be noticed, and it was the girl who finally yelped at their looming presence in the room. She shuffled away, extricating herself from him and crawling into a corner of the bed. Before Masseria could move, Mitch had him in a vice grip and pinned against the wall.

Jimmie stepped toward the girl with slow, deliberate movements. Grabbing a robe she had cast aside, he offered her his hand and then helped wrap it around her. His eyes moved up and down her tiny frame, a slow frown spreading across his face. "How old are you?"

"Nineteen."

Jimmie glanced over his shoulder at Mitch who gave a single shake of his head. Jimmie rubbed her arms, softening his tone. "You're scared, hm? No reason to be. If we wanted to hurt you, we already would have, okay?"

She nodded, her eyes flittering from one to the other.

"How old are you?"

"Fifteen."

"Whoa." Jimmie's hands jerked away from her, and he took a step back.

A pace behind him, Mitch chuckled. "Trade?"

Jimmie didn't hesitate, moving away from the girl and slamming his elbow into Masseria. "She's a child, you little shit."

Mitch stepped to the girl, his hand moving to the small of her back as he guided her to the door. "Runaway?"

She shook her head.

"Parents?"

"Dead." She straightened. "I'm doing what-"

"You have to do to survive," he finished. "We get it. No judgment here. Do you want to work here?"

She rolled her eyes at him. "Course not. I'm not an idiot."

Mitch pulled out a stack of bills. "You do drugs?"

"No." She hesitated, eyeing the bills in his hand with uncertainty. "But I can find some if you-"

"I don't." He tucked the money into her palm, topped it with one of Ashli's business cards and then closed her fingers around it. "Call that number. Tell her I said to give you safe haven. Take a cab wherever she tells you."

"But my job-"

"She'll find you a legitimate one."

"I'm...I mean, than-"

"Don't thank me. Get out of here and don't look back." He pushed her out the door then took a slow pivot to face Masseria. "You are one sick pup."

"I didn't know! I swear!"

"Yeah, that's believable."

Mitch sank down in a chair, eyeing him. He was bleeding from Jimmie's punch, blood trickling down his naked body. Alex's name was tattooed in script across his heart and another tattoo hovered just under his collar bone.

"What is that?" he asked, drawing Jimmie's attention to the symbol.

"Sailor's cross, I think." Jimmie shrugged.

Masseria opened his mouth to speak, but Jimmie hit him again, causing blood to drip from his mouth. "He wasn't asking you."

"Do you know who he is?" Mitch asked.

Jimmie had to nudge him to get him to respond. "Yes."

"Then you know why I'm here," Jimmie's voice was calm, icy.

"I only sat with them! For chrissakes, Alex asked me to guard them and I did. They just shopped!"

Both men straightened, realization dawning simultaneously.

"You were in California?" Jimmie shoved his gun into his kidneys, eliciting a scream. "You are the one who held my sister fucking hostage?"

"Well, that's an interesting development," Mitch managed, shaking his head.

"Your chances of survival were slim before. Now? Now they are non-existent," Jimmie spat.

"I know you."

"No, no, Mr. Kerlin. You have me mistaken."

"Well, you clearly know him," Jimmie interjected, shoving him away. "Get your fuckin' pants on."

While he struggled to pull them on, Mitch searched his memory. It was the tattoo that tugged at him. A sailor's cross wasn't a Sicilian thing - more often a mark of the Greeks or Hispanics. He raised his eyes, frowning at his failing when it finally clicked.

Mitch silently thanked Mike for the recent threat of sending him to Guantanamo. Were it not for that, he never would've put the memory together.

"Penny Lane."

All movement stopped. Even Jimmie seemed taken back by Masseria's reaction, and he took a step away. It took a good dozen heartbeats for Masseria to recover and develop a response.

"Not me."

"I didn't ask a question. I know it was you. What I want to know is if someone sanctioned it."

Jimmie glanced from one to the other, waiting for an explanation.

"Penny Lane was a temporary detention camp in Guantanamo Bay. A pretty upscale place designed to convince insurgents to turn spy on Al-Qaeda."

"And you know about this how?"

"AP reported on it," Mitch clipped. "CIA would give them anything they wanted to try and bring them to the American side. Expensive gifts, cars, drugs and women." He glared at Masseria. "And you were caught smuggling in girls, innocent little girls, to do their bidding."

Jimmie blanched. "Are you fucking kidding me?"

"You couldn't have done it alone. What family sanctioned it? Funded you?"

"No one. I just lucked into it. I swear I'm telling you the truth!"

Mitch could see the question burning in Jimmie's eyes, but he knew he would never ask it. That his company might have fronted something so horrific was causing Jimmie's hand to quake. "Was your brother involved in that?"

"Yeah, yeah."

"Alex?" Jimmie managed. "Bullshit."

"No, promise. He ran the whole thing. You know I ain't smart enough to do something that big."

"That I don't disagree with," Jimmie growled.

Jimmie didn't want to believe it - that his money had been siphoned off for something like that. But, after Alex's betrayal, he was ready to accept it. But not Mitch. He lowered his voice to a hiss. "And Jimmie?"

"Sure, sure. We paid him all the money. Just like we was supposed to."

Mitch knew he was lying, but he raised his eyes to Jimmie anyway. Fury radiated off him, his calm demeanor cracking. When Jimmie opened his mouth to defend himself, Mitch pulled out his gun and shot a single round into the man's thigh.

Screams erupted, echoing through the halls, but Mitch's voice was a low threat next to the man's ear. "Mind your fuckin' manners. We're not that stupid."

Jimmie had reached his limit, and Mitch could feel it coursing through him from across the tiny room. "He's not going to tell us."

Mitch nodded, his eyes never leaving Masseria's squirming figure. When he finally spoke, his voice was full of resignation. "It's okay. I already know the answer."

"You aren't going to sulk if I kill him, right?"

"Him?" Mitch breathed. "Not a chance."

CHAPTER FORTY-ONE

Mitch and Jimmie's laughter carried through the estate hallways, and Ashli rushed to meet them.

"Everything okay?" Jimmie asked, kissing the top of her head in greeting.

She nodded, taking his hand and wiping some of the dried blood off his knuckles. "You?"

"Starving but fine." Jimmie smiled. "Guys are bringing food in."

"I got a call-"

Jimmie shuddered which elicited a soft laugh from Mitch. "Mitch can explain that. Fifteen geez. I'm grabbing a shower. Meet you in ten."

When he was gone, she stepped toward Mitch. "And you?"

"Please don't ruin my mood with an interrogation."

Ashli hesitated then stretched to give him a kiss on the cheek. "I took care of her for you."

His hand snaked around her waist, pulling her into him. She gasped at the suddenness of it, then settled the curves of her body against his. With his free hand, he tilted her head, his lips drifting across her neck. "Thank you."

She could feel the power and adrenaline coursing through him, his body knifelike against her softer one. His lips were still at her throat, his hands now exploring up her stomach to her chest. He tightened his palm, cupping her breast and her body arched towards him.

"Ash." His voice was rough, for once his desire completed unveiled.

Outside voices sounded the arrival of the men with dinner.

"Mitch-" she struggled to right herself, get her breath, calm the flush she knew was visible on her entire body.

He accepted his name as a warning and let his hands drop. "Let me change and I'll be down to help with the food."

She nodded. "Are you sure you're-"

He stepped toward her again, his hand drifting across her cheek before pulling her ear to his lips. "That *leccacazzi* got better than he deserved."

She turned her lips to kiss his palm then his wrist. "Then that's all I needed to hear."

"Maturity," he chuckled, "looks damn sexy on you. I'll see you in a minute."

Casting off his suit and trading it for jeans and a white oxford, he appeared in the kitchen moments later. He rolled his sleeves and began separating out the bags of takeout.

"Do you cook?" She asked, nibbling on a breadstick she'd pulled from one of the boxes.

"Me?" Mitch laughed. "No."

"I imagine you as one of those tough guys in movies who softens and starts cooking some swoon worthy meal for his lover."

"Wearing an apron but minus a shirt to show off my manliness?" He laughed again, kissing her head as he passed by. "You've built my pedestal much too high. I burn toast."

"Well," Ashli sighed, "at least you can order a mean take out."

"That I can." Mitch finished unpacking the boxes, spreading everything along the counters. "Grab some for the four of us before I call the troops or there will be nothing left."

She nodded obediently, grabbing boxes for each of them and tucking wine glasses under her arm.

Mitch stuck his head out the door, calling the men for food before moving into the privacy of the back den. Jimmie was already pouring wine and Teddy was doling out the pasta bolognese by the time he sank into the sofa.

"Tell us your life story, Teddy."

He faltered. "Is that an order?"

Jimmie laughed. "It's conversation. Why is everyone so damn terrified these days?"

"Uh, because the two of you scare the shit out of all of us?" he offered and then smiled. "But I'm idiot enough to accept that. So, I'm from the neighborhood, you know-"

Teddy only gave a short rundown of his childhood before starting in on his time in the military. Rather than the dark times, though, he kept them laughing as he regaled them with tales of pranks the soldiers did to keep things interesting. As they finished the meal, he offered to pick up the trash and leftovers while Ashli went for another bottle of wine.

When she returned, she stood quietly for a minute, watching over the trio. Jimmie was flipping through the television with the remote, Mitch was unbuttoning his shirt to relax better, and Teddy was still focusing on his last glass of wine.

"This feels so...normal," she said, handing the bottle to Jimmie and waiting for him to open it. He obliged, and she moved to refill everyone's glasses. "I'd forgotten what normal was like."

"You dream of normal?" Teddy asked. "That seems too boring for you."

"You don't know her very well then," Mitch countered. He accepted the refill of his glass and then took her wrist in a gentle embrace, tugging her to sit down beside him. She hesitated, her eyes flickering to Jimmie but, although he glanced their way, he made no face of protest.

"Let's watch *Godfather*." All eyes flicked to Teddy before laughter erupted from all of them. "Then that's a no? How about Nicholas Sparks?"

They settled on *Requiem for a Dream* but, less than a half hour in, they had to wake a dozing Teddy and send him off to bed. Ashli had stretched out on the sofa, her head resting in Mitch's lap. His fingers drifted through her hair absently; his eyes focused out the windows. The darkness was complete, he could see nothing, but it still didn't change his gaze.

Jimmie shifted in his chair, drawing Mitch's attention. He nodded once to his lap where Ashli lay, still engrossed in the film. "You're okay, right?"

His voice drew Ashli up, her eyes full of wariness. She glanced from one to the other, gauging any discontent, but Mitch gave a single nod.

"I'm good, Jimmie. No ghosts this time."

Jimmie nodded, then stood up and tossed them the remote. "Then I'm off to bed." He hesitated beside them, his gaze focusing on his baby sister. "It's long past time you stop being a victim. Meet me at the firing range at seven."

Ashli drew in a breath, expecting some hint of a joke. Receiving none, she stood to hug him. "I'll be there. Thank you, Jimmie."

He nodded, kissing the side of her head. He raised his eyes to Mitch. "Don't keep her up too late. My sister," he said pointedly, "needs her rest."

Mitch laughed. "I promise not to exhaust her too much."

"Fuck you, Mitch."

"Night, Jimmie."

Ashli watched him leave then turned to face Mitch. "What happened to you two tonight?"

"Male bonding," he said shrugging. "Come here."

She moved to stand in front of him, goosebumps rising on her flesh as he pulled her to stand between his legs. His hands drifted slowly up her bare thighs, over her night shorts, and up to her waist. He lifted her without effort, pulling her to straddle his lap.

"Are you drunk?"

He continued to let his fingers roam across her skin, tracing random patterns along the outside of her thighs. "No."

"Adrenaline filled? Angry? Missing Antoinette?"

"No, no, and yes, always, but not in the way you mean." He lifted the edges of her tank top, his lips slipping over her skin in a fiery trail.

She let out a soft whimper, sinking lower into his lap. "Alex's brother is dead."

"Yes."

"And you are okay with that?"

"Absolutely." Mitch's hands stilled, and he leaned his head back to look at her. "Anything else?"

"Jimmie-"

"Is not a fool. He knows my intentions."

"One more." She let her fingers drift across his face, her palm prickling from the shadow of a beard he hadn't taken the time to shave. "Why now? After all this time? After all my attempts?"

Mitch hesitated. It was a question he hadn't expected. His fingers pushed under her top, trailing up her spine. Her body shifted, pressing harder against his. Her breaths were ragged, shivers causing her body to tremble in his arms. Mitch leaned back, stretching her body up to rest completely on his. He kissed her throat, his lips searing a path to her ear. "Are you telling me no?"

She didn't answer but, instead, reached to pull off her top. In a swift jerk, he grabbed her wrists to halt her.

"Ashli, look at me."

Her eyes were downcast, refusing to meet his intense gaze. His body stilled, his voice like steel. "Please, Ash, I need you to look at me."

When she finally met his eyes, her own were brimming with tears. Confusion etched across Mitch's face but, before he could speak, her lips were on his - tender, caressing, nearly loving. The salty taste of tears mingled with kisses caused him to pull a heartbeat away.

"Ash," he whispered, his breath warm on her throat, "you *can* tell me no."

Her hand brushed across his face just once, her voice a ragged declaration of need. "No, Mitch, I really can't."

Hours later, as dawn began to settle on the horizon, the two lay entwined on Mitch's bed, both reveling in the quiet world they had created.

"This felt like goodbye."

"Maybe it was hello," he murmured, his lips seeking hers once again.

She smiled through his kisses. "Say my name."

"Do you think I've forgotten who's sharing my bed?" He asked then dropped his lips to hover at her ear. "Ashli Marionette Vinetti."

"Again."

He gave a throaty chuckle. "Ash."

She sighed with content, dropping her head to rest on his chest. Her fingers traced along the outline of his muscles. "We should get dressed."

"You are the one with a date on the range. I'm not leaving this bed for hours."

"Is that an invitation to stay?"

He pulled her face to his, his lips caressing the edge of her jawline before finding her mouth. "No. Go spend time with your brother."

"Is that an order?"

"Yes," he answered without apology.

She paused in her movements then let out a long breath. "I like it when you are in control."

He shifted beneath her, rolling her over and pinning her to the bed before she could take a breath. His grip tightened on her wrists, her arms locked in position above her head. He held her there, listening to her racing heart reverberate in the quiet of the room. "Never say that to a man like me. Understand?"

"Ever my protector," she kissed him fast on the lips before moving from the bed to pull on her clothes. When she finished dressing, she turned to find him still watching her intently. She moved to him, her hands slipping down his chest to land on his heart. "I understand."

CHAPTER FORTY-TWO

"Can I ask you something?"

"Shoot."

"Are you training Teddy as your replacement?"

Mitch glanced up from the security panel screens long enough to gauge Jimmie's disposition. "I tend not to plan that far ahead. You should know that by now."

"So you are unhappy here." Jimmie sank down onto the sofa opposite him.

"Why do you assume that?"

"Something Ashli said."

Mitch's mind flew back to their night at the estate less than a month before...when she had accused him of saying goodbye. "Well, that makes it fact, right?"

"She's smarter than you think. More perceptive, too."

"Jimmie, I have never once doubted your sister's inherent qualities. That would be grossly irresponsible."

"So it's true then?"

"You do realize I am scanning security reports to try and find a possible C4 detonator that could level this entire building, killing us both?"

"Yes."

Mitch's eyes narrowed, his fingers withdrawing from the keyboard. "Then why the fuck are you wanting to have some heart to heart discussion about my future employment strategy?"

Jimmie dropped his eyes. "I-"

But it was Ashli's appearance in the periphery that made all the pieces click. He had sent her away first during the evacuation along with the other executive staff. Only Jimmie and Teddy had been stubborn enough to remain behind. But here she was, standing before him sans bodyguards. He crossed the room in two strides to face her. "You. I evacuated this whole building, put lives in jeopardy. I have men chasing down some phantom bomb of your own invention, don't I?"

"Not the whole building," Ashli corrected. "You stayed."

"From you, I expect such childish antics. But you?" Mitch whirled to face Jimmie. "Fuck you. Fuck both of you."

"Mitch-" Jimmie tried.

"You were going to leave! I know it! I could feel it every time you walked in a room. Ever since Toni-"

"You," he breathed, "do not know me half as well as you think." His gaze locked with Jimmie's. "I was *not* leaving. But I am now."

Jimmie was at his side in seconds. "Mitch, listen-"

"To what? How many more times will you allow her desperation to overtake this organization?"

"More times?" Jimmie asked, glancing from one to the other. "What are you talking about?"

Mitch's sardonic laughter filled the room. "She didn't tell you."

"No-" Ashli tried to move between them.

"Shut up," Jimmie growled. "Tell me what?"

"The warehouse in Atlantic City. The reason you never could find any plausible reason or explanation that made sense. Why, after decades of safety, your little sis was suddenly a target needing protection your staff couldn't provide."

Jimmie straightened, silence growing as he pieced together the revelation. "Is it true? And don't you dare fucking lie to me."

Jimmie's anger radiated through the room, causing Mitch to pause. Reassess. Since joining them, he'd somehow forgotten exactly how deadly James Vinetti could be.

"Yes," Ashli whispered. "It's all true."

Mitch knew Jimmie's rage had consumed him. No matter how much he loved Ashli, no matter that he'd spent his whole life protecting her, in Jimmie's eyes she has committed an almost absolute betrayal through her lies. But hurting her would destroy them both and if Mitch allowed it to happen because of his own fury? He couldn't live with that option either.

His hand caught Jimmie's half strike. Quick enough to prevent permanent damage but not soon enough to stop a trickle of blood from sliding down her cheek when his ring made contact. Mitch gave one silent shake of his head, and it was enough to pull Jimmie to his senses. He stumbled backward, ragged breaths causing his body to heave.

"How long have you known?" he finally managed.

"No man deserves that at his side." Mitch shook his head. "It's what brought me into your life in the first place."

"You don't need power. Clearly, you have that. You've turned her down at almost every chance, so it's not her bed you're after. You came out of loyalty to a stranger? That's what you want me to believe? Not for the money?"

"Believe whatever gets you through the night." Mitch closed in on him, his voice a low promise. "But when, in either of our entire lives, has it *ever* been about the money?"

"Mitch, Toni's on line one."

All three whirled at the interruption. Teddy stood before them, seeming calm but as he surveyed the trio, his hand moved to his revolver. "Everything okay in here?"

Jimmie was the first to recover. He pulled out a handkerchief, pressing it to Ashli's cheek, his eyes daring her to flinch. "Family squabble. Get some ice for Ashli, would you please?"

"The corporate line?" Mitch asked, trying to collect himself. He pulled out his phone, scrolling through messages and missed calls.

"Yeah. It came through the toll-free switchboard. International."

"Thanks. That ice?"

"Yes, sir." Teddy nodded before retreating out of the room.

Mitch took a steadying breath before picking up the phone. "Hey, girl, you lose my number?" It only took a few seconds before he dropped onto the sofa, his head dropping to rest on his hands. "Breathe, okay? Just breathe."

Wordlessly, Jimmie and Ashli took up positions on either side of him.

"He took you where?" Mitch sucked in a breath of his own. "Stay put and I'll come down." His eyes lifted to Jimmie's and mouthed "plane." Before Jimmie could start dialing, Ashli was already murmuring orders into her phone.

"The plane's already being loaded. Do you need someone to be there sooner? I can get-" he trailed off. "We'll be there as soon as we can." He clicked off, tossing the phone across the room before running his hands through his hair to keep from lashing out.

"I never pictured Toni as the damsel in distress," Ashli said.

"Jealousy doesn't look good on you," Jimmie spat. "Where are we going?"

"La Sierrita."

Jimmie gave a dark chuckle. "Are you fucking kidding me?" He stared at Mitch waiting for him to say something. Receiving nothing he shook his head. "Of course you aren't. Fuckin' La Sierrita. Terenari has officially lost his goddamn mind."

"I want to help-"

"No," Mitch and Jimmie answered simultaneously.

"I know you both are angry but it's Toni," she argued. "I want to help."

"Jimmie, give us a minute? Give the staff the all clear to return?"

"Sure. You two just have a little friendly chat while I go raise a fucking army," Jimmie grumbled.

Mitch took the cell phone out of Jimmie's hand, keyed in a number, then handed it back. "Call Gino. He'll answer on the first ring."

As soon as he was out the door, Ashli was by Mitch's side. "It's not jealousy. And it's not penance or whatever else you are thinking right now. I really do want to help. You were right. I never risk anything. For her, for you, I will."

Mitch nodded, his anger at her being overshadowed by his fear for Toni. "Not like this. Not for this."

"But-"

"Will you just stop and listen? For once?"

She nodded and moved to sit on the desk to face him.

"I know you want to help her. I believe that. And I know Jimmie likes to keep you in the dark about everything. He, if anyone, is the one who underestimates you. I, however, am not him."

"Okay."

"La Sierrita is a ranch in northern Mexico. Have you ever heard of it?"

"No."

"It's a ranch for flower sales." He dipped his head toward her, waiting for some semblance of recognition. "Auctions really."

It took her a moment to put the pieces together, and he could almost see her sifting through the snippets of memories and gossip she'd accumulated after so many years in this business.

"Human trafficking?" she whispered. "You are talking about selling humans."

Her shell was dissolving, but Mitch couldn't bring himself to offer her comfort. "Yes."

"But you and Jimmie, don't-"

"Of course not."

"But you've been to them?"

Mitch knew she wanted him to deny it, but he also knew lying to her would serve no purpose. If she wanted reality, he was going to give it to her. "They hold them captive, torture them into submission and then put them up for the highest bidder. Sometimes it takes months, sometimes years. There really are no words for the conditions of a place like this."

"And La Sierrita?"

"The most infamous of them all. The largest operation in the western hemisphere."

"Why haven't the police stopped them?"

Mitch exhaled. "Heavily guarded, like a military installation. Government red tape, backlash, retaliation...there are a million excuses really. Truth is, they simply wouldn't have a chance. It would be a slaughter of American troops."

"Then you won't have a chance either."

"So," he ignored her, "there are reasons for you not to be involved. Legitimate ones. On this, I am in full agreement with Jimmie."

"Why would he take her there?"

Jimmie moved from his stance in the doorway to stand beside them. "Because sometimes, a threat is more than enough to make someone submissive."

"Especially at a place like that."

"He's trying to teach her a lesson?" Ashli gasped.

"Makes Jimmie look like a saint, hm?" Mitch chuckled.

"Ashli, why don't you meet us in Dallas? Toni might could use another female beside her once we get back to the states."

"Really?" she glanced from one to the other for confirmation that she was actually being included. When they both nodded, she leaned to kiss each on the cheek before getting up.

"I'll get us all packed. I'll make this all right. You....you two just do what you need to do."

Less than an hour later, they were in flight. Leaving Ashli and Teddy in the back of the plane to tie up loose ends from their unexpected departure, Mitch went to join Jimmie.

"Jimmie?"

He glanced up from the aerial photos of La Sierrita that were spread across the plane's table. "Hm?"

"I have rules for my life. Not many, I admit, but there are a handful."

Jimmie nodded, pulled out two glasses and filled them with each with whiskey. He motioned for Mitch to take a seat across from him. "You once told me you didn't technically have a sister. You were referring to Toni, weren't you?"

"Yes."

"When you were little, you must've fought like hell. Throwing dishes, you said, right?"

"Yes, but-"

"Ashli, when she acts like she did, it's like I'm transported back to childhood. She makes me so blindingly furious that I can't see straight. I still see her as this little girl and think nothing of pushing, shoving, pulling her hair. But, I never want to hurt her. Not like that."

"So long as we are clear." Mitch clinked glasses with him. "It wasn't actually betrayal. Well, not of you anyway."

"How do you figure that?"

"Jimmie," Mitch grew softer. "She's terrified this life is going to get you killed. Haven't you realized that yet? It's the only reason she's so damn determined to keep me around. I'm expendable to her...you could never be."

"And therein lies the problem," Jimmie shook his head. "You don't want permanence, and she is determined you accept it."

It was a leading statement, Mitch knew. But not one he was even remotely ready to address. "That is far from the only or even the most immediate of problems." He waved his glass over the papers strewn across the table.

Picking up one of the photos, Jimmie frowned. "Ever been there?"

Mitch nodded. "You?"

"Once. It's been in my nightmares ever since."

Mitch gave a knowing nod, accepting the refill Jimmie offered. They sat in silence as they drank, each lost in horrific visuals from their visits to La Sierrita.

When he finally spoke, Jimmie's voice was only a quiet echo but, as if they were one, Mitch was already anticipating it. "We could do it you know."

"It's suicide. Do you know how many governments have tried? Even the fucking UN."

"Yeah but they have all those pesky regulations and ethics."

"We don't have ethics?"

"My ethics say no human deserves to be treated like that and payback is a bitch. What does yours say?"

Mitch considered, twirling the glass in his hand to let the ice bounce around. Every government had failed, and they had long since stopped trying. Did bullying everyone make them have some right to exist? They believed themselves untouchable...but there *was* one organized foe they had not yet faced. "We'd need an army."

"We have two," Jimmie grinned. "Palmese took your call right away. Answered the phone himself. Pissed it was me on the line but he's offered anything."

"Terenari-"

"Fuck Terenari."

"Yeah," Mitch nodded. "Fuck Terenari."

"You get Gino's guys on the move, and I'll get my guys on charters. Markesi's and Devini's, too."

He only hesitated a moment - what they were orchestrating was, in fact, a terroristic act on citizens of a nation friendly to the US. But it did only last a moment. He clinked his glass with Jimmie's. "Done."

CHAPTER FORTY-THREE

Mitch stepped into the tiny bedroom of the church, causing Toni to skitter toward the wall. She was in his arms in seconds, though, her fists tearing into his clothing. Prying her hands loose, he held her at arm's length, checking her inch by inch for any physical damage.

"I'm fine," Toni assured him.

"You are most certainly not fine. Sierrita gives me nightmares."

"Physically unscathed," she corrected.

"Better," he accepted and waved her to sit on the cot, tugging off his suit jacket and loosening his tie. Sinking into the bare metal chair opposite her, he clasped his hands together to wait for her story.

It was as he expected. Terenari had brought her down and had his men tour her around the facilities. Cell after cell of beaten women and children and a handful of teen boys. Icy showers, rapes in progress, food taunts to starving victims, a nursery full of unattended children...her descriptions were so vivid he had to fight down the vomit rising within him. Terenari had long since disappeared, leaving her in their hands. She finally managed to get out by buying the men time with some of the girls. When she admitted that, when she said aloud what she'd done, it was she who vomited what little food remained in her stomach.

Knocking on the door, Mitch opened it only a crack to issue some soft spoken orders. When they returned with towels, water, and a fresh set of clothes, Mitch began helping her clean up. Although his instinct was to look away as she changed, he didn't: he was determined to make certain she really was uninjured.

"Please say something."

"Drink this," he handed her the water bottle, shaking it as he passed it her direction.

A soft tap at the door caused her to jump, but Mitch opened it without looking, allowing Jimmie to step into the room.

She downed half the bottle as ordered. "Say something else."

"Nothing you could ever do would deserve a lesson like this. Do you understand that?"

"I-"

"Say it."

"I didn't deserve this."

"You did the right thing by calling me." Mitch let his palm drift across her cheek, dropping his lips to her forehead. "For the first time in damn near a decade, you did the right thing."

"I did the right thing," she nodded in agreement. She wobbled a bit, falling against his chest. "Mitch? The water-"

"Yeah, I drugged it."

"I hate you."

"Today. Tomorrow, you'll thank me."

"Still hate you." She tried to struggle against him, but he eased her into Jimmie's arms instead.

"Listen to me," Jimmie tightened his grip around her waist to keep her from tumbling to the floor. "You have two big brothers now, got it?"

"Then I hate you, too." But her voice was a whisper, her tears once again falling. Jimmie moved her to the bed, but she held tight, refusing to release his arm. Jimmie sank beside her, rubbing her head.

"Shh, go to sleep or I'll have to knock you unconscious myself."

"Screw you."

Jimmie laughed, glancing up to Mitch. He stood over them, removing his vomit covered shirt and pulling on a clean one. His eyes drifted away only a second, to check the clip in his gun before tucking it back in his waistband.

But the click had caused Toni to stir. "Stop him," she slurred.

"What?" Jimmie brushed her hair aside to hear her better.

Her broken words were a barely understandable jumble, and it took a moment for Jimmie to decipher it. "Make him leave it. He'll do something stupid. He always does."

Jimmie eyed him, unsure of whether he should move to stop Mitch or continue to comfort Toni. But Mitch was already pulling out his gun and sitting it on the chair, the metal against metal clang causing both Jimmie and Toni to jump.

His eyes met Jimmie's and he nodded. "She's right. She always is. Never forget that."

CHAPTER FORTY-FOUR

H er heart is just too damn big, you know?" Jimmie asked quietly, sinking into the pew beside Mitch. "She cried for hours. Not for her own pain but all those girls."

Mitch nodded but remained silent.

"Masseria...Penny Lane. You said you knew the answer. It was Terenari, wasn't it?"

He nodded.

"She's one strong girl with all the hell he's put her through."

Mitch nodded again.

Jimmie leveled a gaze at him. "Tell me something here, Mitchell."

Mitch knew his words were wrong, knew he couldn't take them back. But he also knew there was no way anyone on the planet would hear them except Jimmie. Jimmie would take it to his grave under questioning from anyone. Of that, Mitch had no doubt.

"I want him dead."

"We are going to firebomb that place. Everyone will be dead."

When Mitch didn't respond, Jimmie let his words sink in. When realization dawned, he sank back against the pew. "Terenari," he whispered.

Mitch raised his eyes to meet Jimmie's, knowing there was no way to take back his pronouncement.

"I'd do anything for you. You know that. But he's head of a family. I can't-"

"I know. But I can." Premeditated murder, Mitch thought vaguely. I am planning and orchestrating the capital murder of an individual human being.

"I can't," Jimmie continued as if Mitch hadn't spoken, "help you until everything is perfectly aligned."

"I'm not asking-" Or maybe I am, he thought.

"You don't have to. I just need time. So does Toni. Give us that, okay?"

Mitch didn't trust himself to respond.

Jimmie leaned close to him. "Mitch, he's not some punk on the street. We do have rules and ethics. But I can make this happen for you, for her. I will. Just don't go off on some half-assed vendetta before then, alright?"

Jimmie slipped Mitch's gun across the pew toward him, but still keeping it in his grasp. "Promise me."

"I will give you time," Mitch assured him. "But my patience with him is a razor thin line. Do you understand me?"

Jimmie released his gun. "Without question."

CHAPTER FORTY-FIVE

M itch?"

"Hm?"

"Have you ever...I mean-"

"I've never hired a prostitute much less bought a person," he assured her sleepily.

"You've worked with people who have?"

"Yes."

"How do you, I mean, how do you-"

"Live with myself?" he asked, rolling over to face her. "I don't. There is no forgiveness for the person I have become."

"You have such a warped perspective of yourself," she argued, shaking her head. "I don't know how even to look at my father anymore. To know he is a part of something like this."

"Is that how you feel about me as well?"

"No."

"What's the difference?"

She hesitated. "You try to make the world better. He tries to make it better for himself."

"That's a damn fine line between the two."

"Maybe," she shrugged. "Maybe only to someone who's walking it."

"Very intelligent response. Are you drunk?"

"I think I'm offended."

Mitch eyed her seriously. "Are you?"

"Not exactly." She gave him a half smile then let her hand trail over his arm and across his bare chest. "They gave me something."

"What exactly?"

"The doctor. Nothing illicit. Something for shock or trauma or something. Or so they said."

"Who is "they"? Tell me you didn't trust some Mexican street corner doctor."

"One of Gino's people. He sent an entire medical team."

"He was worried for you," Mitch hedged.

"I'm not an idiot, Mitch. I know what you and Jimmie are doing tomorrow. I'm not suffering from shock; they just want me unconscious for the whole damn thing. Can't say I'm opposed to that concept either."

Mitch chuckled. "I had no involvement in that, just to be clear."

She nodded, scooting closer and letting both hands trace designs across his olive skin. "Do you remember those girls in the neighborhood? The ones from Guatemala? They sat on the porch of that house, never talking to anyone."

"Yes," he sank back into the covers, putting space back between them.

"Were they-"

"No."

She shuffled a few inches closer, her fingertips grazing across him in small, calculated movements. "How do you know?"

"Borders were much more secure back then. Smuggling drugs was even a difficult proposition. People would've been almost impossible."

"You smuggled drugs?"

He laughed. "Do you even know me at all?"

"Sometimes? Sometimes I think I know you better than you know yourself. Other times? Times like now? I think I could never possibly learn every inch of you no matter the hours I try."

"Is that what you're doing?" he asked, letting his fingers slip down her long hair to twist them at the ends. "Trying to memorize me?"

"Is there something wrong with that?" she asked, tipping her lips to brush against his fingertips.

"About a million things actually," he whispered.

It did not deter her. Slowly, she moved her face to his, pressing her lips into his. He couldn't help returning it, an old childhood feeling rising within him. But just as quickly, the need to protect her overshadowed everything. Taking her face in his hands, he pushed her gently away. "Christ, how I wish you were sober right now."

"It doesn't matter-"

"It means everything," he murmured, kissing her quickly on the forehead. "Jimmie!"

She jerked at the shout, but it wasn't enough to move her off of Mitch before Jimmie appeared.

Jimmie tilted his head to the side. "Don't you two look cozy? Sure you don't want me to come back in say, twenty minutes?"

"Gino's docs drugged her," Mitch explained, sliding out from underneath her.

She flopped onto the pillows. "I am right here, you know."

"Oh, I assure you, I know," Mitch chuckled. Tugging on his pants, he turned to Jimmie. "I need you to step in here."

"Pardon?"

Mitch leveled a gaze at him. "I trust you. Don't make me regret it."

"You're so fucking comical."

"I'm serious."

Jimmie blanched. "No. No way."

"For chrissakes, Jimmie. He's not asking you to take over and screw me. He's asking you to babysit."

"Anyone ever told you, you have a dirty mouth?"

"Blame him." she grumbled, pointing at Mitch before curling up with a pillow.

"No idea what they gave her. She's quite handsy, though. May want to watch for that."

"Gee, thanks." Jimmie frowned. "Guys are next door in the chapel. We've got cots set up in the wings, and they've got that Navy Seal guy you handpicked organizing things."

"I'll send someone over in a couple of hours once she's not-"

"Trying to live out her sexually repressed fantasies?"

"Fuck you, Jimmie," she managed from under a pillow.

Both men laughed, but Jimmie moved to stretch out beside her on the bed. "Come here, kiddo." He tugged her to lay on his chest as Mitch headed to the door.

He turned, his eyes watching her broken form curling into Jimmie's. Leaving her safety in someone else's hands was almost impossible. He tried that once already in his lifetime...and this destruction was only part of that decision's result. He moved his eyes to Jimmie. "Jimmie-"

"With my life, brother."

CHAPTER FORTY-SIX

S he talks in her sleep," Jimmie murmured. "I ordered the guards to stay outside."

Mitch nodded, tossing Jimmie some ammo.

"She has this hero thing for you."

"She'll be over that tomorrow."

"And you? Will you be over it tomorrow?"

"It's just hard to deny her," he admitted, "with that man as her father."

"More than you know, I think."

"Her dreams?" Mitch asked nodding. "I've heard some of them. Sierrita will undoubtedly give her a few more."

"And?"

"Let her keep them. It's the only thing she has that is hers and hers alone."

"But-"

"When she's ready, she'll call us."

"Fair enough." Jimmie smiled mischievously. "She is quite handsy."

"Told you."

"And she wiggles."

"Enough," Mitch laughed, tossing him a Kevlar vest.

"She has this birthmark on her shoulder-"

"BB gun when she was seven," Mitch corrected. "Now, Ashli has this tattoo-"

"Truce! Truce!" Jimmie laughed. He let his laughter die then drew in a long breath. "She knows we're going in then?"

"I wouldn't keep something like that from her." His eyes narrowed. "You did call Ashli, right?"

Jimmie's silence was his answer.

"Jimmie, she's sitting in a hotel room hundreds of miles away, pacing the floor, terrified of getting a call asking her to claim your body. Don't deny her this."

He nodded. "Give me a few minutes? Hold the guys?"

"As long as you need."

CHAPTER FORTY-SEVEN

You survived."

"You doubted?" Mitch frowned, unsnapping his vest and tossing it to the dresser before heading toward the bathroom.

"You two are not as invincible as you think." She moved to help Jimmie pull off his vest and, seeing the blood coloring his shirt sleeve she frowned. Gently, she helped him tug it off and examined the damage. "We need to get these cleaned."

"This felt more romantic last night," Jimmie grumbled as her fingers slid along his arm.

"You two are never going to let me live that down, are you?"

Mitch kissed the top of her head as he handed Jimmie a clean towel to put on his arm. "Not a chance."

"How is it you don't have a scratch?"

"Because he can shoot the whisker off a cat at a million yards."

"Flattery will get you everywhere," Mitch laughed, tossing him the medic kit.

"Is this testosterone filled ecstasy or something?" she asked, taking the kit and pulling out supplies.

Jimmie smiled. "We saved hundreds of lives today, kid. If that's not a reason to celebrate, I don't know what is."

"The townsfolk are having a street party, in fact."

"Can't miss that," Toni grumbled. "They stood by-"

"They lived in fear. Don't mistake that for complicity," Mitch chided, pulling on a clean t-shirt.

"I know the difference," she whispered.

"Yeah," Jimmie squeezed her hand. "We know you do."

"Enough! Stick a bandage on that cat scratch and let's find a tequila bar. There's a worm with our name on it."

Hours later, once Jimmie had disappeared into the arms of a local and Teddy had been dispatched to forward the news of success to everyone, Mitch found Toni tucked into a throng of drunken locals. She was twirling among them with abandon, and it took him several tries before getting her attention. When she finally moved to his side, he offered her an amused grin.

"Do you remember anything?"

"Everything," she assured him, slipping into his arms as they moved passed the throng of street dancers. She pinched him in reproach. "You told me you wished I was sober."

"Are you?"

"No. Not even close," she laughed. "I figured it was safer that way."

"Your knowledge of this world? It breaks my soul," he said, pulling her into dance steps at a quieter edge of the street.

"I just knew you would stay stoic in your resolve. And it would excuse any inappropriate tequila induced moves I decide to make."

"That's putting a lot of faith in my resolve."

"Of course."

Mitch chuckled, letting his head drop to her neck. His lips hovered against her skin, feeling the heat rising from her throat. His lips grazed silkily across her shoulder, her body reacting instantly and curving tightly against his. Before he could prevent it, a soft moan escaped and, sensing an opening, her hands snaked through his hair, pushing his head tighter into her. "For the record, you never have to make excuses with me."

She tensed in his arms. "There's man with a camera."

He continued to tattoo her skin with kisses. "Yes."

"You know?"

"Yes."

"He's yours?"

"Jimmie's."

"Same difference," she grumbled and tried to move away. His hand moved to the small of her waist, locking her in place, his lips never faltering. "You are going to send it to my father. To let him know, this was you and Jimmie."

"Yes."

"You are using me."

Mitch hesitated, his eyes meeting hers. "Do you really believe that?"

She sighed. "No."

He bit her earlobe before kissing the same spot. "Then don't say it. It's offensive."

"Mitchell?"

"Hm?"

"Will you kiss me?"

He laughed. "I am."

"No," she pulled away to make him face her. "A real one. The kind you are afraid to give. Right now."

"Toni-" he frowned.

"Please."

And he couldn't deny her. Slowly, slipping one hand around her neck, he pressed his lips to hers, feeling the hardness and tension in her before she finally let herself go. Her body moved instinctively, melding against his, her tongue slipping against his teeth as the kiss became deeper. Mitch heard the camera click, noticed the flash several more times as her hands explored his body, and then pulled a breath away.

"That," he murmured, "was you using me."

She considered denying it but finally nodded. "Yes, but-"

"No excuses," he reminded. "If kissing me gets your father to ease up on you then so be it. I've been used for much less noble causes."

CHAPTER FORTY-EIGHT

Two days later, Toni had been safely placed on a plane to New York on her way to a "vacation" in Sicily. Ashli had remained a calming influence for the men as they tried to unwind in Houston but Mitch couldn't forget the nagging tug of her betrayal with the casino bomb threats. It was Jimmie who argued in her defense, eventually wearing down Mitch's objections. When he finally returned to her bed, it felt more out of obligation to Jimmie than any desire of his own.

"I feel like I'm cheating on Toni."

"No wonder Vinetti secrets were getting spread everywhere. You really cannot keep your mouth shut in bed."

Ashli gave him a playful slug. "I'm serious. The two of you, your history, just everything. She should be here, not me. I'm intelligent enough to recognize that."

Mitch rolled over to lay on top of her, propping himself up on his forearms. "Then you are intelligent enough to know why she can never be here."

"You are a better man than I ever imagined, Mitchell Kerlin. Do you know that?"

"Not even close."

"You were just this wiseguy that everyone talked about as if you walked on water. I couldn't figure it. What made you more special than everyone else?"

"So you didn't approach me for my good looks, then?"

"I'm serious."

He nodded. "I know you are." He let his fingers ruffle through her hair. "I told you once it all ends where it begins, do you remember?"

"I do."

"Tell me, Ashli."

"Jimmie was so out of sorts. He was going through men every week it seemed like. He wouldn't let me in, wouldn't tell me anything, but I knew. Of course, I knew. It was just this silly wall he had built up. I thought if I could just find one person he could trust completely, one person that I could trust to be beside him and keep him safe forever then-" she trailed off as silent tears began to spill over her cheeks.

Mitch wiped them away, kissing her forehead softly, knowing she couldn't bear to say it. "Then you could leave?"

"Yes. Yes."

"And now? Now, what is it you want Ashli?"

"Was the story true? The one Toni told me about the fire when you were little? How you saved someone, and your life went all to hell because of it?"

"I didn't realize you two were sharing stories about me."

"We tired of the darkness of Sierrita," she explained.

"She likes to tell stories," he shrugged. "It's easier for her to blame the world for my life than to believe the choices I made were my own."

"Were they, though?"

"We are talking about you," he grumbled rolling away from her to climb out of bed and pull on his pants.

Ashli struggled from under the covers, grabbing her robe and tightening it around her waist. She headed for the door but stopped and returned to stand beside him. "Do you know why you two get along so perfectly? You are Jimmie's soul. You make him good. Not just the public appearance political face type of good but the down deep, far in your core, wanting to save the world type of good. What you two did in La Sierrita, what you two accomplished together? It changes everything."

"Jimmie is a good guy."

"No," she said, shaking her head before kissing him lightly on the lips. "But now he wants to be."

CHAPTER FORTY-NINE

I own boats? Why the hell do I own boats? I hate boats."
Ashli stood between Mitch and Jimmie in the decrepit box-
ing gym, her hands on her hips. "Because they use boats to do
the ocean research that brings you in millions of dollars in
Gulf oil stakes."

"Oh."

"Mitch, say something here? It's the freaking governor's
invitation. You can't tell the governor of the largest state in
America no."

"That would be Alaska," Mitch mumbled, tugging the tape
around his wrist off with his teeth.

"What?"

"Alaska is the largest state. Not Texas."

"For chrissakes, it won't hurt us to make an appearance.
We're here for another twelve hours anyway."

Jimmie laughed. "Fine."

"Fine?" Ashli hesitated. "Did you just say fine?"

"Do you want me to change my mind?" he growled. "You take care of arrangements. Clothes, get us a car, whatever. One hour tops and then we are on a plane right after."

"I promise."

The Bell Tower on 34th was one of the most sought after venues in the city. With a look reminiscent of Gino's villa, the ivy-coated stone walls towered high above the partiers. The ball, some Houston tradition in the oil industry, was already in full swing before the trio finally pulled up in the drive. Teddy helped them out of the car, whispering briefly to Mitch and Jimmie about the high level of security that was surrounding the event. It made Jimmie feel more at ease...it made the hairs on the back of Mitch's neck rise. Low profile it was not.

They made their formal greetings quickly, posing for photos that made Mitch cringe and then Ashli led them to a cobblestone walk that edged between the two buildings. The party goers had spilled out here, scantily clad girls seeking out quiet alcoves for romantic entanglements. Mitch took a glass of champagne from a passing waiter, something tugging in his psyche. Teddy was at his side instantly.

"What is it?"

Mitch shrugged. "It's too quiet. Too..."

"Secluded," Jimmie offered from a pace behind. "There are a thousand people inside but hardly anyone here."

"You're just still on edge from Sierrita," Ashli said, borrowing Mitch's glass and taking a sip.

"Maybe." Jimmie didn't sound convinced.

"Nonetheless," Mitch's commanding voice echoed down the corridor, "we're going back in."

"No."

"No?" He whirled on her, but she was already stalking off the opposite direction, away from the ballroom entrance.

It all happened in a moment's breath.

Teddy was moving to follow Ashli when he was grabbed from behind. He spun, his fist dropping the man. Paces away, Mitch saw the knife glint under the gaslights. He intercepted him, kicking him in the chest before whirling to put eyes on Ashli. Two men in cheap black suits had cornered her, but Jimmie would reach her first. His punches were as legendary as others had said and he had one down instantly. The other was pulling a weapon when Jimmie kicked him hard in the groin, dropping him to the ground and pressing his gun to the man's temple.

It was only a scratch. A split second sound of a misstep of a dress shoe clicking against the uneven stone walk. Mitch's eyes focused on the shadows, taking a moment to adjust before he found the one who had stayed hidden...undoubtedly, the one who was the real threat.

"No!" Ashli screamed at the same moment the man lurched from the shadows, gun drawn and glittering in the light. Its aim perfect on Jimmie's back.

Mitch flung himself at the man, taking him down just as his finger squeezed the trigger. Mitch felt the warmth of blood pool around him, ignored it long enough to snap the man's neck in his arms, and then felt nothing. Jimmie's face swam in and out of view, Ashli's screams puncturing the night.

His last conscious thought was voiced unbidden: fuck this.

CHAPTER FIFTY

S top it! Jimmie, please!" Ashli's anger had quickly turned into miserable pleading. It was bad enough Mitch was lying near comatose in the next room. To have this fistfight going on in the middle of the hallway where everyone was staring at them was more than she could take.

She expected hospital security to step in at any minute, but the lineup of mafia wiseguys – both Sonny's and Jimmie's- along the wall seemed to have stalled them in the periphery. Instead, it was a flash of silver sequins that pushed through to stand in between the two bloodied men. Sonny's fist came within inches of Toni's face before he stumbled backward to prevent it from making contact.

"You better be damn glad your reflexes are still good," she hissed.

"Antoinette-"

"Be quiet. Don't you think you've made enough of a scene already? You're just lucky Gino's men have kept the press at bay."

"Gino-"

"Yes. Gino." She turned on Jimmie. "And you better have a damn good explanation for him by the time he arrives. Teddy, give Ashli something, will you? The damn girl is near hysterics."

"Toni-" Ashli glanced at her, any cool business-like demeanor she had in reserve now evaporating. Not caring that they barely knew each other she ran into Toni's arms for the comfort Jimmie had been unwilling to provide. Rather than skirt her, Toni took her arm and led her to a side room a few paces away. Accepting a bottle of water and a few pills from Teddy, she followed Ashli inside and shut the door.

Placing Ashli on the sofa, she waited for her to down the pills before sinking to sit beside her.

"You love him?" Toni asked without preamble.

"No. It's more than that." He's my future, my escape, the key to a new life away from all this, she added silently. She offered Toni a sideways smile. "I swear, I'm not usually so inept."

"I know," she assured her. "I've seen you in action. You thought it was Jimmie, didn't you?"

Ashli was quiet. Yes, for a moment she had. And the relief that flooded through her filled her with guilt. And then she realized the truth – that it was Mitch who had been shot. And her emotions sank into a cavern of fear, knowing his death would solidify her in Jimmie's world forever.

"I've seen the tapes. They went for you."

"No, I-"

Toni's voice was laced with hatred. "I don't give a damn what Jimmie thinks he saw. I don't care what Mitch happens to remember when he wakes. And he *will* wake. I know it was you. And I will never forgive that."

The tears streaming down Ashli's face did nothing to soften Toni's fury. "And make no mistake, I will spend my entire life making sure Mitch doesn't either."

CHAPTER FIFTY-ONE

W here's Jimmie?"

Teddy nodded to an office, its blinds closed. "The doctors offered him space. He wanted privacy."

"Fuck what he wants." Toni strode passed all of them, didn't bother knocking and slammed the door behind her as she entered. Jimmie, his head in his hands, barely lifted his eyes to meet hers.

"You face armed assassins in Sicily. You take on La Sierrita. And then you let this happen here? In fucking Houston in a damn opera house?"

"He jumped in front of me! Christ, Toni, what the hell do you want from me?"

"Tell him he's not a fucking bodyguard! Tell him you want him alive. Hell, Jimmie tell him you need him beside you instead of treating him like a damn hired hand. I don't care what it takes, but if anything happens to him, Gino's going to be the least of your worries."

"I don't need your threats. Don't you think I feel guilty enough as it is?" Jimmie spat. "I sat there holding him as the blood ran out of him. Look at me!" He jumped up to shake her, tugging at his still blood stained shirt. "His blood is on me, *mio fratello*! And where were you? Sitting pretty at the right hand of your bastard of a father while he called in the hit?"

Toni shrank back. "You think my father did this?"

"Know anyone else Mitch has pissed off lately? If he couldn't have him, he was going to make damn sure nobody did. And since you couldn't fuck him to your daddy's side Terenari took the only option he had left."

She dropped to the chair as he continued to rage. It took him several minutes to quiet and even more to finally get his temper under control. When he did, he sank to kneel at her feet. "*Mi scusi. La calma è la virtù dei forti.* Unfortunately," he whispered, "I am not strong."

"*Quando la famiglia è in difficoltà, il cerchio si rafforza.*"

He took her hands in his, kissing them lightly and holding them to his lips. "I am not your father. I don't expect you to take my shit with blind acceptance and a meek nod of the head. Knock sense into me when required and never ever let me talk to you like that again. It's unacceptable. Understand?"

She nodded, squeezing his hand in affirmation. Her voice was like a kitten when she finally found words. "Jimmie, do you think it was him?"

"I don't know," he sighed. "It's just the only thing that makes sense."

"Not since we were kids have I been so…"

"Angry?" he guessed, but she shook her head. Jimmie waited, but it was silent tears that gave away her emotions.

"Scared. Come." He opened his arms, folding her into his embrace on the floor, rocking her gently as her tears continued to fall.

"You knew the world couldn't see this, hm? That's why the anger, the fire, the threats to everyone."

"I can't be his weakness. Or he mine. It would endanger us all."

"He's right," Jimmie rested his lips on the top of her head. "You know far too much about this world we live in."

"He's the only true thing I have left," she whispered. "I can't lose him."

Jimmie pulled her tighter, his own grief melding with hers. "Then we hold something in common."

CHAPTER FIFTY-TWO

In the days that followed, the vigil only continued to grow. Men from across the globe took up residence more to gain respect with Gino Palmese than to offer sincere worries over Mitch's well-being. It infuriated Toni, and only Jimmie managed to prevent her from starting several wars. When the tension between her and Ashli had become too much for anyone to stomach, Jimmie had sequestered Ashli in a nearby hotel. Gino had convinced the hospital to give up one of their conference rooms on another floor and then, without ceremony, kicked everyone up there except for Teddy, Jimmie, Sonny and Toni. Several surgeries later, the news finally came that he was awake. Gino visited him for less than ten minutes before leaving in a huff and, although Sonny spent longer, he wasn't much happier when he stormed back out.

When Jimmie entered, with tentative steps, Mitch held his hand up. "Yes, they blame you. But, yes, they'll get over it. I left them no other option."

He nodded. "I'm-"

"If you say sorry I'll shoot you myself. This is not the first time, nor will it be the last, that I end up like this. We're good so let's not be dramatic, okay?"

"Okay."

Mitch smiled. "I hear you were curled up with Toni."

"Unconscious and yet you still see everything?" he asked. "I assure you I'll ask before making a move on her."

Mitch chuckled and grabbed his midsection from the pain that coursed through him. "That seems like a promise."

"It's a given," Jimmie shrugged. "I'm an ape where a woman like her is concerned."

"A woman like her?"

"You know, one with a brain. They get me every time. And, God, that fiery temper of hers? How can you stand to stay away?"

Mitch waved him off before another fit of laughter overtook him. "Make a move on her. See how far it gets you."

"Mitch," Jimmie sank down to sit in the chair beside the bed. "I ask your forgiveness. I said things to her...things I had no right-"

"She's heard worse."

"You don't understand-"

"You blamed her?" he guessed. "Blamed Terenari for the shooting and then blamed her for not preventing it. Knowing you, you used some pretty colorful language."

"I didn't mean-"

"She knows that. I know that." Mitch shook his head. "You don't understand the life we lived, Jimmie. Nothing anyone could do will ever surprise her again." He dropped his voice. "I took away her future. You could call her a whore a hundred times over, and it would still pale in comparison."

"She has a future, Mitch."

"Terenari isn't a future for anyone. You know that as well as I."

Jimmie tapped the envelope in his hand. "I brought the stills from the security camera and the ones we collected from the press corps that was present. Didn't know if you wanted-"

"Let's see them." Mitch nodded, straightening up in the bed and taking the stack from him.

"I've spent hours looking over them but," he shook his head, "I can't find anything."

Mitch went through them twice and was on a third attempt when Jimmie noticed him wincing. "You need rest, Mitch. It's almost time for your meds anyway. This can wait. You need to see Toni before-"

"This is wrong," Mitch interrupted him, holding out a photo.

"What do you mean?" Jimmie took the photo, looking at it critically. It was a shot from the press corps, clear and crisp. He recognized the carpet from the hallway just before the shooting. Ashli was at the center of the photo, Mitch and Jimmie a pace behind her in a much softer focus. Two other men from the crowd filled out the picture. Jimmie frowned, unable to see anything out of place. "What is it?"

"I don't know." Mitch cringed, unable to get his brain to focus. "The perspective is off. The angles or something. Something about the way we're walking..."

"Okay." Jimmie scooped up the photos and patted his arm. "I'm going to send in Toni and find a Doc for you, alright?"

Mitch nodded. "Yeah, good idea."

"Mitch?" Toni's voice was hesitant. "Jimmie said you were in a lot of pain. I can come back-"

"Come here, girl."

She was in his arms before he had the words out, her tears pooling onto his chest. "I was so scared, Mitch. I thought-"

"Shh," he stroked her hair, his voice calming. "I'm right here. Beat up and sore but that's nothing you haven't seen before, right?"

"Don't be cavalier."

"Toni, I'm going to be fine."

"Promise me?"

He tilted her eyes to his. "I promise."

She nodded and straightened, drying her eyes with the sleeve of her sweater. When she had composed herself, Mitch motioned for her to sit beside him.

"Heard you spent some quality time with Ashli."

"Quality is a debatable description."

"Should I bother to ask?"

"I won't answer, so there's really no point."

"I heard you also fought with Jimmie."

"In private," she admitted. "It wasn't broadcast for anyone else to hear."

"Still not a wise move on your part. You know better than that," he chastised. "And while we're at it, you shouldn't be here. Does Nicolai know where you are?"

"He's here. Came with all the others. He's thrilled to have me at your bedside, and furious Jimmie won't let him see you."

Mitch locked his eyes with her, knowing her thoughts before she said them. "It wasn't your father."

"But-"

"They're wrong. You're wrong," he said gently. "Not that I'd put it past him to try but this wasn't his doing. Even he's not this desperate."

"Yet."

Mitch refused to lie and gave her a single nod of agreement. "Yet."

CHAPTER FIFTY-THREE

Mitch demanded to be released long before the doctors advised it. He knew, the longer they stayed in one place, the more dangerous it was for all of them. Ashli had disappeared from the hotel and, rather than wait on her; Jimmie left a contingent behind to search while he escorted everyone else back to New York. Toni went to Sonny's- near enough to be protected if needed while far enough to keep Nicolai from asking too many questions.

"Ashli brought you into this organization; I realize that. That was a long time ago. A lifetime to some. However, I know your loyalty runs deep. I would understand if you feel some obligation," he paused, "some connection to her-"

Mitch glanced up in the mirror, Jimmie's formal stance catching him off guard. He continued to struggle to replace the bandage on his wound. "What are you babbling about?"

"Ashli has been found," he responded, stepping up and finishing the dressing for him. "With a fed."

Mitch grabbed a shirt and tugged it on, following Jimmie into the main room of his suite. It was an accusation he'd heard a dozen times from Jimmie in the time he'd been with him, but something nagged at him, telling him this was different. He would know, wouldn't he? If she were copping a plea, surely his superiors would have told him. He tried to remember the last time he'd met with Mike but couldn't put a date to it. "No."

"No?" Jimmie hissed. "No? Don't you think I have already searched all other possibilities? Don't you think I've racked my brain with every half ass excuse of plausible rationalization of what she may have been doing?" His hands trembled, his voice echoing his misery.

He tossed a stack of photos at Mitch. They scattered across the table, onto the floor. Without moving, Mitch knew they were real. The badges were unmistakable, the government vehicle plate even reflecting in the camera flash to make it more obvious. He dropped to the chair, crumpling one of the photographs into his fist.

"An affair perhaps. She's been known to do it before. She was being arrested. Threatened. I've been through them all. Do you have something else? Tell me. I'd love to hear it."

Mitch tried to come up with anything that might temper Jimmie's worries, but he had nothing. Ashli, who had brought him into the organization. His boss, who wanted Vinetti and felt Mitch couldn't get the job done. Ashli, who wanted out with such desperation it filled her every waking breath. It wasn't only possible...it would have been foreseeable. If only he'd been paying attention. She had turned and no one, not even him, had been the wiser. How long had she been feeding them information? What of Mitch's deeds had she informed them about? His stomach churned, blood draining from his face. He dropped his head into his hands.

"Mitch-" the anger was still there. Betrayal. Jimmie thought Mitch had betrayed him.

"Had I known," he whispered, "I would have told you."

Jimmie dropped into a chair, his eyes watching Mitch closely. It would be so easy to kill him. He had a gun in his waistband right now. Mitch knew it and yet made no move to leave. He sat immobile, seeming as thunderstruck as Jimmie felt. But Mitch was an exceptionally good liar. The best he'd ever come across.

"Vincenzo."

Mitch lifted his eyes, locking them with Jimmie's. His voice was low, gravelly, filled with the distraught emotions welling within him. "I would have told you," he repeated. And he meant every word.

CHAPTER FIFTY-FOUR

Mitch had few options left at his disposal. By making her own deal with the feds that he wasn't privy to, she had tied his hands within the IOC. Had she not made a deal, he could have called in and had agents whisk her away before anyone had a chance to put a hit on her. Instead, she was going to have to rely on the feds to keep her safe while every mafioso from California to Sicily tried to hunt her down. Mitch knew their moves, their talentless security detail, and the safe-houses they would utilize as they moved her from location to location waiting for the arrest warrants to be issued. As an IOC agent, he could have saved her.

As a member of *la familia*, he could have protected her. He could have brought in Gino's men to keep her safe from Jimmie. He could have called Sonny or even Terenari if the situation was that desperate. Instead, she had spent the last few months making allegiances with them only to betray them. Sure, Gino and Sonny would still never deny Mitch's request for aid. But, her betrayal would keep him from seeking their help.

But as Jimmie's right hand, he knew she didn't have a chance. Over the years, Mitch could think of no one as high up in the organization who was willing to take care of complications on their own. Usually, once a man reached a certain point in the hierarchy, they managed to keep themselves clear of the dirtier tasks of the business. Not just because it kept them above government scrutiny but also because they usually felt they had paid their dues already. Either way, Jimmie's willingness to jump into the fray gave Mitch pause. His devotion to his family was deeper than Mitch had anticipated, and he prided himself on never being surprised.

And yet, as he watched Jimmie sitting on the sofa of his suite, meticulously cleaning his weapon, it was impossible to deny it: Jimmie was going to exact his own justice.

"They're going to kill her, Mitch," he murmured without raising his eyes. "Whichever family gets to her first."

"I know."

"In a very painful way."

Mitch nodded, his fists tightening as he tried to keep the visions of her soon to be inflicted brutality at a minimum. "I know that, too."

"I can't let that happen. I have to let her explain; I have to protect her from the worst-"

Mitch couldn't blame him for leaving the words unfinished. He didn't want to hear them either. His eyes drifted over the photos from his shooting, finally settling on the one that continued to plague him.

When the realization hit him, it was a gut punch hard enough to make him gasp out loud and cause Jimmie to turn his direction. He reached to the other stack, the one of Ashli's rendezvous, and then his eyes locked with Jimmie's.

Mitch held the stack of photographs in his hand, tapping them against the table as he began to second guess himself. It wasn't a smart move, politically or probably even emotionally...but it was the honest move. He slid the two photos across the Jimmie.

"You don't have much time. She's not trying to get a deal," he murmured. "She's already made one."

He turned the photo in the correct position for Jimmie's eyes. It was the photo that had tugged at him, the one that had made his stomach turn with vague recognition. He could understand his own delay in catching it – he had just been shot – but why Jimmie's meticulous nature hadn't recognized it immediately was beyond him. Ignoring the centered profile of Ashli, he tapped his finger on the man in the background. Although not the focus of the frame, his appearance was clear, his identity unmistakable. "Sonny's birthday."

"Son of a bitch," Jimmie exhaled, wrenching up the photo. The spiky red hair, the bad suit, the ugly purple tie, the gun on his shoulder holster that had fired at Mitch without warning...the federal agent Mitch had thrown out of the Verona Ballroom just before the onslaught of government warrants that locked down the entire casino over a year before. "They weren't kidnapping her. They were extracting her."

"Or trying to," Mitch nodded. "If they already have her, the warrants will come fast. You know that."

Jimmie was pacing, moving to stare out the suite's windows. Although he was silent, Mitch could almost see his mood changing from worry to disbelief to anger and, finally, to resignation. "That changes things, I suppose."

"Jimmie, don't do this-"

"Don't do what?" he growled, whirling to face Mitch. "Don't leave her to her own fate? Don't finally do what she's asked all along – to just leave her be? Don't admit a lifetime of protecting her will reward me with a half dozen indictments including one for the murder of a federal agent? No matter that I didn't *know,* he was a federal agent. That plays little into legal matters these days. Don't what, Mitchell? What exactly don't you want me to do?"

"Don't give up on her. Don't choose this life over your own sister. She can't be past reason. Don't betray her just because you are angry at the decisions she's made." Mitch grabbed his arm to try and shake some sense into him. "I know you. You will never forgive yourself if you don't try."

"I betrayed her years ago," he mumbled. "And I've spent the rest of my life trying to make up for it."

"What are you talking about?"

"Nothing. Nevermind." Jimmie brushed past him and moved to the liquor on the counter, taking a long swig from the carafe before Mitch could wrench the bottle from him.

"Tell me or I swear to god, Jimmie, I'll shoot you myself. We don't have time for this shit."

"The fire. When we were kids," Jimmie grumbled, yanking the whiskey out of Mitch's hands. "It was my father. My mom had left, and he had started harassing Teresa. She denied it but I knew it was getting worse and worse, and when I found them alone in her room one afternoon, I pulled my gun on him. I was a bad shot even then," he glanced at Mitch only once before moving far across the room. "Took me several to get him. The whole place was a mess. I was a kid. I didn't know what to do. I put Teresa in the car and then lit fire to the house." He dropped his voice, nearly stuttering as he continued. "She wasn't supposed to be there. She had a dance recital-"

"Ashli," Mitch breathed. "She was in the house."

"I didn't know!" Jimmie yelled, throwing the carafe into the wall and watching it shatter into a thousand pieces.

"You took off with Teresa and left Ashli in the house," Mitch whispered. "The white house on the corner. Blue trim. Gray carpet. Saint Rosalia over the fireplace."

Jimmie turned. "What did you say?"

Mitch ignored him, grasping the doorknob and yanking it open. "Teddy?"

"Yes, sir?" Teddy was already on alert, his hand on his gun when Mitch pulled him into the room and shut the door.

"Get Jimmie a drink then get him on a flight. International. I don't give a damn where."

"Yes, sir."

"Mitch, you can't go after her-" Jimmie took a step toward him, but Mitch raised his hands.

"I've got to find Toni. She's in as much jeopardy as we are and if Nicolai questions her loyalty for even a moment..." Mitch trailed off. "I'll contact you as soon as I can."

CHAPTER FIFTY-FIVE

The family found her first.

"Ashli, we have to get you to a hospital," Mitch tried to pry her from the ground, but her body was suddenly heavy. She was fighting him with what little energy she had left.

"No," she shook her head. "Please, I'm safe with you. Let me stay here," her voice was pleading, and Mitch sank beside her, cradling her head in his lap.

"You were never safe with me," he whispered.

"I'm sorry, Mitch. I had no idea it was you. From when I was a child, that day of the fire. I had no idea."

He shook his head, brushing the sweat soaked hair from her face. "It doesn't matter. That was decades ago. Besides, this life suits me."

"Don't say that. Don't ever say that," she coughed, causing blood to trickle down the edge of her mouth. "You are better than this."

"Ashli," his voice was soft, almost afraid to know the answer, "why didn't you tell me you had made a deal with the IOC?"

"If you knew it would have ruined everything. You wouldn't have been determined to bring him down," she managed.

"You didn't want to betray him. You hoped I would take him down, and you could get out of this without betraying him on your own," he guessed. "You wanted me to betray him."

She nodded, her voice falling into pain filled gasps. "If I'd know...if I'd ever imagined that you were that boy...I owe you my life, Mitch-"

"Please," he begged, touching his fingers to her lips to cut off any further words that would cause him even more emotional trauma. "Let me take you to a hospital."

"So I can recover and die by Jimmie's bullet instead? No," she let her eyes slip closed. "None of us deserve that."

Soft taps sounded beside him, shoes clicking on the bare cement where he and Ashli were entwined.

He didn't bother to look up, didn't give a damn who had been sent to clean up the mess. Feds or mafia – neither was going to convince him to let her die alone. She, who was the most aggravating, insensitive woman he'd ever come in contact with. The devil, he'd called her. But here, broken, dying, welcoming death, he could see her so much more clearly: a child, searching for a way out the only way she knew how. And what she wanted most, freedom from her brother's shadow was now lost on her. She only wanted not to die by Jimmie's bullet. Mitch knew it shouldn't matter to her; death was death whichever way it came but to her, it was a last gift.

Jimmie had spent decades killing to protect her – she would not allow him to have her death on his shoulders as well.

"Mitch," a tender touch landed on his shoulder, "we have to go."

"Go away," he grumbled. But the voice was pleading now. Unyielding. Silken fingers slid under his chin, forcing him to look up. "Toni-"

"The police are on their way. Gino's men-"

"Gino?" he shuffled, trying to comprehend. "You can't be here," he managed.

"And neither can you." She tugged on his arm, but he was still holding tight to Ashli's limp body. "Mitch, look at me," she whispered, dropping to her knees and clasping his face into her hands. "She's gone. Please, we have to go."

He nodded, allowing her to drag him forward. Sirens somewhere close echoed into the recesses of his mind, and he dropped into the passenger seat of the car Toni led him to, its engine still running. He dropped his head onto the seat back, ignoring the blaring rock music and squeal of tires as she tore out of the alley. He needed to be doing something. Directing her, telling her where to go, how to drop the car. Finding a place where he could get cleaned up so that passersby wouldn't be staring at the blood now raining off him. How could she possibly have lost so much blood in such a short time? Wasn't that impossible?

"Get out," Toni's voice was low, commanding. "We need to change cars. Quickly," she urged, tugging on his arm and moving into another vehicle with darker, midnight tinted windows. "Are you hurt?" she asked tensely, her hands moving over him with lightning speed.

"Knife in my side," he mumbled. "Rest is all Ashli's."

She hesitated a moment, watching him, then tapped on the glass in front of her. "Take us to the hotel on Palisade. You know which one?"

"Palmese's airstrip?" the driver asked, his voice much calmer than Toni's.

"Yes." She turned to Mitch as the driver's partition rolled back up. "Gino's plane is already on the ground, but we've got to get you cleaned up first."

He nodded, dropping his head into his hands. She tried to slip a drink into his hand, but he shrugged her off, his thoughts finally starting to become clear. "Where's Jimmie?"

"Erice," she responded, taking the glass and swallowing the contents herself. "He arrived a few hours ago. Gino's men are picking him up and taking him to the estate."

"Exile," he managed with a tight laugh. "And yet we've done nothing wrong."

"No one is likely to believe that," she returned and fingered the slice through his now blood red shirt. "Who uses a knife these days?"

"Hm?" he asked then noticed her movements. He offered her a half smile of reassurance. "It was all he had left when I got done with him."

"I suppose that's something," she huffed. "Come," she took his hand in hers as the car slowed to a stop. "Let's get you cleaned up. I need to call Jimmie and Gino and let them know I found you."

He stopped at the back stairwell as he tugged on the long overcoat the driver offered him. "They sent you to find me?"

"Don't you dare blame them," she hissed. "I volunteered when we realized you weren't coming to see me but to go after Ashli. What were you thinking? You're a damn blessed fool sometimes, do you know that?"

"I was almost-"

"In time?" she returned, pushing him into the service elevator and punching the top floor. "Gino was right. Your hero mentality clouds your judgment. Do you think if you got her away there wouldn't be another attempt and another and then another? Lord, Mitch, even Ashli knew that."

"I hate this," he managed as she pulled out a card key and opened the door to Gino's personal suite. "I hate that you are now part of this."

"I have been part of this since the day I was conceived," she spat, turning her back on him to pick up the phone. "Go get cleaned up."

CHAPTER FIFTY-SIX

Toni tossed uneasily in the slender bed aboard Gino's plane. Ashli was gone. Jimmie and Mitch were now relegated to Sicily for who knew how long. Her father would soon miss her. Or perhaps not. There was no way to know his mindset these days. Should she tell him she had left to help Mitch, he would be thrilled. But that felt like betrayal...like telling him even the tiniest sliver of information about Mitch and Jimmie would be a personal betrayal against them both. Hadn't the two already had enough of that?

She kicked off the covers in frustration. How could she possibly sleep with everything that had happened tonight? Images flooded her mind: Mitch drenched in blood; the broken look on his face when she'd torn him away from Ashli's body; his distraction; his obvious guilt over having failed to protect her; his hatred for Toni having been the one to retrieve him. Not hating her exactly, although that was how he made it feel, but more that he had entrenched her even further into a world he wanted her to have no part of.

A slight movement at the edge of her vision caught her off guard. Now she was seeing things; she cursed herself as she glanced at the clock. They would be landing in just a few hours...where had all that time gone?

"May I come in?"

Mitch. From somewhere in her darkened room, he was there. Her stomach fluttered. How long had he been watching her? "Of course."

He moved slowly, as if in a daze. She could see no visible scars on him, and his hair was only ruffled from the hand he kept dragging through it. His shirt was open, a white bandage no bigger than her fist the only indication that the night's events had even occurred. But he wouldn't meet her gaze, and that told her enough. He sank in front of her, burying his face in her lap. Her hand hesitated in mid-air before resting on the top of his head. He wasn't crying, wasn't even emotionally spent by the look of him, but the resignation of the night's events seemed to have enveloped him. She wasn't sure how long they stayed that way - his exhausted face pressed into her bare legs, but she couldn't bear the thought of pushing him away for even a moment.

His soft breathing had almost lulled her to sleep when she felt it...the soft, silky slide of his lips along her flesh. His hands slid across her thighs, pushing the already short fabric of her slip higher up. He didn't ask permission, didn't even glance her direction for approval and that alone gave her chills. His mouth traced slowly along her skin, first sliding up one thigh and then down the other as he nuzzled her gently with his growing beard. Her breath caught in her throat as he scooted her further back on the bed, his hands drifting aimlessly along her curves as he shifted his body to lay on top of her.

His touch was light, almost irritatingly so, and she gripped his shirt tightly in her fists in an attempt to pull him toward her. Her movement accomplished nothing, though, not even a change in his breathing pattern as he continued to slip his tongue along the curves of her neck. His fingers tightened around her breasts, causing her to let out a tiny gasp. His mouth moved to cover hers, the pressure of his lips on hers and his hot breath causing her almost to suffocate under his demands.

He undressed casually as if stepping into the shower, his movements seeming painstakingly slow. She wanted to grab him, pull his body into hers and show him the desperation with which she wanted to be with the man he kept so hidden. But, he would have nothing of it. His caresses were smooth but not tentative, the self-assurance that normally aggravated her now causing her breath to stagger in her throat. She let her fingers slip along the muscles in his arms, across the sharp angles of his shoulder blades that arched rhythmically as he moved. He leaned down, his lips brushing against hers as his body moved with a slow, calm rhythm just for her.

He only moved when she breathed...a hypnotic action that seemed to draw her deeper into him. She had no idea how he managed such serene control over himself, but his gliding movement touched her more deeply than she ever imagined possible. She felt a warmth grow in her lower abdomen and sucked in a breath as he let his fingers trail down her side to crook her leg up toward him.

Even in her frazzled state, she could sense her perception becoming more acute- the metallic creak of the bed underneath them; his calloused hands rubbing on the back of her neck; the river of chilled air drifting across his shoulders from somewhere high up above; the thump of his heart pressing into her flesh; the medicinal stench of his first aid treatment being overtaken by his smell of sweet gun oil and salty sweat; the slight tickle of his long hair as it swayed against her face with his movements; the tremble in his already exhausted muscles as he tried to hold on long enough to get them where they needed to go.

She could feel him shift position, moving his arms underneath her shoulders to cradle her head in his hands. He had no energy to kiss her but dropped his face on her shoulder, his labored breathing hovering at the hollow of her throat as he used his new position to entwine them so deeply it tinged on painful.

"Breathe, girl," he ordered quietly, his command veiled with a tinge of concern.

How he had noticed such a thing in his exhausted state was beyond her. That he could block everything out and be there only for her made her weak. Tears welled at the corners of her eyes as she tried to ignore him. She didn't want to breathe. She knew a single breath would cause the feeling to end; oxygen would rush over her, and she'd no longer be able to stave off the feelings he had caused to well within her. She wanted to prolong it...to lock out the real world for as long as she possibly could manage, to keep it just the two of them – a tiny sliver of life where there was no blood or death or broken ties of loyalty.

She caught his eye uneasily, his ice blue eyes darkened to the color of piercing steel, looking far deeper into her soul than she thought possible. He knew.

He knew what she was afraid of and what she wasn't. What she wanted to escape from and what she longed to have. He understood that by holding her breath, she was prolonging the sensation of true living that he had welled within her. He had recognized how desperately she feared the lost dreams her father had stolen from her.

Dreams of simplicity – days of sunshine watching her children play in the front yard; a happy marriage not tinged with death where hours were filled with common everyday things like washing clothes and dishes and baking bread – things she remembered her mother doing in childhood. She knew he could see her fear of never feeling this way again – and it terrified her. As tempted as she was to stay here in this place forever, he was telling her it was impossible and that she had to move on. She had a choice, but it took his words to convince her to make the decision.

"I'm here, girl," he whispered, pulling her into a reassuring embrace, "just let it come."

She sucked in a desperate breath, her sobs punctuated by ragged gasps as he quickened and allowed shudders to overtake them both. She clasped to him, unwilling to let him move away. He rubbed her head gently, her body trembling with uncontrollable sobs from both fear and the effect he'd had on her.

He traced the curve of her waist as he felt her heart slow and her emotions return to normal.

"Ask me, Toni. I'm only giving you limited time to come up for air."

Whether it was a threat or a promise, she wasn't sure. She considered the many things she wanted to ask him – about his past, her past, Gino, Jimmie, even Ashli – but none seemed to be appropriate after the tender, almost reverent lovemaking they had just shared. "Are you alright?"

His hand traced lightly down her face, slipping across her jawline, his fingertips brushing loose curls away from her glimmering eyes. "I'm stronger with you beside me," he whispered, his lips barely brushing hers, "and yet, a thousand times weaker as well."

His lips traced hers without touching them, her ragged breathing giving away her impatience as he continued to explore the curves of her face with his lips. He could feel her pulse race beneath him, her lips becoming more demanding, and her touches more aggressive. When she shifted her body to lay over him, he pulled inches away. "I'm not," whispered, "and you should know that going in."

"Mitch," she smiled, "I knew that the moment you first arrived in San Francisco."

CHAPTER FIFTY-SEVEN

He kicked at the cobblestones, lagging a few paces behind the others as they meandered through the ever-narrowing passages of Valderice. He inhaled the fresh scent, the salty breeze that managed to waft away all the odor from the nearby fields where goats were rambling loose across the countryside. He raised a hand in greeting to a grandmother, accepting a fresh orange from one of the children he supposed lived in the tiny hovel she called home. All the houses here were of stone, crumbling remnants that had been whitewashed with age. What he remembered as dark brown and cinnamon colored were now the lightest shades of beige and khaki. He smiled as Toni drifted back to his side, letting Gino and Jimmie walk on ahead. A few paces behind them, Gino's entourage, was following, their footsteps so quiet even over the pebbles that Mitch had to constantly remind himself that they were actually there, and danger had still not passed.

"Gino is telling stories of a Halloween massacre," she said with a lopsided grin. "I decided his morbid tales are ruining the

beauty of such a place. He told me I should come be philosophical with you."

"Not me," he laughed, offering her a slice of the orange he
was peeling. "Not today anyway."

"Not enough alcohol for philosophy?" she queried, letting
her arm slip through his.

"No alcohol yet," he admitted. "Although I'm told Gino has
lunch planned for us at a nearby vineyard so we'll all likely be
soused by the time we get back to his house."

"Gino called Nicolai," she said quietly. "Told him if he had a
problem with my being here to take it up with him and leave
you alone."

"And he replied?"

She shrugged. "He offers his condolences for the loss you
and Jimmie have suffered and prays that the federal situation
will be quickly resolved in favor of Vinetti Industries."

"How diplomatic."

"Yes, he's nothing if not *diplomatic*," she mumbled.

He let his hand rest on hers, tightening it around his arm. "I
give, Toni. I don't understand your fury at him. Not about this.
This was not his doing." When she didn't answer immediately,
Mitch stopped mid stride and turned to face her. "Or am I mistaken?"

He eyed her intently, confused for a moment at her silence.
She was fingering the locket around her neck, the one with the
Terenari family crest on it, the one he had forced her to put
back on before they disembarked the plane in Sicily. She refused to tell him why she had ripped it off, to begin with, but
he wasn't going to allow her anger at her father be displayed

for everyone to see. At least in public, she would be a loyal daughter.

A loyal daughter. Mitch's mind raced with the obscure comments she had made to him since their reunion. How Nicolai was no longer honorable, how she had been witness to his misdeeds, how she knew without question that Nicolai would stop at nothing to get what he wanted. And it had all started with a single unsolved murder almost 10,000 miles from where they now stood.

"How long have you know Nicolai killed Coppell?" he asked.

A dam broke instantly in her emotions, and her words came fast. "I didn't know you would join the Vinettis. I had no idea. Nicolai had no idea. He had counted on you coming to him after Coppell's death. You retreat to familiar; that's what he said. He'd made sure you weren't even in the country so there could be no question about your involvement in it but those stupid cops...and then Ashli stepping in from nowhere. Everything happened so fast. Instead of moving you closer, he forced you to Jimmie's side. None of this, not you being shot, not Ashli turning, not where we stand at this moment, would have happened if it weren't for Nicolai and his damned determination to always come out on top."

He placed a hand on her to calm her. "Make no mistake, girl, I am at Jimmie's side by choice. Not by any turns of fate or foiled intentions of your father. My current situation is a result of my own actions and no one else's. Never forget that."

"And me?" she whispered. "Is it a decades old promise, memories only, that keep you beside me?"

Mitch sighed, knowing what she wanted to hear and knowing there was no way he could offer it. He couldn't and wouldn't love her – no matter how easy it might be for him to do so and how difficult the battle to fight it was. But she was the one constant in his life. The one thing that shone through despite all the lies and betrayal the mob and the IOC dealt him. He couldn't love her, but he wasn't willing to lose her either.

Cupping her face in his hands, he kissed her forehead and then dropped his lips to her ear. "I am beside you because some fates are impossible to fight."

"My complicity in Coppell..." she trailed off and then tried to straighten herself to face him. "Were it not for me, I think, this all could have been prevented."

"Your complicity?"

"I was there," she whispered. "He made me go along. I hadn't been back at his side long, and I think he meant it as a test of sorts. I didn't even know who Coppell was at the time – had no idea of your connection to him." She was shaking now, her body trembling as she tried to voice the thoughts jumbling through her. "We were alone in the room with him. It happened so fast. He was in his pajamas; they had little gold fleur de lis all over them. And the blood, it was everywhere. Nicolai's shot went straight through the back of his head. He didn't even slump over. It was just..."

"Oh, lord, girl," Mitch mumbled, pulling her into his arms as her emotions finally broke and her anger turned into tears. The more she cried, the more his fury at Nicolai grew. That he would involve her in such a thing, that he would force her to witness such a thing...did the man have no redeeming qualities left in him?

"It won't happen again, I assure you."

The growl in his voice caused Toni to straighten, putting things back in their rightful perspective. "Don't, Mitch. Don't give him ultimatums. It will only make things worse."

"I will not allow him to destroy whatever humanity you've managed to hang onto while at his side. If you think different-ly, then you don't know me at all."

"I do know you. I know you are going to demand he keep me out of things. I know he'll act as if he didn't realize his ac-tions were wrong, apology profusely for it and then I'll be left to pay for it."

"If he lays a hand on you-"

Toni's hands moved to his chest, touching him gently to try and calm his fury. When it failed to work, she pressed closer to him, her hands reaching to caress his face. Her voice was a tiny whisper as she stretched to tiptoes. "You are my best friend. Even when I hated you. Even when I hadn't seen you in any more than a dream for a decade. Don't ever risk something that will take that away from me. Promise me."

When he failed to respond, she shook him slightly. "Prom-ise."

Even though it killed him, he shook his head. "I can't. I will protect you, no matter the cost."

CHAPTER FIFTY-EIGHT

Mitch twirled the wine bottle in his hand, reveling in the silence the vineyard garden offered. He had managed to slip out of the lunch early, while the others continued to dine on farm fresh quiche, Roma tomatoes and copious amounts of white wine. It was the first time he had been alone since before Ashli's death. All of them – Gino, Jimmie, Toni, Teddy – seemed determined to keep watch over him as if he was suicidal. They'd even hovered as he spoke with Sonny, asking him to make the arrangements to have Ashli cremated and her body sent to a private location where they could hold a memorial service without stepping foot in the States.

He knew they meant well – hoping that their presence would keep his guilt at bay. But no amount of alcohol or crass jokes could accomplish that. Even Jimmie had been allowed time to mourn, but none seem to feel that was Mitch's place...none seemed to realize the demons of his own that he was trying to fight.

"It was Vinetti," Mitch sighed, not raising his head as he heard Gino's heavy footsteps come up behind him. "That night. When I was just a kid. Jimmie shot his father and set fire to the house. He pulled Teresa out, never realizing Ashli was inside. It was Ashli that I pulled out of that burning house."

"Yes."

"Why didn't you tell me?"

"So she could destroy even more of your life?" he asked, dropping onto the wrought iron chair across from him. "You were sent off for the crime or have you forgotten? Do you remember what it was like, Mitch? To say goodbye to your mother, me?" his voice dropped to a mere whisper. "Antoinette? Do you remember?"

"Every time I breathe."

"Protecting you will always be my weakness, Vincenzo. I won't apologize for it." His land lay gingerly on Mitch's knee. "I know you. You would have joined Vinetti years ago if you knew it was her. Just like your mother, you want to save the world."

"You don't want me with Vinetti?"

"What I want matters little. You and he are good for each other. I can see the changes you have brought in each other. A man needs that to stay alive in this world. Your choices are your own. Just like with Antoinette."

The shuffling behind him caught him off guard, but the citrus smell was a giveaway. He had no idea how long she'd been listening to their conversation, but Toni had joined them. Worlds were colliding, and he was just too tired to give a damn about covering his tracks. He turned his head her direction, just quick enough to see Gino move and place a hand on her to keep her in place.

"I think, perhaps, he could use the two of you right now."

And then Mitch saw him. A pace behind Toni, his face blanched to the starkest of whites, Jimmie was leaning against the wall in stunned silence. Even with Mitch's own grief, he knew Jimmie's was a hundred times deeper. "Sit down, Jimmie."

But he seemed unable to move. It was Toni's soft touch that led him onto the patio and helped him drop into the chair Gino had vacated. Without bothering to ask permission, she slipped to sit beside Mitch, snaking her hand into his.

"I don't understand," she admitted. "I remember the fire. I remember you and Gino arguing with your mom in the kitchen. I remember the day the police showed up and arrested you."

"You threw trash cans at the squad car," he interrupted with vague awareness.

She frowned. "But you saved someone and went to jail for it?"

"They believed it was an initiation of sorts," Gino provided, then chuckled. "Which he failed, of course."

"That's why no one knows of any connection between the two of you. He got caught and never made it into your family," Toni guessed.

"Except those of us right here," Gino nodded. "That secret has kept him alive. If Mitch is trusting you enough to be here, then I assume he feels you worthy of entrusting his life."

"Bit dramatic there, Gino," Mitch grumbled. "You aren't the only reason people want me dead, remember."

"You saved her, though," Toni argued, shaking her head. "You should've been a hero."

"I'm no hero. Especially not Ashli's." Mitch quieted, closing his eyes and dropping his head to the back of the patio swing as the memories flooded through him again.

It was Jimmie's calm voice that broke the silence. "Don't blame yourself for the choices she made. You didn't dial up the IOC, Mitch. She did this all on her own."

It was a reprieve. Jimmie didn't blame him for Ashli's death. He didn't blame him for anything. Although kind, the words offered Mitch little solace. He had failed her not once but twice. Perhaps even more times if he counted the opportunities he'd had to get her away from Vinetti Industries since he'd been in their employ. Jimmie might forgive him, but he knew he'd never forgive himself.

Mitch glanced across the group. It was time to lay the few cards he could on the table...they deserved what tiny bit of honesty he could offer them. "It was Nicolai that killed Coppell."

Incredulous eyes turned to look at him, but it was Jimmie who found the words first. "What?"

"Toni was there," he nodded toward her. "He forced her to go along."

Gino was at her side in an instant, prepared to offer comfort, but she merely shook her head. "He believed Mitch would come to his side once Coppell was out of the picture. I don't know why he's so adamant about it. He has a plan bigger than Mitch, I'm sure." She gave them an apologetic look. "But I'm not privy to it."

"The table," Gino surmised. "He knows how deep Mitch's loyalty can run, believes he can use that childhood tie to unseat me."

Jimmie nodded. "That makes sense. That's why he tried to use Toni, why she was so important to his plan. You were inseparable until Gino broke you apart."

"He believed Mitch would retaliate and join him against Gino." Toni shook her head. "But he never anticipated-"

"Ashli," Jimmie exhaled. "He underestimated her. As we all did."

"And the IOC?" Gino asked.

"Also my father. He had someone tip them off about Markesi and Mitch's connection to him led them straight to Vinetti Industries."

All behind my back, Mitch thought with only temporary resentment. He couldn't blame the IOC for trying to get the job done. He had obviously been failing miserably at it. Even he could see that now. He wouldn't be surprised to learn that his "accidental" shooting had been staged as well – an attempt to get him on the sidelines so they could get Ashli out and take Vinetti down while he was incapacitated. The mafia and the IOC, he reminded himself, were more alike than they both realized. To know that he was still affiliated with both almost made him vomit.

But to know that neither knew about his liaisons gave him some measure of comfort. His ties with Gino and now Jimmie kept him well protected in the mob, and the IOC wouldn't consider him dispensable until they knew for sure he wasn't on their side...they couldn't afford to lose someone as deep undercover as he was. Right now, that was the only security he had.

And it was much too precarious a situation in which to have Toni involved. He sighed, rising to his feet, and extending his hand toward her. "Come, Antoinette, I could use a walk."

CHAPTER FIFTY-NINE

Mitch sank onto a crumbling wall, a former patio of a home that had been long since taken over with wild orange vines. They draped around them, hanging over their shoulders but he ignored them and slid his fingers into hers, pulling her to stand between his legs. His hand swept to her waist, his hands raking gently against the cotton fabric of her dress. Curls of hair fell over her shoulders, brushing against the edges of his face. He inhaled deeply, memories coursing through him.

"I've wondered," he mumbled. "You smell so much like this place. Every time you're near, I'm transplanted back. To this tiny village to which you've never even been. It was nonsensical. More than once it has made me believe I was going insane."

Trembling hands slipped into his hair, her fingers knotting at the bottom of his neck as she pulled him in closer. "Gino," she explained. "Every year for my birthday he sends me a basket of perfumes and soaps made by the locals. Fresh oranges, sea water and-"

"Black violets," he nodded, nuzzling her neck. His lips traced the arch of her neck before comprehension dawned and he withdrew his lips from her fragrant skin, his hands clenching into fists against her back. What would it hurt if he gave in? A fling amidst one of the most beautiful villages in all of Sicily. No one would blame him; no one would ever even have to know. All the frustration, the exhaustion – everything could be erased by the passion he knew she possessed. He lifted his eyes to her, the trusting, childlike eyes he had memorized nearly two decades before. A single night could erase many things...but not if she was the girl. He had already made this mistake once. He couldn't allow himself to do it again.

He dropped his head into her chest, pulling her tight so that his arms overlapped around her waist. She was trembling, he could feel the shivers running up her spine as he held her. He waited, embracing her until he felt her breathing return to normal. When it finally did, he tugged her down to sit beside him on the ledge, folding her hand into his.

"You brought me here to say goodbye," she accused with a resigned sigh. "Will you always think me a little girl?"

"I will always think you, someone who needs protecting," he corrected. "It's who we are. It's the world in which we live."

"So I'm not attractive. That way, I mean," she shook her head in confusion. "I've wondered. Not about you but others. Then men I've known, they always back away as if I'm-" she trailed off, unsure of the word.

Mitch glanced at her, the perplexed look on her face resembling the child he knew so well. He had not mentioned it, the fact that he had taken her virginity on the night of Ashli's death. She was so accomplished in so many ways it had never occurred to him that she was innocent where men were concerned. He had considered talking to her about it, attempting to counsel her with some wise words of wisdom but he'd found his own emotions too rattled to even broach the subject. Instead, he'd befriended her as they had been when they were kids, hoping at the least he could teach her how life was meant to be so that she wouldn't make the same dire mistakes in her relationships as Ashli had. But her words now, the revelation of truth that her father had so mercilessly destroyed her self-esteem without even intending to caused his heart to ache.

When she was a child, she had never been afraid to ask him anything. She turned to him for dating advice, makeup, the clothes which looked best on the boyish figure that she swore she'd never grow out of. She'd even sought his advice for the color of ribbon to put in her hair. He had told her once, in a self-absorbed adolescent moment, that her ribbons didn't matter because she'd always look like a toad. He'd never seen her wear ribbons in her hair again.

He lifted her hands to his lips, kissing them gently. "Were you a stranger, I would ravage you right here."

"Really?" she looked doubtful.

"I'm not the noble creature you suspect," he laughed. "The bed, the beach, this rocky ledge – I'd tear your calico to shreds and consume you as if I hadn't eaten in years." He watched her reaction but rather than relief it was something he couldn't quite decipher. He chuckled. "Have I frightened you now? Will you stay far away?"

"On the contrary," she murmured, "you have intrigued me."

"Oh, Lord." He threw his head back in laughter. "You are an exasperating woman."

"Now," she leaned closer to him, her eyes twinkling, "have I frightened you?"

"Indeed." He nodded, locking her face in his hands and kissing her quickly on the lips. "You have terrified me more than any other soul on the planet."

"And will you stay far away?" she asked grinning, taking her hand in his and pulling him back onto the main road.

"Doubtful. I'm not nearly that smart." He let his hand slip into hers as they walked. "Do you remember when I used to hold your hand when you crossed the street?"

"Of course." She smiled, leaning toward him conspiratorially. "Do you think the local donkeys are planning a drive-by?"

"It's not you," he said quietly, tugging her forward so he wouldn't have to look into her eyes as they walked. "The men. It's your father they fear. It has nothing to do with you. You understand that, don't you?"

She was quiet, swinging their hands back and forth as they walked. The silence was beginning to worry him but, as if she knew he had reached his limit, she sighed.

"I understand that I will always be in his shadow. I will always be Nicolai Terenari's daughter. I don't understand why that must be my burden to bear. I didn't ask for it or even desire it."

"We all have a past that haunts us, Toni. Do we judge ourselves because of it or do we move on and make amends?

"Is that what you're doing, making amends?"

He smiled, refusing to answer. "Your father is a dangerous man but not an unlovable one. Your mother found a reason to love him."

"He's not the same person," she argued.

"And that makes forgiveness impossible for you?

"Yes. No. I mean-" She stopped, spotting Jimmie rounding the corner toward them. "I'm sorry. I just don't think I understand. You are being philosophical."

"Is this a private party?" Jimmie stepped from one of the crumbling buildings, his eyes bright.

"Just coming to look for you. Come, let's go this way."

Mitch led them farther down the road to single home set back from the road. Unlike all the others, this one had remained livable. It was still old, its age showing clearly, but someone had taken the time to restore it and keep the overgrowth at bay.

"This was your home?" Toni asked, tucking her arms into Mitch's and Jimmie's as she stepped to walk between them. "Before America, I mean."

"I was born here," he answered simply. "And I lived here until my father died."

"Dare I ask how he died?"

Mitch chuckled, leading them through the tiny home and onto an even smaller garden in the back. Grass had taken over the former vegetable garden, but a grouping of small orange trees still stood strong. "You likely already know."

He sank onto one of the remaining ledges, trickles of rocks dropping to the ground with his weight. He fingered one of the overgrown bushes nearest him. "My mother tended these oranges. They were her joy, she said. Her hands forever smelled of citrus. Gino would come by in the afternoons, and she would give him handfuls to take back to his wife. He tried to pay her for them, but my mother wouldn't hear of it. God's provisions couldn't be bought, she told him. But he found other ways to pay back her kindness. Sending men to fix the leaking roof while she was gone for the weekend to visit family. Or sending people to harvest the field in the dead of night, so she woke up to baskets full of a garden's worth of food."

"He loved her," Toni guessed.

Jimmie shook his head, reaching to pluck an unripe orange from the tangle of vines. "Loving her would've made her a target. Gino would never have allowed himself such a weakness."

"You don't allow or disallow love, Jimmie."

Jimmie laughed. "Don't be childish. Do you think the men of *la familia* are bachelors by choice? We are born alone and will die alone. For us, admitting loving someone is like signing their death certificate."

As soon as the words were out of his mouth, Jimmie regretted it. Mitch's eyes flashed away, the torn look on his face sending a surge of memories through Jimmie's head. What had Gino said when they were fighting over Toni?

"Did you learn nothing from your mother's death?"

"Of course, Gino. But I'm not irresponsible enough to fall in love with her."

Had that been what happened? Had Gino fallen in love with Mitch's mother?

As if Mitch had read his thoughts, he shrugged at the unasked question. "Either way, they were both married to others. His wife died during childbirth while they were still young. And my father," he hesitated, "my father was more a professional drunk than a father."

"Your mother never mentioned him," Toni murmured. "When you came to America, she never once mentioned his name in the hundreds of hours we spent together in your kitchen."

Mitch nodded, his voice a low, quiet hum of memory. "America was to be a new place and a new beginning. A place where her son could find freedom from the shadows of the men she believed would both save and destroy him."

He was silent, waiting for them to understand. He expected Toni to understand first, to know him with inherent ease, but it was Jimmie who understood first. "Gino killed your father."

Mitch gave a single nod then raised his eyes to bore into Toni's. "We each have our burdens. It's how we address them that determines the person we shall become."

Jimmie looked from one to the other. It was obvious Mitch was attempting to teach her a lesson. Something that, he suspected, the both of them had learned but she still had not. Why else would Mitch have bothered to tell him something so personal, so immensely private, that no one the world over was privy to it?

Mitch wouldn't look at him; he was intent on Toni. She was touching a locket hanging low on her neck, her other hand grazing along the stone remnants of the cottage. Jimmie straightened, the fingering of the jewelry around her neck making things fall into place for him. He stepped toward her, placing his hands on her shoulders.

"Your father is a despicable man. I won't bother to pretend I hold any fondness for him. But you," he dropped his forehead to hers, "you may be his blood, but you are nothing like him. I would accept you by my side at any time."

CHAPTER SIXTY

They, are your allies?" Gino's voice was quiet, contemplative. "They are the ones you have chosen to be at your side? Your most trusted confidantes?"

Mitch nodded, his eyes meeting Gino's but only briefly.

"A man who would sacrifice his own blood and the enemy's daughter?"

Mitch had no response for him. His words were true, his admonition coming only from the concern Gino felt for Mitch's safety. He knew Gino would accept whatever decision he made, would already fathom consequences that Mitch himself could not yet realize. But it was not as if he planned this. He had not gone willingly into any relationship with Jimmie. Ashli had done that for him. That it had turned into something far more meaningful than either imagined was not by any conscious effort on their part.

Toni was a different matter entirely. Gino had anticipated their connection as children. He had known it, planned for it, and done his best to shelter them from the pain their friendship would bring. After all the years of work, Mitch was now destroying everything Gino had so meticulously crafted...by simply allowing her to be at his side.

He glanced to where Jimmie and Toni sat, their heads drawn together in quiet whispers – no doubt trying to piece together the puzzles of his bewildering life story which must have only grown murkier with the recent revelations. He chuckled at their furrowed brows, causing them both to glance his way.

They smiled, an almost identical sheepish grin at having been caught in their gossiping. And yet, neither made any move to apologize for it, only dropping their heads back together to continue their dissection of his existence.

He considered Gino's nonverbal warning, knowing how dangerous his liaison with the two was. His ties to Gino, an impending war with Terenari, the aftermath of Ashli's death – all would pale in comparison to the murderous swell that would occur if the IOC were to learn of his decision.

"Mitch?" Gino's eyes were on him, patiently waiting for Mitch's internal struggles to cease.

"They are my family, Gino."

Gino's guiding hand was light on Mitch's shoulder, his fingers tightening with a calm, learned reassurance. "Then when the war comes, from whichever direction it may blow, they will be mine as well."